THE ABACUS PRIZE

LOVE, LIES AND MURDER IN THE IRS

BY
ARLENE KAY

A GRACE QUINN MYSTERY

To my friends and former colleagues who inspired this series.

Thank you.

CHAPTER ONE

"LAS VEGAS! I hate that place. It's vulgar and crass, a cultural wasteland. The airport doesn't even have a book store!"

I couldn't believe my ears. Surely Mary Hagan was toying with me. She knew that I loathed hellish temperatures especially when combined with cold fish like the American Association of Actuaries. I bit my tongue to avoid saying something that would ruffle her platinum bob. As Mary often observed, she was my superior and I was her indentured servant. Serf was a more accurate description in the feudal world of IRS executives.

"Really, Grace? It's America's playground, second only to Walt Disney World. Most people would kill for this assignment. Besides, the convention organizers specifically asked for you. That's quite an honor."

My boss was the picture of innocence, beaming her saccharine smile my way. No sarcasm not a trace of malice. That made me both suspicious and panicky. Maybe she didn't understand.

"We've had some very bad publicity lately," Mary said, shaking her head. "IRS needs to spruce up its public image. These people are our customers after all."

"They're *Actuaries*, Mary. They get off watching reruns of *Dr. Who*. They make CPAs look exciting."

Mary Hagan arched one brow. That was actually a pretty good trick since her brows were impeccably shaped. Too late, I recalled that she was a CPA herself.

I began to backpedal. "Not that accountants aren't good company. In fact some of my best friends ...."

"Save it, Grace." Her smile tightened. "Apparently, you really wowed them last year. Don't be modest. I've seen the tapes. The audience looked positively mesmerized."

"They weren't mesmerized. They were catatonic. They sat there calculating my life span, which won't be long if I have to spend another week with those geeks."

Mary patted that perfect bob and frowned. As she bent over I caught a whiff of her signature fragrance, Fleurisimo. It was French, exclusive and expensive—things that Mary Hagan prized.

"Well, I guess I could ask Jacobs," she said, "but he's not the public speaker you are Grace. Of course as I said some people consider this assignment a perk."

"I'll cover all his projects while he's away. You know me, boss, I'm a team player."

There was that smile again. My cat had that expression whenever he cornered a mouse.

Mary tapped her pen on the desk and sighed. "You know this may actually work out. Jacobs was scheduled to cover Continuing Professional Education for CPAs next week. CPE for CPAs—kind of catchy don't you think? It'll be the perfect fit for you." Her honey-scented accent deepened. Evil can easily hide in a pretty face.

The trap was sprung and I'd walked right into it. She handed me a purple folder with my name and that catchy title right on the front. "It's here in D.C., over at the San Simone. Isn't that convenient?"

I was a beaten woman, outmaneuvered by one of my own sex. For the past two years I had dodged that gaggle of pencil pushing geese, gloating when my colleagues drew the losing hand. Now I was paying the price—in spades.

"But I'm not a CPA," I whined. "I'm not even an accountant. You know how cliquey that bunch is. They'll never accept me."

Mary grabbed her briefcase and headed out the door, pausing for another parting shot. "Nonsense. You'll win them over right away. Stop fighting. Try using charm for a change. After all, you've got plenty of time. What are you—thirty-one?"

I nodded dolefully, visualizing the pain that awaited me.

"This is a learning experience, Grace. Keep that in mind. Oh, I almost forgot to tell you. I know how you love antiques. Guess what?"

I couldn't even begin to guess. Maybe they had an ossified pocket protector on display.

"The hotel is hosting the unveiling of the Golden Abacus. It's solid gold, fifteen hundred years old and priceless. A real coup for D.C. The Chinese guard that thing with their lives. Haven't even displayed it for 200 years." Mary sighed at the mere thought of it.

That bit of information intrigued me and provided a scintilla of hope. Maybe this gig wouldn't be so boring after all. I gave her a plucky, can-do grin and watched as she strode confidently out the door with her stilettos clattering.

◊ ◊ ◊ ◊ ◊

It was late and I was hot. Not in the sexy, hey look me over way but in the sweaty, make-up melting disaster mode. Summers in the nation's capital were a bad time to wear pantyhose let alone Big Hair. Thank God I had the good sense to carry my towering heels and chug along in sensible shoes. The San Simone was the grande dame of D.C. hotels with a vast lobby filled with couches, gilt objects and faux antiques. I had just enough time to hit the ladies' room before joining the other merrymakers at the opening social. As I scuttled toward the door I heard my name. A woman with admirable lungs, impaired diction and very few inhibitions was screeching at me.

"Grace Quinn, what in the hell happened to you? Looks like you were rode hard and put away wet, girl!" Before I escaped, she clasped me to her bosom in a rib-crushing hug.

It was hard to ignore Maude Morrissey, try as I might. Her towering frame and bold red locks made her quite a showstopper. Years before in another lifetime Maude and I had been colleagues at the Internal Revenue Service. She left and became one of the most quoted members of the tax press. I stayed and became a junior executive assigned to the Washington headquarters to pay my dues.

I edged toward the rest room pantomiming distress. Undeterred, Maude followed me through the door, talking non-stop.

"I never expected to see you at a CPA shindig, Grace. You said ...."

"Never mind what I said, Maude. That was ages ago. I've matured."

"Huh!" she snorted, "A likely story."

I hunted for a brush and started making repairs. Some people regard me as a make-up slut. I can't resist any product that even hints about improvement. The same applies to clothing. The term clotheshorse has been bandied about quite freely by my sober-suited colleagues. Style savvy is a no-no in an organization that values anonymity, blending in, and downright dullness. Maybe I need different friends.

Actually, I didn't look too bad. My blonde locks were waved not frizzed and my makeup was salvageable. I wore a slash of lipstick and a pink linen dress that was born to be wrinkled. At least that was my story.

"Have you seen it? It's sublime!" Maude babbled in ecstasy

"What in the world are you talking about?"

"The Golden Abacus." Maude's moon pie face tilted skyward rendering her temporarily speechless. Unfortunately. I was not.

"Oh, the accountants' wet dream. Nope. Haven't seen it but I plan to."

Maude bellowed like a rabid moose. "Grace Quinn, you have a way with words. You just gave me a great headline!"

I panicked. Thoughts of a rapid and unpleasant end to my executive career spun in my brain. I pictured Mary Hagan's stiletto heel piercing my unprotected throat and the shame that would taint my entire family as they mourned my future.

"Wait a minute. Maude, come on. I was just kidding."

"Ah, Grace, don't sweat it. The readers of *Tax Chat* want a 'G' rated column. Now social media is a different story. That bon mot is tailor made for Twitter, maybe even Facebook." She finally took pity of me and relented. "Don't worry. Your secrets are safe. Besides I'm on the trail of a real story that will shake them all the way to Capitol Hill. You don't mind if I steal your cute little line though? Just for chit-chat."

Maude squeezed my shoulder and stomped out the door in search of bigger game.

It was the last time I saw her alive.

The Exhibit Hall was packed with a crowd of nerdy folks desperately trying to network with Power or what passed for it. Both genders favored Brooks Brothers to the exclusion of trendier garb. Although their attire was sober most participants were not. Who knew accountants were capable of such hilarity?

In the center of the room encased in thick impregnable glass was the real star of the evening—the Golden Abacus. I moved closer. The ancient beauty glowed with the patina of age and the lure of long ago secrets. The gold exterior, measuring only eight inches, rivaled the luminescence of the sun. A beautifully printed placard described its provenance.

"The Chinese abacus is also called a Suanpan. The Golden Abacus (circa 1200 AD) was constructed of solid gold and presented to the Imperial Emperor of the Ming Dynasty. Westerners first viewed it in 1903, shortly after the Boxer Rebellion. It later disappeared until being discovered in the private collection of Henrich Himmler. The German government repatriated the Abacus to China in 1957. This is the first American showing."

Wow! No wonder Maude was impressed! I pivoted and found myself face to face with something equally splendid. The handsome man of color was a ghost from a thousand dreams. It was none other than Jonathon Grey, my dear friend and first mentor.

"Grace! I never expected to see you here. Let me look at you." Jonathon Grey took my hand and studied my face. "Same beauty. You haven't aged a day."

My Irish ancestry betrayed me with a full-face flush. His praise warmed my heart, soul and other body parts too personal to mention. It also stirred libidinous feelings I'd suppressed for way too long.

"Jonathon. I thought you senior partners were too busy to mix with the common herd." Not my finest line but it's hard to be clever when your heart plummets to your basement.

He trained sexy bedroom eyes my way. "Of course not. I volunteered to fly in just to see the Abacus. Now if I'd known that *you* were going to be here, I would have really fought for the chance."

Jonathon was still a stone fox. A quick survey of his face and form confirmed that fact. He wore a Brioni suit like an elegant second skin and hadn't lost those tight little ....

"Grace, have you seen any of our other old friends yet?"

My pleasant inventory of all things Jonathon was interrupted. I blushed even more as I tried to recover. "As I matter of fact I was just waylaid by Maude Morrissey and have the bruises to prove it."

A pained expression flitted across his face. At least I think it did. Jonathon's reaction was so fleeting that I couldn't be sure.

"I'm meeting with Maude later on," he said. "All kidding aside, why are you here? I know it isn't just to rub shoulders with the accounting crowd."

"My orders are to mingle, staff the IRS welcome center and conduct two seminars on business taxes. In other words to show executive commitment whatever that is." I shrugged. "Hey, it beats slumming with the actuaries."

Long ago, Jonathon and I had been involved in a particularly grisly murder case in Chicago. He left the IRS and I moved on to Houston. The memory was so vivid it seemed like only yesterday. I looked at him and bravely tried to act as if he were just another guy.

"So, how is everything in Chicago?"

"Fine. My son is a CPA, you know. He finished law school at Northwestern and just had to go work for one of the big firms— no government jobs for that boy."

"He could do worse than to imitate his dad. By the way, Mr. Money-bags, how does it feel to be independently wealthy now?" I stepped back a few paces to give my libido a rest.

Jonathon grinned. "Well, you know me, my needs are few ...."

"If you want some suggestions on how to spend it, I'm always available." My pathetic attempt at humor fell flat. Our eyes locked and my knees felt a tad weak. Fortunately, we were saved by the ear-piercing shriek of the microphone.

We both turned toward the podium as an elderly gent in bold stripes began to speak. I recognized Cyrus Worthington, the quirky director of the Smithsonian. Despite his eccentricities he was quite a catch for this delegation of pencil pushers. Cyrus had long ago realized that a career in the world of philanthropy required more than a PhD. Hard cash and impeccable social connections were equally essential and he had married both.

"Ladies and Gentlemen, what a pleasure."

The origin of Cyrus's British accent baffled even his intimates. One wag suggested that he was the bastard son of an impoverished nobleman. His critics maintained that he had immersed himself in Masterpiece Theater and taken it to heart.

"On behalf of the Smithsonian, I want to introduce the guest curator of Asian Artifacts at the Beijing Museum, Dr. Jie-ling Chow. She has graciously accompanied the Golden Abacus, a priceless national treasure to our country as part of a cultural exchange."

Cyrus gazed fondly at Dr. Chow and said with a rakish glint in his eyes, "I'm sure you will agree with me that Jie-ling herself is a priceless national treasure as well."

What do you know? Surprisingly enough the old goat still had some life in him after all. Nervous titters flooded the room as the audience shifted uncomfortably. Dr. Chow was very poised and as her name "Jie-ling" suggested, quick witted.

"Thank you so much, Dr. Worthington. Your kindness overwhelms me. Please call me Jie. It is so much easier for my new friends."

Unlike Cyrus, Dr. Chow spoke English effortlessly and without any accent. I noted that she had gotten her professional degrees from Stanford, so she was no newcomer to the States. She was a trim, attractive woman of about my age with suspiciously black hair and a perpetual smile that set my teeth on edge.

Like a born trouper, Jie-ling launched into prepared remarks about the Abacus, its history and meaning to the Chinese people. I managed to crane my neck and scan the crowd without being too obvious. Several familiar faces nodded at me but Maude was not among them. Since she was pretty hard to miss, I supposed that Maude was pursuing the "Big Story" she'd hinted at.

Finally, the program concluded and the crowd stampeded for the bar. Free drinks trump culture any day particularly for the money-hungry green eyeshade crowd. Jonathon joined the pack, hastily excusing himself with a promise to meet me later. I felt the need for a stiff drink and a stab of desire for a cigarette. Even after ten years of abstinence, I could still remember the taste of that last butt. Maybe it was like sex—a dim but delicious memory.

I joined the long line at the bar and idly eavesdropped. Three men in front of me were engaged in a heated debate. I recognized one as Evan Braddock, the tax manager for Avalon Industries. He was a tall, balding man of middle years with a vastly inflated sense of self and a talent for stating the obvious.

Government employees were a lesser species to him as he had once explained to me.

"The really sharp guys are in the private sector," Evan intoned in the big brassy voice I loathed. "They compete in the big leagues and take the risks. The ones who play it safe work for the government."

I didn't know his companions. One of them was glaring at Evan with bulging eyes and clenched fists. Dare I hope he would flatten dear Ev? Probably not. Corporate combat rarely included fisticuffs although the occasional stab in the back was not unknown. The other guy was young, tall and fit with a suit that screamed deep discount. It would never make the grade in the boardroom but in this sea of polyester it passed with flying colors. The poor fellow, who I named Cheap Suit, was obviously a government employee. His tacky faux leather folder also proclaimed that he was an IRS employee.

I leaned closer to study him. He did look familiar but I just couldn't place him. When all else fails, eavesdropping is a skill that comes in handy. I am a skilled practitioner of that art.

"She KNOWS," said clenched fist. "What are we going to do?"

Braddock glowered at him. "Pipe down, and keep your cool. Everything's under control." Just as the conversation took an interesting turn, the IRS guy swiveled around and spied me.

"Do I know you?" he asked. "Aren't you some kind of executive?"

Yeah, I'm some kind of executive, dufus, the kind who knows you're up to no good!

I recalled Mary's emphasis on charm so instead of smiting him, I smiled graciously and extended my hand. "I'm Grace Quinn, and you are ...?"

Cheap Suit mumbled a greeting and grasped my hand in his sweaty paw. Braddock curled his lip and snarled a minimally civil greeting. The third guy stayed mute.

"We have to go, Ms. Quinn. So nice to see you again." Braddock hustled his buddies from the line and out the door leaving me very curious.

CHAPTER TWO

I tried to mingle but it wasn't easy. Several fellows chatted a bit but their minds weren't on taxes. That's the disadvantage of having a smiley face badge pinned conspicuously to your chest. You can't prove anything. Guys might be trying to read your name when they lower their gaze well below your neck. If their intentions were honorable, this crowd had a galloping case of eyestrain! Lord save me from horny geeks with calculators.

"Hey Grace, c'mon over here! It's great to see you!"

I stared into the big blue eyes of Therese Harding, a friend from yester-year.

Even though she's a CPA, she had somehow lost the memo about being a serious and deadly dull being. Therese was a hoot!

"Oh my God, I'm so glad to see you. How come you look so young?"

Therese grinned, "Girl, you see before you a poster child for the marvels of clean living. Take a closer look."

It isn't polite to gape but my mouth hung wide open. Therese looked a good decade younger than her real age. Since she brought up the subject, I got personal.

"Okay, what did you have done? You really didn't need anything."

Women are quite adept at peddling that line of pure bullshit. I didn't fool Therese for one minute.

"Nothing." she said complacently. "I cleansed my body of all toxins, fasted, and started working out." Therese pulled a compact from her purse and studied her face. "Why? Do you think I should my nose done?" she asked. "I knew it! It's awful, isn't it?"

"Absolutely not," I said. "You know I consider myself a nose person, and yours is perfect."

I'd commissioned some nose work myself a while back and believe me, I've studied every kind of proboscis.

Therese quickly glanced around her. "So what have you heard about the big scandal?"

"Scandal? Which one. Every day seems to bring another. Man do I hate twenty four-hour cable news."

"You know, the Tax Shelter mess. I hear that some very big names are going down. Idiots of course. They should have known someone would catch them."

"What! Is it anyone we know?" I hate being out of the loop on gossip. Maybe under the velvet claw of Mary Hagan I was losing my touch.

"Believe it or not, one of the dunderheads is a former IRS executive. Not the sharpest tool in the executive shed, but not a bad guy either ...."

"WHO? WHO?" I was beginning to feel like an owl.

"Harry Hawkins for one. Most of the others are private sector guys.

"Harry! I kind of liked him, even though his IQ was zoo-quality."

Therese giggled. "Well one of the other names floated around is definitely *not* one of your favorites."

I refused to beg. Therese finally tired of the waiting game and spilled her guts.

"Kelvin Cates—don't you just love it?"

"You mean the clown prince of Examination. He's too dumb to even know how to cheat. He probably thought it was legit."

Kelvin Cates was a member of my executive class. He frequently skated on ethical thin ice but his brainlessness gave him a built in diminished capacity defense. He was a big, bumbling jock who annoyed the hell out of me.

Therese tilted her chin in warning as someone pulled up a chair.

"Ladies, may I join you?" A well-built man in his forties with truly great hair made himself comfortable. The dancing eyes and sly smile belonged to Brett Roberts, another graduate of the IRS. I'd worked with him years ago in Houston.

Therese gazed fondly at Brett. "It's about time some handsome man rescued us. Sit down right here. I'm going to go get another drink so don't you run away." She jumped up, and headed, glass in hand for the bar.

"So what have you been up to, Grace. Sick of being a public servant yet?"

"When I am, you're the first person I'm going to call, Mr. Roberts. It's really nice to see you again."

"Well, just remember. I'm like the IRS collection policy—FIRM BUT FAIR—emphasis on the firm part, ma'am."

Brett was a tease. I happened to know he was very happily married with two small children.

"Just you remember the other collection saying, ONE CALL DOES IT ALL."

We both shook our heads, and chuckled at the old comedy routine.

"Hey Brett. I saw Jonathon Grey a while ago. Aren't you working at Stratton-Miles with his son?"

Brett's face darkened. "You know how much I love that old boy but his son is a whole different kettle of fish."

"I don't understand."

"Christopher Grey has none of his father's social graces," Brett snorted. "He's a smart kid, who's also a smart-ass. He may not be quite as smart as he thinks he is either. I'd hate to see Jonathon caught up in something."

"He's in trouble? Chris, I mean." I held my breath, fearing what would come next.

Unfortunately Brett clammed up and unlike Therese he was good at staying silent.

I tried a diversionary tactic to loosen him up.

"Guess what? I ran into Maude, almost literally. She was incoherent, blabbering about some big story she was going to break. Something that would shatter lives, end careers, etc. It's probably just Maude fudging the truth again, but she was pretty convincing."

Brett looked shaken. "If that nosey bitch is involved, you can bet it's something big. She's been sniffing around Stratton and a couple of other firms asking things."

"What kind of things?" Suddenly I flashed back to Evan Braddock and his musketeers, and Therese's hints about tax shelters.

"Oh, nothing. Listen Grace, forget I said anything. You know how this industry thrives on gossip. Look, I gotta go. Keep cool." Brett patted my arm and loped toward the door leaving me more curious than ever.

Therese came to the rescue juggling two Cosmopolitans in her hands. "Hey, where's Brett-man" she said. "I wanted to talk to him."

"I don't know. We started discussing Chris Grey and he got all weird. Then I mentioned Maude Morrissey and he freaked. Therese—what the hell is going on?"

She gave me a sharp look. "You mean you really don't know? Chris Grey left Stratton six months ago. He hooked up with a boutique law firm that renders advisory opinions on tax shelters and other shady deals."

"So what if it stays legal? Shaky but legal. Besides, I thought that whole tax shelter mess was over with years ago."

Therese gazed speculatively at me. "You'd be surprised. The big boys found greener pastures but a few bottom feeders are still milking it. You know what a thin line it is and there's always an audience of suckers who believe that bilge. Ripe for the picking."

My heart sank. If Chris Grey joined a rogue firm he could be in big trouble. Those schemes were fighting words to the IRS and they pounced on offenders with big government feet. Bad guys often brandished a legal opinion from some smarmy law firm saying their approach was A-Okay. I hoped Chris Grey wasn't mired in that kind of mess. Jonathon, the soul of rectitude, would be devastated.

"Could Maude really be on to something?" I asked.

Therese coughed delicately. "You know what her record is like. Hardly pristine. She's probably rooting through the forest like a truffle-seeking hog. On the other hand even a blind pig can find the occasional truffle."

"That's really mean." I had to admit it was a great visual though. "Hey, let's go find Maude and chat her up. She may let something slip."

"If there's liquor involved she'll cop to the Kennedy Assassination." Therese was no big fan of Maude's but she was a good sport. "I suppose it wouldn't hurt to try."

"Great. You take the Regency Room and I'll cover the Exhibit Hall. Meet you back here at nine sharp."

Off we went, dodging the occasional grab and ignoring catcalls. A Security Guard sporting a frown and a sober navy blazer had planted himself outside the Exhibit Hall and blocked my path. He caved quickly and unlocked the door when I flashed my smiley badge at him.

The cavernous Exhibit Hall was deserted—all 40,000 feet of it. The one exception was the Abacus. It looked even more impressive bathed in half-light. Oddly enough its aura of mystery reminded me of the time I'd seen the Mona Lisa. I was overwhelmed, uncertain whether or not to genuflect or bow.

The mood was shattered by a dainty cough. I screamed and whirled around to face the elegant Dr. Jie-ling Chow.

We were both embarrassed. Dr. Chow touched my arm and said in her soft, precise voice, "Please forgive me—I ... I was keeping vigil. I didn't mean to frighten you."

"You're Dr. Chow. I'm Grace Quinn, from the IRS. I hoped to meet you, but not this way."

"You work for the IRS?" Jie-ling seemed frightened or at least ill at ease. Not an uncommon reaction to be sure.

She quickly regained her composure. "I did see your name on the program but you're so young for such an important post."

Did I mention how charming Dr. Jie-ling Chow could be? I revised my initial assessment of her and smiled. "Thanks. I had the same thought about you."

Her words about "keeping vigil" sounded strange. After all, the hotel had plenty of security. Wait a minute—scratch that. Other than the few rent-a-cops in blue blazers I hadn't seen a visible police presence. Maybe they were undercover trying hard to mimic the ill-fitting attire of the convention crowd.

"Have there been problems with the Abacus, Jie-ling?"

Her expression was guarded. "Not really, I'm just a bit anxious. After all it's my responsibility and if anything happened ...."

Something about Dr. Chow rang false. Maybe it was the rictus grin that never reached her eyes or the whiff of subservience she radiated around any available man. That helpless act evaporated instantly when a woman appeared. I chided myself for being culturally insensitive but stood by my assessment.

Jie-ling must have read my mind. She shifted uncomfortably and blurted out the truth.

"It's my fault! I tried to save money by hiring only a few guards. Now I'm terrified that something might go wrong. My family would be ruined!"

"Is the case wired to an alarm or something? It must be. And that glass thing looks mighty strong." I always believe in using technical terms whenever possible even though I'm a total Luddite where technology is concerned.

Jie-ling shrugged. "I'm probably being foolish, Ms. Quinn. Don't mind me. The Abacus should be fine until tomorrow. After that it goes to the *Freer* for a month and becomes the Museum's problem instead of mine. Besides, Dr. Worthington said not to worry about anything. Please excuse me."

She whisked gracefully toward the exit without a second glance or a parting word, leaving the vigil to me. It was obvious that Maude wasn't there so I decided to check out the information booth I would staff the next day. It wasn't hard to find. By ignoring the slick high tech offerings of the private firms, the low-rent blue and white eagle of the Treasury Department stood out like a beggar at the feast. The IRS of all organizations could never sponsor something that looked like a waste of the Taxpayer's money. The Press loved to trumpet anything that put us in a bad light and lately they had uncovered a number of faux pas.

I found the stodginess of our exhibit rather comforting. The old booth looked both ageless and stoic, chock full of pamphlets, flash drives, business cards and paperclips that were already obsolete. We couldn't dispense nifty little keepsakes like the private folks but we freely gave advice. In return, most people gave us a wide berth.

The creaking of the Exhibit Hall door announced Therese's arrival. She had an extra spring in her step that meant only one thing. Her perpetual quest for a suitable mate must have been successful or promised to be.

"I couldn't find Maude anywhere," she said. "Isn't that just like her? When you want to find her she vanishes and if you try to avoid her, she's all over you."

"What kept you, then?" I summoned my mean teacher look.

"Oh, I ran into Lon Wesson and couldn't get away." Guilt suffused her face but Therese hung tough.

"Didn't you and he have a *thing* at one time?"

Therese curled her lip. "Must you remind me? Our encounter was brief and I do mean brief. Talk about your minute men! His wife can have him. Come on let's go eat. I'm starving."

We left the hotel and sauntered towards the Dupont Circle area. A slight breeze made the evening marginally cooler and the stroll bearable. We agreed on Italian food and claimed a table on the patio of Tomate's, a restaurant known for large portions and reasonable prices. I was studying the menu when Therese grabbed my arm.

"Grace—look across the street."

I fumbled in my purse for my glasses. Myopia is my middle name but so is vanity. By the time I was actually able to see anything the street was deserted.

"Well, what did I miss?"

"It was Maude, and you'll never guess who she was with?"

Guessing games bore me. Easier to surrender than play along with Therese. "Okay. I give up. Who was she with?"

"Christopher Grey—and he didn't look happy!"

"Which way did they go? Maybe we should follow them."

"What? Are you crazy? They got into a cab, and besides I'm famished."

Therese was right. Just because I love mysteries, and just because I once had a small but significant role in solving a murder it didn't make me Hercule Poirot or even Miss Marple.

We ate a fabulous carb-laden meal and wandered back to the hotel full of guilt. I was ambling down the long corridor toward my room when I realized that my notes for the big speech were missing. Damn! The San Simone has 880 guest rooms and despite the convention and routine business traffic, it felt deserted. I wasn't keen on tramping around the place in the dark looking for my notes. On the other hand, an audience of 900 very literal minded accountants expected me to deliver a rousing speech. The choice was clear.

I tried the Regency room where a cleaning crew was valiantly trying to tidy up. No notebook there. It had to be in the Exhibit Hall at the IRS booth. That meant meandering through 40,000 feet of dead space by myself. I thought of calling Therese but it seemed silly and cowardly.

Oddly enough the doors were unlocked and only the exit signs were visible. The friendly man in blue had vanished too. I shuddered, revisiting every creepy thriller I had ever read.

Even the Abacus was cloaked in shadows. So much for Dr. Chow's vigil and security fears. I moved toward the center of the room and stopped short. Part of the glass container was shattered and shards of glass littered the floor. The Abacus, bathed in a ghostly light, was the lone sentry. I crept toward it with my heart beating a frantic tattoo. Someone had tried very hard to yank the treasure off the pedestal. If only I had my cell phone! The damn thing would have come in handy for once.

I crept toward the door and sprawled headlong onto the floor next to the corpse of Maude Morrissey. Screams caught in my throat as I stared into her eyes. Maude looked strangely at peace, illuminated by the dull glow of the emergency exit. A glass obelisk protruded from her heart and a crimson pool seeped into the carpet. A rustling sound ratcheted my adrenaline to overload, leaving my brain strangely disconnected from my legs. I couldn't move, couldn't even scream. I felt no pain from the glass fragments. An inane phrase kept popping into my brain: dead space, dead space.

A familiar voice spoke from the darkness adding to the nightmare. "Don't be afraid Grace. It's me."

As he stepped toward the Abacus, I saw the face of Jonathon Grey.

CHAPTER THREE

I blinked my eyes and tried to focus. Slowly, sensation returned and I struggled to regain my sea legs. Jonathon reached out and steadied me.

"Easy Grace, you're bleeding."

I glanced down, puzzled by the rivulets of blood that stained my leg.

"You're in shock, let me get you to a chair."

"Jonathon, what ...?"

As she had in life, Maude commanded the stage slumbering silently, oblivious to everything. I couldn't tear my eyes away from her. Everything seemed so odd—for the first time in my recollection her mouth was shut. Maude consumed every molecule of oxygen in the room even though she no longer breathed the air.

Jonathon found me a seat, and stood silently at my side. For once his legendary poise deserted him and he seemed as lost as I was. I caught his eye and saw confusion, and yes, a hint of fear and uncertainty.

"What happened? Who hurt Maude?" I couldn't bring myself to say murdered.

"I don't know. Maybe it was an accident." Jonathon was lying. We both realized that an accident was quite impossible. I fought to suppress a giggle and lost. It was a prelude to hysteria and so tasteless that I shuddered.

"Maude always wanted a big story," I said. "Now *she's* it. She'll need a *ghost* writer."

Jonathon ignored the levity and walked slowly toward the main door. "I'm going to get help. Can you stay with her, Grace?"

I really had no choice. Besides, the room was empty so I wasn't in any danger. Before he exited, Jonathon spun round. "You're going to have to trust me. I had nothing to do with Maude's death."

I desperately wanted to believe him. He had mentioned a meeting with Maude when we spoke earlier but it was Chris Gray who Therese saw arguing with Maude. I wondered where Chris was now.

Time had no meaning for me. I ran the gamut of emotions from fear to lethargy as I waited for help. Suddenly, the door crashed open as Jonathon returned accompanied by a very bewildered security guard with torn blue blazer and bruised forehead. The poor man kept rubbing his head and mumbling.

"Grace, this is Mr. Kingman, the guard ...."

"Private police." The man corrected Jonathon forcefully.

Jonathon nodded and continued. "Mr. Kingman responded to a radio call shortly before midnight."

"And I got clobbered!!" Kingman interrupted. "I'm not feeling so good." He swayed and would have fallen had Jonathon not pushed a chair under him.

"Easy does it. Are you okay?" As he grasped Kingman's shoulder, I noticed a wide red stain on Jonathon's suit that hadn't been there before. Blood and Brioni don't mix. That's a fashion tip worth noting. I angled my body away from him and closed my eyes.

Despite the chaos, his voice was the same rumbling baritone I knew so well. "Don't worry, Grace. The police are on their way. They'll know how to handle this."

Kingman suddenly glimpsed Maude's hennaed toe protruding from her leather sandal. "Oh my God!" he gasped. "That's a body! Someone died." This time he did faint. He flopped flounder-like on the floor and lay as still as Maude's corpse.

At that moment the police arrived—two patrolmen flanking a trim blond man wearing a trench coat just like in the movies. His was well tailored more Burberry than rumpled Columbo, but the impact was the same.

"I'm Lieutenant James Clarke," said Trench Coat. He had a clipped prep school accent that seemed out of place in an

American cop. British novels feature police inspectors from the monied classes but Americans not so much.

James Clarke seemed very much in charge and cool, almost glacial. He pointed at the uniforms and issued a brisk command. "You two secure the crime scene. I suppose *this* guy is still among the living?" He pointed to poor Kingman. "Paramedics will be here soon to sort him out."

I straightened my shoulders and gave Clarke the big-eyed look. Apparently I failed to impress him since he stared rudely at my torn hose and bleeding leg.

"Did you mix it up with the deceased?" he smirked. "Let's start by getting your names. You first." He pointed at me and flipped open his notebook.

"My name is Grace Quinn." I forced myself to quit while I was ahead. It didn't faze Clarke at all.

"Good for you. Now tell me, Grace Quinn, what are you doing in the middle of a crime scene?"

"I came for my notes, for my speech tomorrow. You see I work for the IRS and ... "

Clarke raised his hands palms up. "Stop right there. My night's already ruined and *this* I definitely don't need."

I bit my lip and glared at him. Just what I needed—another tax hating cop. He'd probably made hash of his last return and had at least three ex-wives clamoring for alimony and child support.

Clarke turned to Jonathon. "Are you with the IRS, sir?"

Jonathon stayed calm. "My name is Jonathon Grey. I'm a former employee as was the victim, Ms. Morrissey."

"You *know* her?" Clarke exclaimed. "This may be my lucky day after all. Okay, you go outside with Officer Rhodes, and you, Ms. Quinn, stay with me."

I'd had no time to coordinate stories with Jonathon but I resolved to brazen it out and put Clarke firmly in his place. He switched on a tape recorder and lit a cigarette. When I stared pointedly at the "no smoking sign," Clarke ignored me.

"How well did you know the deceased?" He made that simple question sound like an accusation.

"I used to know her quite well but it's been years since we were close."

"You had some kind of cat-fight, did you?" The man sounded positively giddy at the prospect of cornering his prey. "Probably over some man."

"Certainly not. That's an incredibly sexist remark!"

Clarke ignored me again. "Then, what happened, Ms. Quinn? Enlighten me."

"I don't know. We just drifted apart after she left the Service. I did see her earlier tonight though."

"And?" Clarke took another long draw on his cigarette. "What was the victim doing at this shindig?"

"Maude was a member of the tax press—a reporter for *Tax Chat*."

Clarke choked back a laugh. "You mean someone actually pays to read that kind of stuff? Don't bother to answer, Ms. Quinn. I'm sure you find it tax issues fascinating. Okay, so what did she tell you?"

I recounted my conversation with Maude including the remark about the big story.

Clarke leaned forward in his chair. "What did she tell you about this big scoop? I need specifics."

"Nothing. I just told you that."

"Don't get huffy, Ms. Quinn, after all this *is* a murder investigation. How did your knees get all bloodied? Rendering first aid, were you?"

I explained my unfortunate tumble, a mishap that seemed to amuse Clarke.

"It's no wonder with those shoes," he said, pointing toward my stilettos. "They could be the murder weapon."

"Hardly, Lieutenant. I believe the glass shard protruding from her body solves that riddle."

Clarke leaned back and shook his head. "You think you're pretty smart, don't you, Ms. Quinn? Probably watch a lot of cop shows and solve every crime. Read thrillers too. Well get this straight—withholding evidence in a homicide is a felony."

"What evidence?" I summoned my sweetest smile for Clarke.

"Where was Mr. Gray when you came into this room?"

"I don't know."

Clarke narrowed his eyes. "Like hell you don't. No more games. You come clean with me on anything and anyone who even might be linked to your friend's murder. Or else."

"You don't scare me," I said with more bravado than I felt. "Now, may I go?"

Clark waved me toward the door after delivering one parting shot that compounded every cop cliché I'd ever read or watched on the tube.

"Go on. I know where to find you. Just don't leave town."

I stumbled out of the room almost gasping for air. This wasn't the first corpse I'd ever seen but it felt very personal. Maude had never been my best friend. Far from it. But she had been a part of my early life and we shared a lot of memories. I'd just finished graduate school when I joined the IRS, and Maude and I were sworn in, and introduced to the wonders of bureaucracy on the same day. Frankly I often considered her obnoxious and spiteful. But like her or not, the Maude I knew was a force of nature not some ungainly corpse sprawled on a hotel floor.

I glanced at the ornate bronze clock on the wall: 1:00 a.m., too late to call Therese or God forbid, my boss. Mary Hagan would have a cow when she heard about this. IRS people have a morbid fear of bad publicity and a murder would certainly qualify. She'd probably blame me for getting involved. Like I had a choice!

Where in the world had they taken Jonathon? I lurked near the elevator hoping to run into him without being spotted by Clarke. The elevator pinged, announcing the arrival of a disheveled Cyrus Worthington with his shadow, Jie-ling Chow. Cyrus was perilously close to hysteria a condition I was all too familiar with.

"The Abacus!" he gasped, "Did they take it? Oh my Lord, what am I going to do?"

Jie-ling clasped his elbow and guided him toward the Exhibition Hall. She glanced my way and stopped. Poor Cyrus almost took a header but he steadied himself at the last moment.

"Why are you here, Ms. Quinn?" said Dr. Chow. "Is the IRS involved in this somehow?"

The hour was late but this babe with her impeccably tailored suit and perfect hair annoyed the hell out of me. I smiled with just a hint of malice. It was either that or give her a shot in the chops.

Cyrus eluded her grasp and began pounding on the door.

"Let me in," he bellowed. "I must find it!"

Out of compassion and a dash of curiosity I called to Cyrus.

"Dr. Worthington, don't worry. The Abacus is safe."

That stopped him and the Ice Princess in their tracks. Worthington plopped down on the nearest chair and put his head in his hands. Jie-ling became Miss Congeniality.

"Tell us, please Ms. Quinn, where is the Abacus. Dr. Worthington got a call about a robbery and of course we came immediately."

"Apparently someone attempted to steal the Abacus. It's case is bloodied but unbowed." I suddenly remembered Maude, and felt sickened by my glib comment. "There was an ... incident, a crime."

Worthington's head popped up like a turtle's. "Yes, yes ... but the Abacus is all right?"

"Someone was *murdered*, don't you get it?"

Jie-ling Chow blanched. "Who was it? Was it Mr. Kingman?" She turned to Cyrus, "He's our security guard.

Neither of them seemed especially concerned. After all, the Abacus was their priority.

"You should probably speak with Lieutenant James Clarke. He's inside the Exhibit Hall."

Clarke was just the man to staunch a hysterical curator and Dr. Chow would appeal to his protective side. I'm sure he fancied himself a knight errant or some sort of super hero.

It was 2:25, and I was exhausted. I stumbled to the elevator, found my room, and fell into bed fully clothed. I had just gotten drowsy when the phone rang. DRAT! For once, Jonathon's mellow tones failed to move me.

"Grace, I have to see you. What's your room number?"

"412," I mumbled.

"Fine, I'll be right up."

Great. I had five minutes to make myself presentable.

By the time Jonathon rapped on the door, I'd managed to restore some sense of order to my hair and clothing. Even murder didn't justify poor grooming.

Unfortunately he was not alone. Chris Grey filed in ahead of his father and stood with clenched hands and lowered eyes. Brett was right, Chris had none of his father's grace. He was tall, well over six feet, with closely cropped hair and grey-green eyes. Obviously, he inherited some good habits from dear old dad, because his frame was lean and muscular. Unlike his father, however, he wore a perpetual sneer.

Jonathon closed the door and took my hand.

"Grace, I'm so sorry to bother you but this is important. Have you met my son, Chris?"

"Nope. Haven't had the pleasure." I grabbed the limp hand that Chris Grey extended and smiled.

His manner was decidedly sullen. Maybe it was a habit he'd picked up selling sleazy tax shelters to the great unwashed. Or maybe it was a legacy from his mother.

"I don't know what we're even doing here, Dad. No offense, Ms. Quinn."

"Chris, Grace is a friend! She has a right to know where we stand. Unless I'm very much mistaken, this Inspector Clarke is pretty sharp."

I waved them to the only two chairs in my room. Despite some of my past fantasies this was no ménage à trois.

Chris Grey clutched the arms of his chair in a death grip. "What did you tell the police? How much do you know?"

I ignored his poor manners as a favor to Jonathon. Perhaps they don't teach civility in Law School. Jonathon leaned forward and put his hand on his son's shoulder.

"Grace, I didn't kill Maude. In fact, I got there just before you did. I was supposed to meet her at midnight but I was late. She was already dead."

"You don't have to explain anything, Jonathon. You could never harm anyone." I turned toward his surly son. "On the other hand I had dinner at La Tomate, and *you* were there with Maude, Chris. You two caused quite a little scene."

Chris moved the edge of his chair, tapping his toes. "What did you tell Clarke?" he asked. Those grey-green eyes were glued to my face.

Jonathon looked ashen as he turned toward his son.

"For heaven's sake, Chris, what's going on? Grace ...?"

"I was with a friend but don't worry I didn't tell Clarke anything. Not yet. He seemed more interested in *you,* Jonathon."

Jonathon and Chris exchanged glances. Maybe it was the hour or the memory of poor Maude's corpse but I grew weary of social courtesies and polite evasions.

I stood and spoke directly to Chris. "Word is, you might get indicted. Did Maude have some dirt on your firm?"

Chris held himself as taut as a spring. "I don't have to tell you anything," he said.

"We're here to get Grace's help. Stop acting like a spoiled kid, Chris." I'd never seen Jonathon quite so grave. He sat upright in his chair; soldier straight, staring at his son. "If you won't tell her, I will. Chris left Stratton about a year ago and got a position as in-house counsel to Tax Champions." Jonathon's voice was flat and unemotional. He might easily have been reading from the tax code.

"Isn't he a bit *young* for that level job? I asked. "What is he, four years out of law school?"

Chris spit out his words. "You're pretty *young* to be an executive, and I don't see you apologizing. Or is it different when you're white?"

"Whoa—hold the phone. Chris, you are out of line here!" Jonathon's voice shook with emotion "Let's be calm and discuss this rationally."

"I'm sorry Chris," I lied. "It's just surprising. General Counsel slots usually require a lot of experience."

"Yeah, well they're a young company and they wanted someone progressive not some old fogey. Anyhow, they had an older guy from one of the big firms as their primary legal advisor."

I didn't dare look at Jonathon. We both knew that Tax Champions was on the IRS hit list. Chris Grey must be terribly naïve, or thoroughly corrupt. Either way if the feds started crawling all over that outfit, the legal advice furnished by young Mr. Grey could land *him* in jail while the empty suit from the big law firm simply faded away. What a chump!

"Okay, how did Maude fit in? Was she going public with something?"

Chris swallowed hard, and looked at his father. Jonathon nodded.

"She had a source giving her inside information. Tax Champions grossed over $100 million bucks last year, and Maude wanted to blow the whistle. She called it a pyramid scheme, a fraud."

"I've read your promotional materials," I said. "You do make some pretty wild claims."

Jonathon cleared his throat. "Grace, you know that several retired IRS executives are on staff there. People who used to be respected."

I recalled what Therese said. "I hope you don't mean Harry Hawkins or that fool Kelvin Cates."

Jonathon averted his eyes. "Harry and Kelvin are both involved. The point is that Maude was blowing this thing all out of proportion. She could have ruined Chris."

I felt ill. Jonathon had neatly outlined a great motive for both him and Chris.

"Jonathon, is that why you arranged a meeting with Maude—to plead with her?"

"To *reason* with her."

Chris leapt up and started pacing.

"Come on Dad, it's no use. Anyhow, it's none of her business. Let's go."

This arrogant young ass was cruising for a bruising. Chris probably inherited his social skills from his mother—a congenital defect! For Jonathon's sake I said nothing.

Jonathon walked over and stood before me.

"I'm sure Lieutenant Clarke will question all of us again tomorrow. If you could just—don't lie of course—but maybe stall him."

I couldn't stand the bruised look in Jonathon's eyes, or his air of defeat. Suddenly it hit me!

"Hey, there's something else to consider here. The Abacus. Maude might have blundered into a theft-in-progress. After all, someone *did* try to steal the it."

Jonathon brightened a bit but Chris maintained his stony stare.

I took Jonathon's hand. "Maybe the police can chew on that theory while we explore other options."

His eyes widened. "Wait a minute, Grace. The last time you got involved in a murder you were nearly killed! I can't let you take that risk."

"Oh don't worry," I said. "That was years ago. I've learned a lot since then." I handed Chris a pad and paper.

"Chris, you need to make a list of everyone involved in this Tax Champions mess who is here this week. That's a good starting point. Jonathon, why don't you chat up some of your old cronies and get any gossip they've heard."

"What about you—what are you going to do?" Chris Grey's tone had thawed a bit.

He was actually quite handsome when he wasn't snarling or sulking.

"I'm going to immerse myself in Chinese culture. I've always been fascinated by the Ming period."

As they filed out the door, I rapped Chris on the arm.

"Oh and Chris, don't forget to mention what you were doing with Maude this evening. It's bound to come in handy."

As I fastened the lock, I heard him swearing softly.

CHAPTER FOUR

I knew absolutely nothing about Chinese art, culture or the Ming dynasty. My plan was to learn enough to ingratiate myself with Cyrus Worthington and his shadow Jie-ling Chow. The solution was almost too easy: Research. I got top marks in graduate school for my research and that skill would come in handy now. I needed to acquire a thin veneer of knowledge, just enough to look reasonably conversant with the Abacus and its origins.

The opening session of the conference had been postponed, so I had the time to do a bit of sleuthing. The best place to get a crash course was at the Smithsonian's Asian artifacts center right in D.C. I trudged over to the Dupont Metro stop, and clutched the handrail as the escalator stairs slowly descended the steep steel mountain. D.C. veterans called the Metro the "Vertical Commute." Personally, I've always liked the anonymity of public transportation—no fishing gratuities out of your purse, or enduring inane conversations with illiterate cab drivers. I would arrive at the Smithsonian metro stop with a minimum of bother.

The Smithsonian complex includes a bewildering number of buildings. A uniformed guard gave me reasonably clear directions, and I soon reached a door labeled, "Asian Pacific American Program." What a mouthful! Carefully, I wedged open the door, prepared to bolt in case I had invaded official space.

"Good morning. May I help you?"

A stunning Chinese man in his thirties looked up from his desk, smiled warmly, and stood. I think he was Chinese—I *know* he was Asian and incredibly handsome, possibly the best-looking man I had ever seen. Tall, dark and gorgeous, what's not to like? I forced myself not to stare. He was probably used to that and something told me it was the wrong move. Besides my mission had nothing to do with romance. This was strictly business.

"Hello. I'm not sure this is the right place to go. I was hoping to find reference material on the Ming dynasty and some of the current cultural exhibits."

"We don't have the material right here but I can get you started. Please sit down. My name is Patrick Fong, by the way."

"Hi Patrick. I'm Grace Quinn."

I observed that Patrick Fong was a shade over six feet and very fit. He had a full head of thick black hair and dark, dancing eyes. Correction. His eyes were mesmerizing. I revised my cover story and opted for the truth or a reasonable facsimile.

"Actually, I saw the Golden Abacus yesterday and was fascinated by its history. I want to learn more if I can."

"Really," he said. "You probably don't know this, but someone tried to steal it last night. The story broke on Twitter not the *Post.*"

I had a couple of choices here—act surprised, spill the beans or improvise. I opted for door number three—half-truths and evasions.

"No kidding! I bet you know Dr. Worthington, and of course, Dr. Chow. I met them yesterday. This must be awful for them."

He coughed, almost as though he were snickering. "You're right. In fact I'll be joining them shortly. Everyone's quite upset as you can imagine."

Patrick Fong folded his arms and waited. His bright eyes were alight with curiosity and I don't think he totally bought my act. It was too late to jump ship so I plunged right in.

"Exactly what does the Asian Pacific American Program do? I've never heard of it before."

"Oh, it has a very broad mission. Most of us are volunteers who spend a few hours helping out. The organization encourages cultural exchanges and the like."

Patrick Fong had a particularly sexy mouth with a full lower lip that begged to be kissed. I gave myself a mental shakedown. *Good grief, girl. Don't be foolish.*

I stared at him, trying to keep focused. "You're not really a museum guide, are you?"

"Oh no. I'm a Fed like many of my fellow Washingtonians." Patrick nodded politely at me as if my question was foolish. "Do you live here Ms. Quinn, or are you a visitor?"

I hesitated, zeroing in on his hands. They were exceptionally large and well shaped with long tapering fingers. Some women believe that big hands equate to the size of other appendages and pleasurable pursuits. Personally, I'd had mixed results. Call me a skeptic.

I tried to regain my poise. Men simply don't affect me this way. My co-workers were mostly male and I'd learned to ignore their appearance especially when sex reared its ugly head. Oops. *Bad metaphor, Grace. Get with the program.*

The amused glint in Patrick Fong's eyes suggested that he had read my mind. He was probably used to idle speculation and unrequited lust—the rogue. Despite a few unfortunate encounters in my past, I was neither a groupie nor any man's love slave.

I recalled a passage on strategic retreat from Sun Tzu's *Art of War*. That seemed particularly appropriate under the circumstances. According to the Master, it was sometimes wise to resist attractive bait and regroup one's forces. This was one of those times and Patrick Fong certainly fit the bill when it came to attractive bait.

I pasted a faux smile on my face and rose. "What a coincidence. I'm a Federal employee too. I appreciate your time, Patrick, but I better head back to my convention."

I had to escape before he became too inquisitive. There was something about this wildly sexy man that was making me sweat.

"Maybe I'll see you over at the San Simone, Grace." Despite his nice guy manner, I sensed a hint of steel behind those dreamy eyes.

"I'll look forward to it. Nice meeting you."

I opened the door and walked briskly to the subway. Patrick Fong had handed me some brochures about the Freer and Sackler Museums and their Asian Art exhibits. Come to think of it that's where the Abacus was bound when the cops released it. Today's expedition proved that private detective wasn't a sound career choice for me. I wasted precious time and learned almost nothing for my trouble except that I was sorely in need of a man's touch. I'm usually the one in control, a dominatrix of taxes, capable of bringing strong men to heel. Grilling accountants was a snap compared to facing a guy with film star looks and quick wits. On the other hand, I'd never met an accountant who was anything like Patrick Fong.

When I reached the San Simone, the lobby was bustling with hungry guests. I quickly scanned the sea of faces hoping to find Therese among the throng.

"Ouch!" I yelped as a fingernail stabbed my back.

"I thought I might find you here. Let's grab a chair and have a nice chat. We'll drink some sweet tea." Mary Hagan looked like an ad for Vogue. Her makeup was subtle, her platinum bob gleamed and I detected just a whiff of Creed in the air. By comparison I felt and looked like a frump. My sensible walking shoes and windblown hair were no match for the smooth perfection of Mary Hagan. She immediately came to the point.

"Okay, now spill! What's this about Maude? Did you really find her body?"

"How come you know about that?" I asked. "It's not even in the *Post* yet!"

Mary gave me a pitying look and went on the offensive. "Grace, Grace, must I remind you that I was once part of Inspection? Plus, you shirked your obligation to report this to me. What was that all about?"

Oh right, the Treasury Inspector General outfit, a brand of secret police that rivaled the KGB. The creepers and peepers as those in the know called them. Mary had proudly served in that nest of vipers and always flaunted it. They were tied in to the local cops, the FBI, and every other security force in the country. Too bad. James Clarke probably clicked his heels and genuflected to the Fed gods before taking any action. He seemed to have a healthy distaste for IRS. On the other hand all blood ran blue in law enforcement.

Mary Hagan tapped her well-shod foot. "Grace, while we're young, please."

I gave my boss a mostly accurate account excluding any mention of the Grey clan and Patrick Fong. Mary leaned back and slowly sipped her tea.

"You know, I never really warmed up to Maude," she said. "A while back she adopted two kittens from a shelter, kept them for two years, and then ditched them like yesterday's trash. They weren't "convenient" she told me, without the slightest trace of conscience."

Mary and I both loved animals. I had to agree that Maude was a selfish bitch who was probably capable of anything— including blackmail. *De Mortuis nil nisi bonum,* or so they say. I've never subscribed to that tactic of whitewashing the dead. Besides whoever devised that phrase didn't know Maude Morrissey.

Mary's smile was smug as she went for the kill. "I'm surprised you didn't mention Jonathon Grey. I heard he was with you."

"Oops. I forgot. Jonathon had an appointment with her. He got there about the time I did."

"Hmm. His son's name has been popping up a lot in hallway conversation. I'd steer clear of them if I were you, Grace. Could mean trouble."

"Jonathon has been wonderful to me. He's my friend and mentor for years and if you think ...."

Mary held up her pinky. "Okay, I get the message but be careful. The Commissioner is giving the keynote speech today and let me tell you, he takes no prisoners when it comes to these shenanigans. Word to the wise." Mary pushed her glass away and rose. "Good luck with your seminar. Keep me posted." She glided away without a backward glance.

I put my elbows on the table and clutched my aching head. One loathsome fact of life in IRS was the inbred paranoia and willingness to cut off anyone tainted by even a whiff of scandal. I'd seen fine people abandoned by their colleagues over nothing more than a whisper. Loyalty meant something to me. I refused to cave to the gods of ambition.

Three hours of sleep were simply not enough! My mental fog lifted as I heard my name.

"Grace Quinn, where have you been? I've been scouring the hallways for you, girl." Bright blue eyes and a sunny smile lit up Therese Harding's face. She was just too perky for my present state of mind.

"Go away. Leave me alone."

"Are you kidding? Give me the full scoop on Maude. This is soooo exciting."

I jerked upright. "Therese, this isn't some thriller. Maude was murdered, and believe me it was *not* pretty."

"I heard she was nude. Was she raped?" With her mouth slightly agape and her eyes lazering my face, Therese reminded me of a raptor in mid-flight.

"NO! At least I don't think so. The autopsy findings haven't been released. And she was fully clothed, for your information." Therese folded her arms and gave me her patient look.

"They're calling you the "Typhoid Mary" of the IRS, you know. After all, you do seem to attract corpses."

I felt my blood pressure rise. "That is so unfair! Can I help it if I'm a victim of circumstance?"

Therese was unrepentant. "What about the Abacus? The police have cordoned off the Exhibit room and old Cyrus Worthington is hopping mad. Dr. what's her face is circling the room like a buzzard."

Hmm ... so Jie-ling Chow was still here. Maybe I could engineer a chance meeting and ...."

"Grace, you're zoning out again. You know, maybe we should tell the cops about Maude and Chris Grey last night. They looked pretty intense."

I had to play this scene very cautiously or Therese would suspect something.

"Well, I didn't see anything. If you recall, you were the witness. I guess you could track down the detective in charge. He's probably somewhere in police headquarters."

Therese wrinkled her nose. "It was probably nothing. I don't want to waste my time chasing after some paunchy cop with donut dust on his coat. Maybe I'll just wait to see if they ask anything."

"Good idea. To answer your question, the Abacus wasn't stolen. Someone beat on that Plexiglas case and shattered it but the Abacus survived."

"So what was Maude doing there? Probably skulking around hoping to witness a crime. You know what a busy-body she was."

Therese knew Latin, but didn't subscribe to that old bromide either. Forget about saying only good things about the departed.

"I meant to ask you. Who could fill me in on this Tax Champions mess? Mary says the Commissioner is speaking today and I want to sound informed."

Therese gave me a level glance and shook her head. "Tell the truth, Grace. Chris Grey *is* mixed up in this and you want to help Jonathon. You were always hot for him."

Blood rose straight to the roots of my hair. I tried and failed to maintain a dignified silence. "Come on, help me out. Who should I talk to?"

Therese gathered her things and checked her watch. "*We* should talk to Brett Roberts. Let's get going. After all you have a speech to give in ten minutes."

I hustled toward the auditorium, deep in thought. Most people fear public speaking. Not me, I've always had a natural gift for it. When I reached the podium, a sea of eager faces awaited me, with open notebooks and pens poised to record each pearl of wisdom.

Fortunately the crowd was livelier than usual and before long they were laughing and nodding at the appropriate times. Most of the 600 seats were filled but I could only see the first row. I was the warm-up act for the Commissioner. My mission was to rouse the group and keep them focused on the immortal message: "Tax compliance is every American's duty."

I recognized a few old friends and at least one new face planted front row center. The sinewy form of Patrick Fong heightened the sex appeal of the audience by 1000%. I was thrilled but puzzled. What in the world was he doing there? Most Americans would rather be barbecued than listen to a discussion of federal taxes. Even I felt filled to capacity after an hour or so.

After fielding several questions, the session ended on a positive note. I glanced up from the microphone and there he was.

"Ms. Quinn, I enjoyed your presentation. Most informative. Entertaining too." Patrick lowered his voice to a near whisper. "May I speak with you for a minute?"

"Sure." In my confusion I spilled a sheaf of papers all over the stage. He bent over to help and succeeded in cracking his head against my skull. So much for foreplay.

"Are you okay? I'm so clumsy, I should never have been named Grace."

He chuckled, picked up my briefcase and helped me down the steps. "Do you have time for coffee? I'd like to talk with you about last night."

"Why are you so interested? Idle curiosity, personal or professional reasons?"

"A bit of all three," he said with a grin. His smile was captivating and I was fairly sure that he knew it.

Just then, Therese joined us. "Hey Grace, I found Brett. He's free right now."

Her eyes widened as she sized up Patrick Fong. Who could blame her? He put every other male in the room and possibly on the planet, to shame.

"Hi, I'm Therese, a friend of Grace," she said, giving him the blue eyed stare.

Patrick handed me my briefcase and shook her hand.

"I'll leave you ladies to your appointment. May I phone you later, Grace?"

"Sure. Nice seeing you again."

I watched him stride up the aisle with the grace of an athlete. He was indeed a fine specimen of the Asian Pacific American Program. Maybe I could apply for a guest membership.

CHAPTER FIVE

Therese gave me a vicious jab in the ribs. "Earth to Grace. Remember our meeting with Brett? While you're at it, tell me everything about your admirer over there. He's *gorgeous!*"

"You think every man under eighty is cute. Anyway, I just met him this morning."

"So what? Sometimes that's enough."

Before Therese renewed her attack we reached Morsels, the hotel's casual restaurant.

Brett Roberts was wedged in a corner table for three trying to look inconspicuous. He waved as we entered the café and pulled out our chairs. Brett had a hunted look that told me Therese had trapped him into this tutorial.

"Grace, what happened to Maude? Everyone's upset over it." Brett was a Southern gentleman who wouldn't pry unless I encouraged him. With Therese around, I didn't need to say a word. She could barely contain herself.

"Do you believe it, Brett?" she said. "Maude got bopped on the head and Grace found her!"

I didn't correct anything she said. Nobody needed to know the real cause of death. Even I had my doubts.

Brett grimaced. "My God. Maude was annoying but that's unbelievable."

"Grace will find the killer, won't you Grace?" Therese gave me her sunny smile.

I was perilously close to becoming a murderer myself. If looks could kill, Therese would have died on the spot. I turned to Brett.

"Look, Brett, I need, an outline of some of these pyramid schemes and any other dodgy things they're pedaling. Just a sketch, strictly informal."

Brett cleared his throat, and glanced around uneasily. "I want to help, but it's really all speculation. I don't know anything for sure."

Therese snorted. "That's bullshit! You're the one who told me about Tax Champions, Brett. Come on. GIVE."

He shrugged, and took a deep breath.

"Remember, I'm just speaking in generalities here. The concept is simple and elegant. Tax Champions found a market share that was virtually untapped. They made a big play for the wage earner, 'home business' crowd. Do you know how many taxpayers that covers?"

Therese's eyes bugged out. "Wait a minute, you know how few of them are really entitled to those deductions. Why that's criminal!"

Brett grinned. "Just think of the potential targets. Millions of everyday Joes who think that rich guys get all the breaks. Seems like every politician from the President on down squawks about the middle class getting screwed by Uncle Sam. Tax Champions is doing something about it."

The audacity of the scheme stunned me. Its theme was an updated version of 'only the little people pay taxes'. Clever marketing and ambiguous language sounded plausible. The appeal to class resentment made it irresistible.

"Naturally, some home business deductions are perfectly legal. But Tax Champions claims to halve the average Joe's taxes by writing off food, entertainment, vacations—you name it." Brett shook his head and smiled ruefully.

Therese snorted. "Okay, assuming even some of this was justified, what business are these people going to write off? I mean they have to have some kind of business even if it's shaky."

"Exactly! That's where the pyramid scheme comes in—they set up home-based businesses selling the same tax evasion schemes to thousands of other suckers. Their sales managers bring in more recruits, who bring in more. You get the drift."

I watched Brett as he talked, and remembered his comments about Chris Grey.

"Brett, how much does it cost to become one of these sales managers?

"I understand they charge in the neighborhood of $5,000 bucks upfront, with monthly fees for administrative expenses. Multiply that by the thousands who sign up, and you get a nice healthy profit."

Therese got an aha moment.

"Wait a minute. Are you telling me that former IRS guys like Cates and Hawkins agree with this nonsense? I mean, they were never geniuses but at least I thought they were honest."

Brett cleared his throat. "They say these are genuine for-profit businesses and there are plenty of legitimate businesses that rely on a similar structure."

I felt sick. "Yeah, but those businesses sell tangible products, like cosmetics, or cleaning products. This sells nothing. I've heard it called Tax Alchemy."

Therese turned and stared at me. "Naturally, they have legal counsel, some attorney who tells them how close to the line they can go."

I couldn't meet her eyes.

Brett yawned, and crossed his legs. "I think we all know at least one of their lawyers, don't we, Grace?

Therese yelped. "Chris Grey. Who would have ever thought that the son of a straight arrow like Jonathon Grey would be telling yokels they could write-off their nauseating trips to Disney World. Talk about the magic kingdom!"

"Hold on," I cautioned. "We don't know Chris has done anything illegal. And where did Maude come in? Was she really zeroing in on Tax Champions, Brett?"

"I only know what I hear," Brett said. "Chris did a lot of bragging after he left Stratton. Said he was making half a million big ones. I told you, Grace that kid is just too damn puffed up. Jonathon's kid." Brett shook his head in disgust.

"Tell me, have you seen either Harry Hawkins, or Kelvin Cates around?"

"I haven't," Therese said. "If I had, I'd run the other way anyhow. Cates always was an idiot."

Brett frowned. "Yeah, I saw Harry last night. He was hanging around the front desk, waiting for someone. Grace, why are you involved in this mess anyway? Is it some special assignment for new Executives these days?"

"I told you this is strictly off the record. I owe it to Maude to help find her killer."

Brett stood up. "Young lady, that is the biggest pile of horse pucky I've heard all day. You didn't like her any better than the rest of us did. Take my advice and leave everything to the police. There's a shitload of money involved in this thing and that can turn people nasty."

Therese jumped in. "It probably had to do with that Abacus anyway. Maude thought she was some kind of crime-busting reporter instead of a stringer for a third rate tax sheet."

She almost convinced me. Then I saw James Clarke silhouetted in the doorway. He pointed to me and headed straight for our table.

"Oh Grace, you have another admirer. Who is he?" Therese asked.

"Lieutenant James Clarke, Metro police. Didn't you want to tell him something, Therese?"

"Nope. I'm out of here. Three's a crowd and all that."

"Let me join you," Brett chimed in. "And Grace, remember what I said. Leave it to the cops."

Lieutenant Clarke had a ghost of a smile on his face as he watched Therese and Brett make tracks.

"Was it something I said?" he asked. "I hope I didn't interrupt your meeting."

Clarke pulled out a chair and sat down. Like most cops, he positioned himself with his back to the wall and pulled out a notepad.

"Are you ready to sign a statement, Ms. Quinn? You've had some time to think about it, in case any details may have slipped your mind."

I lied without compunction. "I really can't think of anything else, Lieutenant."

I'd been a manager too long and deceit was second nature to me. I smiled brightly to compound my sins. Clarke matched my smile and upped the ante.

"I asked because a witness has come forward who says that Jonathon Grey had a dispute with the victim. A heated dispute."

"I can't imagine Jonathon Grey losing his temper with anyone, let alone Maude. We all knew her and yes, she was tedious. But if that were a capital crime we'd have to eliminate half the Congress."

Clarke laughed. "Very clever. Now tell me everything you know about Christopher Grey."

It seemed that Clarke had been a very busy boy indeed. He'd assembled some damning information and made shrewd guesses in a very short time. On the other hand, maybe he was bluffing.

"What about Chris Grey?" I asked. I put a tight leash on my tendency to talk too much. Clarke had to show some of his cards if he wanted a response.

"I had a very informative session with the editor of *Tax Chat*. He told me that the victim, Miss Morrissey, had the inside track on a financial scandal that would rock the tax world. Do you know anything about that?"

He was toying with me. Unfortunately, I'm a lousy poker player.

"I told you before, Lieutenant. Maude said she was pursuing a big story but she never described it. And frankly, knowing Maude, I figured that at least half of it was pure fantasy."

Clarke patted the pack of cigarettes in his shirt pocket. It seemed to calm him.

"Your friend never mentioned Christopher or Jonathon Grey?" he asked.

"Not last night."

He pulled out reading glasses, and perched them at the end of his nose. Despite his snarky side, I had to admit that James Clarke was clever.

"What do you know about a business called Tax Champions?"

"Nothing official. Like everyone else I've heard some rumors."

Clarke sighed theatrically. "Ms. Quinn, we're at an impasse here. I know that Christopher Grey works for that company. I also know that you and his father are *close.*"

"What are you implying? Jonathon Grey is my friend and has been my friend for a long time. *Nothing more.* I'm surprised you traffic in gossip, Lieutenant."

If Clarke wanted a reaction, he'd gotten one. He flashed the peace sign, and leaned forward.

"Gossip is a cop's best friend. Didn't you know that? Relax, Ms. Quinn, I'm not trying to pick a fight. Besides, another old friend of yours filled me in on you. I think you remember John Jacob Wilson of the Chicago PD."

Wilson! That was another lifetime ago. I actually grew to like the old codger a lot even though he never appreciated all my efforts.

"What else did he tell you?"

Clarke smiled. "Oh, this and that. For one thing he described you as 'curious' shall we say."

"I'll bet he said nosey."

"Well, let's just say that he mentioned how helpful you were in solving that murder. Why won't you help me?"

"I'll help in any way I can, but I don't know anything. I hadn't seen Maude Morrissey in years. I have no idea who her enemies were or her friends for that matter."

Clarke leaned forward. "Ah, but you can find out. You're part of this crowd. You have contacts I simply don't have."

He probably thought that appealing to my vanity would work. As if!

"Lieutenant, if you want information about Jonathon Grey, ask him yourself. He doesn't lie. And while you're here, what about the Abacus? Surely the motive for Maude's murder was related to that. Accountants don't batter a priceless relic. Let me tell you. They'd be too afraid of a casualty loss!"

Clarke ignored my little tax joke. He stared icily at me and tapped his cigarette pack again.

"I have someone checking out the museum end of this. Give me credit for a few brains, Ms. Quinn. The victim was either an innocent bystander or the prime target. Right now I'm voting for option two. She left some notes at her office that link this Tax Champions thing to her murder."

I felt a little finger of doubt snake down my spine. Self-restraint was never my strong point—I had to ask.

"What did the notes say?"

Clarke exhaled forcefully. "That's classified, official police business."

"Then why are you so focused on Jonathon? What proof do you have?"

"Miss Morrissey was a very organized lady. She listed all her appointments and cross-referenced them to her assignments. They were on her computer, tablet and smart phone."

Clarke paused theatrically as if waiting for applause.

"So what?" I said. "How does that implicate anyone."

"What I see, Ms. Quinn, is a woman bent on protecting her *friend*. As it happens, the victim listed her last appointment of the evening. At the time of her death, she was meeting with Jonathon Grey."

I swallowed hard and bit back a retort.

Clarke studied me grinning like a particularly vile Cheshire cat. "Interesting coincidence, isn't it?" he said. "Maybe that will jog your memory about last night."

"You have my statement. I suggest you question Jonathon Grey personally concerning his whereabouts."

Clarke leaned back in his chair. "Are you familiar with the quaint concept we call 'accessory after the fact'?"

"Vaguely." I studied my manicure in a blatant show of indifference.

"In the District, you get the same penalty as the murderer himself. Not very nice. They don't have nail salons in the slammer, you know." Clarke nodded at my hands.

"Are we finished Lieutenant?" I asked. "I have work to do."

"That's all for now. Enjoy your conference." He snickered as he sailed out of the room.

Meanwhile, I was surfing a rising tide of panic. Jonathon and Chris needed to hire an attorney. Wait a minute—Chris *was* an attorney that's what got them involved in this big mess. I gathered my things and headed for the ballroom. The police had relocated all the booths and exhibits in an outside area until they released the crime scene.

The exterior of the room was festooned with bright yellow tape. The word *crime scene* was written on it in bold black letters just like in the movies. I noticed a crack of light coming through the front door. Maybe I could take a peek at the Abacus. I stole up to the door on tiptoe. Just as I reached for the knob, I heard a sound.

"Excuse me."

I whirled around straight into the muscular arms of Patrick Fong.

"Grace! This is a surprise," he said. "Maybe we can have that coffee, after all."

Oddly enough, I was startled but unafraid. His grip felt strong and comforting. Much better than I cared to admit.

"I wanted to see the Abacus one last time," I said. "For cultural reasons."

He gave me that half-smile again. "Naturally. I think I may be able to arrange it. Dr. Worthington is in there now. Come on."

We climbed through the tape and headed for the Abacus. Someone had removed the dented case, and the sun shone directly on the artifact's golden face. The Abacus was breathtaking; Patrick Fong was a close second.

Cranky Cyrus Worthington was engaged in a heated discussion with a uniformed guard. "Listen to me, my good man, that will not do! This is a national treasure. Do you want to start an international incident?"

The 'private policeman', stared at Worthington and cracked his gum. Cyrus's face turned an alarming shade of puce as he shouted. "Stop chewing your cud, you imbecile! I demand action!"

I wondered where the imperturbable Jie-ling Chow was. Cyrus could certainly use some help.

Worthington saw us, and held out his arms.

"Oh Patrick, there you are. I can't seem to communicate with this Neanderthal. We need more security for the Abacus. But he won't listen … " Cyrus staggered back into his chair. He retrieved a pillbox from his pocket and put a tablet under his tongue.

Patrick Fong moved swiftly to steady the older man. The guard did nothing.

"Cyrus, calm down. I'll make sure you get round the clock coverage for the Abacus. Nothing can be moved for another twenty-four hours but we can certainly arrange protection."

"Oh thank you my boy." Color slowly returned to Cyrus's cheeks. "I knew the State Department would understand."

State Department! I narrowed my eyes and folded my arms. Patrick Fong was more than the average Fed he claimed to be. He looked up and grinned sheepishly.

"So you're from State?" I asked.

Patrick nodded. "Yes, I'm a cultural attaché. I coordinate Asian exchange programs."

"Oh. Just another art history major in search of a mission."

"Something like that," he said.

Cyrus cleared his throat. "Excuse me, who *are* you, young lady?"

Obviously the old goat didn't recall my kindness from last night. Not surprising since he appeared to be missing a significant number of brain cells.

"We met last night, Dr. Worthington. I'm Grace Quinn."

Cyrus squinted through his pince-nez. "Are you with the State Department too?"

"She's with the *IRS*, Cyrus." Jie-ling Chow materialized from nowhere, teetering on stilt-high heels. Her tone was decidedly frosty.

"The *IRS!*" Worthington's mouth formed a perfect circle. "But what ...?"

"Grace is here as my guest, Cyrus. Don't be concerned." Patrick turned toward Dr. Chow and smiled. "Oh Jie-ling. Good to see you."

She minced up to him and clasped his hand. There was that whiff of vulnerability again.

After a few minutes, Patrick retrieved his arm from the Dragon Lady and made our excuses. "I better get to work on the security arrangements." He beamed at Jie-ling, and said. "You couldn't be in better hands now, Cyrus. I'll check back later."

Patrick grasped me by the elbow and steered me toward the door. Something was fishy, and it wasn't in the state of Denmark.

CHAPTER SIX

"State Department?"

Patrick Fong met my gaze and shrugged. "It's a respectable post."

"Most cultural attachés are really CIA. Or so I've read."

"You've been reading too many thrillers, young lady. Besides I'm not a Senior Executive like you. You're the big deal."

"Don't patronize me, Mr. Fong. I don't need your approval."

There was that warm smile again. Too bad he was lying through his big white teeth.

"I wouldn't think of it, Ms. Quinn." He headed for the elegant Marquee bar and gestured toward a stool. "Is this okay?"

"Fine. Fine. Just pick some place where we can have privacy."

Patrick raised his eyebrows. "Really! We can always go to your hotel room."

"In your dreams! I'm interested in history—the history of Cyrus Worthington, Jie-ling Chow, and the Abacus exhibit. This whole thing seems odd and it may be connected to Maude Morrissey's murder."

He grew serious. "Let the police do their job. After all, they're professionals."

"Does that mean you won't help me?" I asked. "That's okay. I totally understand."

Actually it was *not* okay at all, but I had to remain poised.

Patrick grabbed my hand. "Grace, cool it. I'll share whatever I can. There's nothing that mysterious anyway."

"Give me a sketch of Cyrus Worthington, I've read the basics in the *Post,* and on Google but what's he really like?"

He paused. "Cyrus comes from one of the oldest, most respected families in Virginia. The Worthingtons used to be a big deal—definitely the product of Mayflower stock. Most of his family is gone now and he devotes himself to his real love—Asian artifacts."

"Where does he live?" I asked.

"Why? Planning to pay him a visit?" Patrick seemed to enjoy taunting me. "He lives with his sister in one of those baronial pads in Cleveland Park."

Cleveland Park, one of my favorite places, was a neighborhood of beautifully restored homes not far from the National Zoo. If Cyrus had one of those brownstones, he must have some major bucks.

"Where do you live, Grace?" Patrick asked playfully.

"I'm currently homeless."

"What!" He feigned shock. "Poor baby."

"It's true. I'm on temporary assignment to Washington so I live in a hotel room. Not that it concerns you one bit. Let's get back to Cyrus Worthington."

"Okay."

"So Cyrus had the right social connections and education to land himself at the Smithsonian."

"Don't forget money," Patrick said. "It's a sine qua non in the museum world. If you don't have it yourself, you better have generous friends who do."

"What other personal things do you know about Cyrus?" I asked.

His voice had an edge to it. "I don't feel comfortable gossiping about his personal life."

This was no time to be squeamish. Faint heart never won fair—well, you get the idea.

"How about Dr. Jie-ling Chow. She's quite a character," I said.

"Jie-ling, sweet Jie-ling."

Patrick seemed to be testing me. I remained strong by biting my tongue. Hard.

"Jie-ling has a Chinese father and an American mom. She chose to live and study in China and she's fiercely protective of her country."

"Which one?" I asked sweetly.

"China, of course," he said. That naughty Mr. Fong put his arm around me and gave me a little hug. "Do I see claws, Ms. kitty-cat?"

I have to admit this was the most pleasant interrogation I'd ever conducted. I ignored the hug and removed his arm.

Focus, Grace, focus.

"What's her part in arranging this exhibit?" I asked, "She seemed very nervous about the security details. I'm positive that she lied to me."

"It's a *very* big deal. It could make or break her career."

"Patrick, this is important. Did Cyrus or Jie-ling ever mention Maude Morrissey?"

His face was impassive, harder to read than the Rosetta Stone. "Not that I recall. I've got to make some phone calls. Are you free for dinner?"

"Tonight is the big awards dinner. The Commissioner is the key-note speaker and I have to be there."

Patrick shrugged. "Sounds fascinating. Oh well, there's always tomorrow. I'll ring your room."

He threw a twenty down on the bar and headed for the door. Before exiting he spun around and blew me a kiss.

◇ ◇ ◇ ◇ ◇

I try to avoid banquets. Most are long and boring, full of windy speeches and cheap awards. Add 800 accountants in penguin suits to the mix and the evening is excruciating.

I sauntered around the ballroom observing the hi-jinks of the happy hour crowd. My goal was simple—find and interrogate the Greys, pere y fil. I had dressed with particular care in a cornflower blue suit that screamed innocence and maidenly charm. Most of the guys towered over me despite the five-inch heels I had unwisely chosen. As I passed the doorway, an arm thick as a birch branch grabbed my waist. The pleasant somewhat foolish face of Harry Hawkins beamed down at me. Harry was a nice fellow—hardly a stellar performer—but a decent guy, and as luck would have it his pudgy fingerprints were all over Tax Champions. Opportunity was knocking.

"Grace, you're more irresistible than ever," he joked. "Come home with me and I'll show you my calculator."

"Harry, Harry, Harry. It's a tempting offer but your wife might object." I deftly removed his arm, and patted his shoulder. "Since you're making big bucks these days, you can buy me a drink."

We leaned against the bar, and sipped our drinks. Harry 's slurred speech told me he had a big head start on me. Perhaps his guard and his inhibitions were down. Carpe Diem.

"Awful thing about Maude," he said. "Must have been some druggie."

"Oh, I don't think so Harry. After all, the Abacus was almost stolen."

Harry's eyes grew misty. "I kind of liked her, even though she was a pest. Maude was always a fighter. Had to get the last word in."

"Harry, Maude mentioned Tax Champions to me. Sounded like she was on the trail of something big."

"Nah, she was just fishing. Tax Champions is solid."

I swallowed a drop of my cosmopolitan. "I saw her just last night. How about you?"

"She called me ... " Harry shifted uncomfortably. " Why do you ask?"

"I was the one who found her, you know. It's hard to forget."

Harry blanched. "She was wrong, Grace. Prowling around our office, contacting customers was wrong. Maude never could learn to keep her mouth shut."

"It's shut now, Harry, and I think Tax Champions is right in the middle of everything."

"Murder!" he yelped. "No, we're not like that. Read our materials. We're just trying to give the little guy a chance."

"To do what—evade taxes? The police think Maude was going to blast you guys in her column—something about a pyramid scheme."

Now Harry looked a little green around the gills. "I didn't touch her, Grace, I swear it. You see ...."

A shove from behind jostled Harry, spilling his drink.

Oh, excuse me, old boy." I turned and saw the toothy grin of Kelvin Cates. Cates was that rarity—a CPA with social skills. Personally, I detested him. He was my least favorite classmate from executive training, an opportunist who left as soon as he could to mine the private sector.

"Kelvin, what a surprise. How are you?" My voice rang with forced cheer.

"Ah, little Gracie. Still clawing your way to the top, I see."

I longed to plant my five-inch heel between his beetle brows but I settled for a brief smile instead. Cates was the dunderhead of our class who thought that schmoozing substituted for grey matter. He was a natural for Tax Champions.

"Kelvin, I was just telling Grace how Maude..." Harry froze as Kelvin glared at him.

"I'm sorry to interrupt but we've got to go, Harry. Our boss is waiting for us. Anyhow, the banquet's starting."

"But Kelvin—" Harry gave me a sheepish grin, and gulped down his drink. "Catch you later, Grace," he said.

"Sure, Harry."

I watched them head for the exit. Cates gestured, Harry shook his head. Even a tuxedo couldn't spruce up some guys.

A splendid exception to that rule soon appeared. Jonathon Grey in a tuxedo, straight from the Armani showroom, was a sight to behold. He grabbed my elbow and said, "Let's take our seats. I have news."

We chose an unoccupied table at the back of the banquet hall. As soon as we were seated, Jonathon leaned over and handed me a folder.

"I got this from one of my contacts at Justice," he said. "Maude was badgering him about Tax Champions. It's a list of questions she sent to DOJ. Some of them are pretty scary."

I scanned the list while Jonathon continued. "Most of the guys I spoke with think that Tax Champions is toast. Kelvin and Harry are being interviewed next week, and the smart money says an indictment will follow."

"What about Chris? Is he in danger too?"

Jonathon's eyes clouded. "I couldn't say."

"Where is he? I hoped he might have some news for us."

Jonathon clasped his water goblet. "Listen, Grace, you've got to believe me. Chris is not involved in Maude's murder." He lowered his voice. "And neither am I."

"Have you spoken with Lieutenant Clarke?" I asked. "Jonathon, he's really zeroing in on you and Chris. I'm worried."

The empty seats at our table started filling up. Several old pals of Jonathon greeted him warmly and started chatting. He leaned over and caught my eye.

"Later," he said.

I forced myself to ignore the folder Jonathon had given me. The Commissioner's speech was positively riveting, even though I'd heard it at least five times. A successful executive has to perfect an expression of benign rapture. I call it the Nancy Reagan stare. I'm pretty sure that the Commissioner's harsh words about illegal schemes hit home, especially with the Tax Champions duo. The crowd buzzed uneasily—someone's ears were burning.

Our dinner was the bland fare so beloved of conventions everywhere. It was barely edible, but I noticed the diners shoveling it in as though it were manna. A brief tribute to Maude followed the dreary awards ceremony. While others bowed their heads, I scanned the crowd. Kelvin Cates was whispering to Evan Braddock. I could just glimpse the grins on their self-satisfied faces. Suddenly, a new player stepped to the podium.

Lieutenant James Clarke introduced himself and addressed the crowd.

"I'm investigating the murder of your colleague, Maude Morrissey. I would appreciate hearing any information that would help us find her killer."

Clarke reeled off contact information and left the stage. The audience sat in stunned silence while the waiters cleared the tables.

The accountants' ball ended with a bang.

Most of the merrymakers headed for the hotel bars to drown their sorrows on the company's dime. Jonathon was busy so I elected to follow Kelvin Cates. He was velcroed to the odious Evan Braddock whose claque included Cheap Suit and Clenched Fist from the first social. I wished I could identify Cheap Suit. Since he was an IRS employee, he had to work in the corporate tax arena but why was he close to Braddock, and Cates, former Execs with questionable ethics?

The four guys bellied up to the bar and ordered a round of drinks. Braddock seemed relaxed tonight but Clenched Fist was ready to explode. His finger stabbed the air as he sputtered something I couldn't quite catch. Cates attempted to placate him by a friendly pat on the back, a gesture that earned him a murderous stare. Cheap Suit hung back. His shoulders were hunched, his lips buttoned. What a quartet!

I edged closer to the bar. Eavesdropping isn't easy in a crowded club but I heard Cates say the magic words: Tax Champions.

"I'm not worried at all," he said. "Our situation just got a hell of a lot easier."

"What do you mean?" barked Clenched Fist.

" ... Morrissey." I almost fell off my chair! If only I could hear the entire conversation.

Braddock turned toward Cheap Suit. "I presume you got it, Devon."

Cheap Suit hung his head. Save me from a man who mumbles! His reply was inaudible, but it got a loud reaction.

"WHAT!" No more Mr. Cool for Braddock.

Kelvin Cates lost his toothy grin. "Where is it?" he hissed. "Do you know what you've done?"

Cheap Suit nodded. He looked both miserable and frightened

Clenched Fist curled his lip and advanced on him.

"Okay, who's the mole?" he asked.

Cates and Braddock looked puzzled. "I thought we had that covered," said Braddock.

"You mean you still don't know?"

Cheap Suit shook his head.

Clenched Fist pounded the bar. "Amateurs!" he snorted.

They formed a tight circle, and lowered their voices. I couldn't hear a thing.

That's why I shrieked when Mary Hagan crept up on me. She patted my hand, and pulled up a chair. The woman was down right intimidating with her perfect hair, makeup, and expensive scent.

"Did I interrupt anything, Grace?"

"No, well that is, I was just ...."

Mary smiled with complete confidence. "You were snooping, weren't you? Learn anything?"

"Nothing conclusive," I said. "I know those guys are up to no good but I can't pin it down. The guy in the embarrassing suit has to be an IRS employee."

"Of course he is. That's Devon Hall. He's a criminal investigator." Mary looked smug.

"You're kidding," I said. "Most CI guys are kind of hot but that guy is pathetic."

I looked at Mary. "How do you know him, anyhow?"

She paused. "You'd be surprised at the things I know, Grace. Unlike you I am a CPA. I get around."

I bit back my reply. After all, Mary was my boss. Besides, I was stunned to learn that Devon Hall, aka Cheap Suit, was a special agent consorting with low lifes. Maybe Maude had trusted him, confided in him. Maybe he killed her.

"What's that thing?" Mary asked, pointing to my folder.

"Oh, just some paperwork." I smiled brightly. If only Mary would give up.

She held out her hand. "Let me take a look."

I had no choice. I reached into my bag, grabbed a folder, and surrendered it to Mary.

"This is no big deal," she said after reading the contents. "It's just the outline for your speech. You'd think it was the Golden Abacus."

I laughed weakly. "You know what kind of worry-wart I am."

Some day soon I would tell Mary everything. The precious pages that Jonathon gave me were neatly pinned to the floor by my five-inch heels.

Therese's arrival saved my life. She and Mary shared a politely concealed enmity that prompted Mary to make an excuse and leave.

"I don't think she likes me," Therese said. "Probably thinks I'm a bad influence on you."

"Like I need any help. Wait a minute while I get something." I leaned under the table and retrieved Maude's list of questions. "Move over and read this."

Maude's forthright style blared out of the page. She knew something was up and wasn't shy about showing it. The Justice Department probably ignored her, or sent some vanilla response. "I am in receipt of your letter—blah blah blah."

Therese's head shot up. "Look at question number two—*Are you pursuing a criminal investigation against Tax Champions and/or it's principals?* Maude knew they would stonewall her on that. Oh my God, look at question number five—*Will you recommend disbarment of Christopher Grey, General Counsel of Tax Partners?* Jonathon must be bullshit about all this."

Maybe that explained the sudden absence of Chris Grey from the banquet. Things looked grim for the Tax Champions crowd—or did they?

"Therese, look over at the bar. They look pretty complacent don't they?"

She craned her neck, unfortunately she also squealed. "Do you believe it! It's creepy Cates and his gang."

Evan Braddock heard her. He slid off his chair and headed our way. I snatched the papers off the table and stuffed them in my bag.

"Well, what a surprise. Look Kelvin, it's Grace Quinn and her friend Therese. Ladies, may we join you?" He planted himself next to Therese.

Cates lumbered over but Cheap Suit and Clenched Fist remained at the bar glowering.

Before he got comfortable, I rose and gathered my things.

"Sorry guys but we're late for another meeting. Feel free to use the table."

Therese stayed rooted to her seat. "I think I'll stay awhile Grace. It's been ages since I chatted with Evan and Kelvin."

I didn't know what to do. As a rule, Accountants are too unimaginative to commit a murder, however, the Tax Champions crew had shown amazing aptitude for creative accounting. Therese might be in danger.

"Call me as soon as get up to your room, Therese. We need to talk."

She gave me a wave and a half-wink. "Don't worry Grace, I trust these guys." Cates preened and Braddock smirked. Macho roles didn't often come their way.

I wondered what connection there was between Braddock and Tax Champions. If he was involved, he'd kept a very low profile. I trudged to my room, and flopped on the bed waiting for Therese to call.

CHAPTER SEVEN

Sunlight was streaming through the drapes when I awoke. Oh my God—Therese hadn't called! She might be lying in a ditch somewhere. Of course there was the remote possibility that she was lying in someone's bed. Better the ditch than the hairy arms of Kelvin Cates.

I grabbed my robe and rang her room. The brring, brring, brring, of the phone drove me mad. Just as panic set in, I heard a pathetic croak.

"H-u-l-l-o."

"Therese! Are you okay?"

"Grace? What time is it?"

"Seven-thirty."

"In the morning?" She yawned loudly. "I didn't get much sleep."

"Are you *alone*?"

Another yawn. "I am now," she said.

I had neither the time not patience for seamy details. "I'll meet you for breakfast in an hour," I said. "Be there—it's important."

It took me at least that long to get presentable. Today, I decided to wear black. It showed proper respect for the dead and it was very slimming. I felt like an avenging angel, if angels ever wore black, that is. I had just touched the doorknob when the phone rang again. Damn, it might be Jonathon. I dashed back, stubbing my toe in the bargain. Scatological terms spewed from my mouth. I grabbed the receiver in time to hear a muffled voice.

"Stay out of this, Bitch, or you'll join your friend."

"Who *is* this?" I couldn't even tell if was a male or female voice.

For once in my life I was speechless. I sat down as blood rushed to my head and my heart pounded. Is this what a heart attack feels like, I wondered? The phone rang again. I stayed frozen, terrified of hearing that horrid voice again.

Get a grip, Grace. Remember your Shakespeare. "Cowards die many times before their deaths, but the valiant never taste of death but once."

I slowly reached for the phone praying that it was a wrong number.

"I'd almost given up on you," said Jonathon in his pleasant baritone. He paused and waited for my response. "Grace, are you *okay*?"

"Not really. I'm meeting Therese for breakfast if you'd like to join us."

"Why don't we meet for lunch? I think the seminars break about twelve-fifteen."

Buck up, I told myself. After all, you can't suspect Jonathon of anything.

"Sounds good," I said. "Where are we meeting?"

I heard Jonathon chuckle. "How about Kramerbooks? I doubt that we'll run into any of the tax crowd there. Chris will join us."

How fitting! Maude loved that bookstore. Maybe her spirit would inspire us.

After a concentrated effort on my person, I rushed into the dining room. Therese was already seated, looked remarkably perky. Perhaps a night of dissipation was just the tonic she needed. She smiled lazily at me, daring me to ask.

"Just tell me it wasn't Cates or Braddock," I begged. "Anyone is preferable to them."

"Are you kidding—those creeps! I dumped them early on. No, it was someone else entirely. Quite a surprise, actually."

I held up my hand. "That's enough, I don't need particulars."

"What you *need*, Grace is some quiet time with Patrick Fong. Believe me, *I* wouldn't pass that up."

"I'm sure you wouldn't. Be serious for a minute, I want to tell you something."

I described my mystery caller.

"WHAT!" Therese grabbed my wrist. "What are you going to do, call Clarke or...."

She ran out of ideas pretty fast. "You don't suspect Chris Grey, do you?"

"It could just as easily have been one of your playmates from last night, you know."

Therese exhaled. "You're right. That's just the kind of slimy trick those toads would try. But look on the bright side. You're getting someone nervous, so you must be on the right track."

"I haven't done much," I said. "It could just as easily have been Jie-ling Chow or even Patrick Fong. Cyrus is too feeble to make threats. Besides that faux British accent would give him away."

"Oh!" Therese wiggled with excitement. "I almost forgot to tell you. I did some sleuthing myself last night. You know that guy you call 'Cheap Suit'."

"Devon Hall" I interrupted. "I found out he's a Special Agent."

"Anyhow, you'll find this very interesting. He's one of the agents working the case on Tax Champions. I heard him mention it."

"What! Talk about a conflict of interest! What else did you find out?"

Therese looked insufferably smug. "I only heard bits and pieces. They thought I was loaded but of course I can out-drink any man."

I'm not sure it was anything to brag about but Therese did have the proverbial hollow leg.

"And ... " She was driving me nuts. Finally after I almost reached the breaking point, she continued.

"They kept muttering about a recording. Something like that. Whatever it is, it's incriminating, and I think Maude had it."

Therese has a very sharp mind. Despite her eccentricities she'd done better than I had at ferreting out clues.

" Here's what stumps me. Why kill Maude, when everyone and his brother say that Tax Champions and all it's deck hands are sinking fast anyway? Look at these." I handed her the questions that Jonathon gave me last night.

Therese rapidly scanned the paper. "Old Maudie was right on target for a change. I think I have the answer to your question."

It was my turn to gape. "Tell me, for God's sake."

"It's very simple, Grace—intent. Every prosecutor must prove intent if he's going to get the bad guys. Maybe Maude got hold of a disc, e-mail or something that directly links Cates and his gang to an illegal scheme. Harry Hawkins might have been duped, he's dense enough, but Kelvin Cates and Braddock are crooked. I wouldn't put anything past them.

"Even murder?" I asked.

"Especially murder," she said.

The first session was a panel discussion entitled "Ethical Issues for the Tax Professional." These events are normally a real snooze that substitutes long rambling monologues and mind-numbing charts for informed dialogue. This time might be different. Two of the participants, Evan Braddock and Brett Roberts were sworn enemies. Brett loathed Braddock and usually snubbed him so perhaps sparks would fly. The moderator was my boss, Mary Hagan. She entered the room in a swirl of Creed, perfectly dressed and coiffed. Mary had plenty of experience skewering contractors at the Defense Department so accountants were much easier prey.

She started the session with a bang! "Let's discuss the ethics of tax shelters," Mary said, smiling sweetly. "We all know that some are completely legal, some are murky, and others are shams. Would anyone care to comment?"

Evan Braddock colored, but said nothing. A stout woman from one of the major accounting firms doffed her glasses, and grabbed the microphone.

"Our firm is completely opposed to any transaction that even skirts the law," she said pompously. "We deal only with major corporations not the mom and pop crowd."

A young Hispanic man interrupted her. "Oh, so you mean that a client base of small businesses is inferior. I resent the implication."

Braddock added his two cents. "I believe that the most egregious transactions involve large corporate taxpayers, Violet. In fact, two corporations were indicted only last week."

The attacks stunned Violet and left her speechless. She replaced her glasses and turned toward Mary for help. Mary on the other hand seemed to be delighted at the sprightly discussion. She smiled encouragement at the combatants and proceeded to throw gasoline on the fire.

"I believe Mr. Braddock has a point but I'm interested in your thoughts about aggressive marketing techniques, especially those that target less sophisticated taxpayers."

No one took the bait, but a hand went up near the front of the room.

Mary nodded. "State your name and the firm you represent, please."

"I'm Christopher Grey and I represent Tax Champions."

There was a collective gasp. Chris Grey wore a well-cut charcoal suit with a crisp blue shirt. His tie was power red, his mood—combative. Oh my God, poor Jonathon.

Mary leaned forward, her eyes glistening. "Mr. Grey, what is your point?"

"I'm tired of self-righteous hypocrites who twist the tax law for fat-cats but sneer at helping the little guy. We're pioneers, social engineers who give everyone a fair shake."

Brett was the first to respond. "That's a new twist on it, Chris, but I wouldn't take it to court."

The audience shifted nervously. Adrenalin junkies and hard bodies were in short supply.

Evan Braddock sneered. "You guys sure have taken it to the bank though, haven't you Chris?"

That did it. Chris Grey was a guided missile aimed straight at Braddock. He bounded up the stairs and leapt at Evan Braddock.

"You double-crossing son of a bitch," Chris yelled.

Braddock jumped to his feet and doubled his fists. "Bring it on, big man," he said.

The drama ended prematurely when Mary Hagan wedged her five-foot frame between the combatants. Chris stopped short and Braddock staggered to his seat.

"Gentlemen, please," she said. "Who thinks that accountants are boring?"

Chris backed off, took his seat and sat glaring at Braddock. When I turned to check the time, I saw Therese at the back of the room wildly waving her arms. What in the world! I slipped out of my chair and headed for the door. One look at her face told me there was trouble.

"Grace, come here," she said. "You're *not* going to like this."

"What are you talking about?" I asked.

Therese looked around and lowered her voice. "The cops just arrested Jonathon Grey."

"That's ridiculous, Jonathon didn't kill Maude. Clarke knows that. They probably just took his statement."

Therese shook her head. The expression on her face was solemn.

"I don't think so. Clarke and a swarm of uniforms surrounded Jonathon, and led him to a car. That sounds like an arrest to me."

"Yeah, but did they handcuff him? They always do if they're arresting someone."

Therese peered over her reading glasses. "And you're basing this on what—*Law and Order* reruns?"

Actually I was thinking more of the classics—*Kojak*.

"We've got to *do* something," I said. "Let's find Clarke. He can't just grab an innocent man and arrest him."

Therese held out her arm. "Wait a minute—don't you think Chris Grey should know that his father's in the pokey?"

I knew Mary Hagan would have a fit if I interrupted her session. I turned to Therese.

"*You* go get him. Take him a note, or something. Just don't let anyone else hear about it."

Therese shifted from one foot to another and bit her lip. "Grace, I don't think we should get involved, especially with Chris Grey. He's vicious."

I spun around and stared at her. "This is for *Jonathon*, Therese, don't be such a wimp. And since when are you afraid of anything? You almost seduced Kelvin Cates, for God's sake."

That sobered her up. Therese narrowed her eyes and stormed back into the seminar. She returned with an obviously shaken Chris Grey.

"Is it true?" he asked me. "What she said, my father ...."

"Apparently," I said coldly. "Isn't it time you spoke up?"

I don't think he even heard me. Chris Grey kept shaking his head and mumbling something about a mistake. Before I could question him, he raced down the corridor and out of the hotel.

"Well, you handled that like a pro," Therese said. "Even I could do that."

She was right. Now we were back to square one—find James Clarke.

I didn't have to go far. By the time we reached the elevator, he was there.

"I've been looking for you, Ms. Quinn," he said. "It's time for that statement we talked about."

Clarke pointed to an empty chair and sat across from me. He stared at Therese. "May I help you, miss?"

She vacillated between curiosity and fear. Fear won out.

"Actually, I was just leaving." She gave Clarke the smile reserved for any presentable male and strolled toward the elevator.

Clarke adjusted his tie, took out his notebook and clicked his ballpoint. The man gave new meaning to obsessive/compulsive.

"Where is Jonathon Grey? What have you done with him?"

Clarke smiled and ignored my question. "Remember Ms. Quinn, *I'm* the one who gets to ask the questions here. Let's start by revisiting the night of the murder. When did you first see Jonathon Grey?"

"Should I have an attorney present?" Television shows came in handy once in awhile.

Clarke's smile broadened into a sneer. "You tell me. Do you intend to tell the truth this time?"

"About what?" I asked.

"Let's stop fencing, Ms. Quinn, or, may I call you Grace?"

"You may *not*—unless of course *I* may call you James."

Clarke was not amused. I felt a decided chill in the air.

"Look Lieutenant, I've been brow-beaten, sneered at and threatened. I'm not in the mood for parlor games, so if there's nothing more ...."

"Threatened! What are you talking about?" Clarke started tapping his foot.

"Last night someone phoned my room and told me to buzz off or I could end up like Maude."

"Probably a prank," he said.

"I took it *very* seriously."

"Did you recognize the voice? Was it male or female?"

"It was muffled," I said, "more like a hiss than a voice."

Clarke leaned forward. I could tell by his eyes that he was worried. They turned from blue to a stormy grey when he was agitated.

"Where was Jonathon Grey when you found the body?

"Behind me, I think."

"You mean, you don't *know?* Don't you see, Ms. Quinn, you could be in danger. Stop withholding evidence."

I was suddenly exhausted. Mary's session had ended and the corridor was flooded with curious accountants. Even the odious Evan Braddock craned his neck, hoping to eavesdrop.

"Honestly Lieutenant, I was in shock. I remember Jonathon calling out to me and I think he came from behind me."

Clarke gave me a speculative glance. His manner cool and impersonal.

"Describe his behavior," he said. "Jonathon Grey seems like a pretty cool customer."

"He was shocked and horrified of course. We both knew Maude."

"Did he mention how he got blood on his jacket sleeve?" Clarke wasn't smiling now.

"I think it happened when he bent over Maude's body to feel her pulse. Or maybe it happened when he helped me up from the floor. My leg was bleeding you know, from the glass."

I didn't lie; I just didn't volunteer any information.

Clarke patted his pocket for the phantom pack of smokes. "Why was he in the Ballroom anyway? Did you arrange to meet him there?"

"Hardly, Lieutenant. I only went there to get my handouts. You know, for my speech."

He crossed his legs and scrutinized his notes. "You mentioned this 'big story' that Ms. Morrissey was writing. Was it about Tax Champions, the company Christopher Grey works for?"

"Maude never told me."

"I know that Jonathon Grey had a meeting with her. You know it too," he said.

I tried to be patient but Clarke was becoming tedious.

"We already discussed this. What's different now? Why did you arrest Jonathon Grey, the least violent man I know?"

Clarke paused. "I guess it's okay to tell you this. We got the fingerprint analysis back on the murder weapon—you know, the shard of glass."

I steeled myself for what promised to be very unpleasant news.

"You see, Ms. Quinn, the only fingerprints on that murder weapon belong to Jonathon Grey, and the blood on his suit belonged to the victim, not you."

I exercised my right to remain silent.

"Just for the record we haven't arrested Mr. Grey. Yet. But I have a theory. I think he went there to protect his kid. Most fathers would do the same. Things got heated—I hear Ms. Morrissey had quite a temper—and he killed her in the heat of passion." Clarke sighed. "Even a gentle man can be driven to murder with the right provocation."

Clarke asked a few more perfunctory questions about Maude then stalked away leaving me to brood.

CHAPTER EIGHT

Things looked grim for Jonathon, but he hadn't seemed worried at all. Was that the glow of innocence or the resignation of guilt? Despite my pledge I'd done almost nothing on the Abacus angle and I doubted that Clarke had done much either. Suppose Maude had interrupted the botched robbery? According to Patrick, the value of the Abacus was incalculable. That added up to a lot of incentive for criminal mischief. Maude was stabbed with a glass shard, therefore the theft must have preceded her arrival. It had no hallmarks of professional thieves—they would have gotten the Abacus. That left amateurs like Jie-ling Chow, Cyrus, and even Patrick still in the running not to mention the inept private cop, Bert Kingman. Maybe he wasn't as dumb as he seemed. I sunk down on a velvet sofa cushion trying to think.

When I glanced up, Patrick Fong was walking toward me. Damn, that man didn't walk, he *glided* like a panther! A toned, muscular jungle cat primed for action.

"Grace, I've been looking all over for you. What's the matter?"

"Everything." I considered squeezing out a tear but rejected that as too cheesy. Besides, Patrick Fong wasn't that easy to fool. The man acted downright cynical at times.

He sat next to me and put his arm around me. "Don't worry. Maybe I can help."

He had the most beautiful almond eyes. If only I trusted him more.

"My friend Jonathon Grey has been arrested for Maude's murder, and I know he's innocent."

Patrick's face was stony. "If he is, there's nothing to worry about. Let the police sort it out."

He sounded like a broken record—an annoying, scratchy record.

"I think it's all about the Abacus, and you know more about it than you admit."

Patrick swore softly. "Come on Grace, give me a break. The Abacus is none of your business. It's a State Department matter."

I glared at him. "You said you wanted to help—put up or shut up."

Patrick shook his head and laughed. "Okay, what do you want to know?"

"If someone stole the Abacus, how hard would it be to dispose of it?"

He wrinkled his brow. "It could be done of course but not easily. When there's a murder attached to a theft, the stakes are high."

"I've heard that some private collectors aren't too picky about those things."

He dropped his arm and compressed his lips.

"Well?" I said. "Surely the State Department has stoolies, or something."

"Stoolies!" Patrick hooted. "Where the hell do you get these notions from—comic books?"

As it happens, I'm an enthusiastic student of mysteries but I wasn't about to divulge that. They all used stoolies, confidential informants and the like. I folded my arms, and stared at him.

"Would it have to be an inside job?" I asked. "Jie-ling Chow seemed pretty worried."

"Jie-ling—give it a rest. She'd be too worried about messing her hair." He cupped my chin. "Nah, there were a lot of people involved in the exhibit—shippers, hotel employees, insurers, a whole assortment of suspects. I think you're a tiny bit jealous of Jie-ling."

"Don't flatter yourself. I have absolutely no reason to be jealous."

I felt flustered but I forced myself not to react. Patrick Fong was deliberately trying to bait me.

"Have you questioned Kingman, the rent-a-cop?" I asked.

His response was terse. "How many times do I have to tell you? *I* am not the police. I haven't questioned anyone nor do I intend to."

"Okay, don't help me. I'm pretty resourceful."

Patrick nodded ruefully, "That's what I'm afraid of. Look, if I help you—just this once—will you forget this detective business?"

I crossed both fingers and looked at him. "Of course. Come on, let's go check it out."

"Wait a minute. I don't even know where Kingman lives."

I hate smugness but sometimes it seeps into my soul. "I know," I said.

"But, how ...?" Patrick raised his chin and frowned.

"All employees are required to fill out W-4s when they're hired. I contacted Capitol Security Agency and verified Kingman's home address with them. It's a matter of tax compliance, you see."

Patrick was temporarily speechless. "But that's illegal!" he growled. "No wonder people hate the IRS."

"Slightly unorthodox but not illegal. I am authorized to ensure that businesses comply with the law. Come on, we're wasting time. Let's call a cab."

"I have my car here. It's faster."

We hoofed it out of the hotel and into the adjacent parking garage.

Patrick led me to a sleek BMW sedan and held the passenger's door open for me.

"Nice wheels," I said admiring the plush leather seats and super stereo system. I expected a stream of cool jazz instead of Kenny Rodgers singing the beautiful love song, *Lady*. The enigmatic Mr. Fong was even more interesting than I'd thought. Was a touch of the romantic woven into that impenetrable façade?

His mood was somber as we headed over to northeast D.C. On him somber was sexy rather than tedious, a pleasant change from the earnest CPAs that surrounded me.

Most people with sense avoided the Northeast quadrant of the city with its teaming crime rate and squalid conditions. An hourly worker like Bert Kingman had few alternatives. He lived in a scarred, dispirited brownstone with debris littering the lawn and cracks pitting the sidewalk. Frankly I welcomed the presence of a man in this scary neighborhood especially one who looked like he could handle himself in a fight. Most CPAs could only whack an assailant with the Internal Revenue Code or bore him into submission.

I heard Patrick grumbling as he locked his car. "Nobody better touch this baby," he muttered. Unfortunately, he wasn't referring to me.

I ran up to the battered entry way as a man exited. Naturally he held the door for me, as I knew that he would. Very few men suspect a woman of nefarious deeds, a sexist carryover that confers a distinct advantage. I checked the mailboxes for Kingman's apartment number—3G—and headed up the stairs.

Patrick joined me with a sour look on his face. "Grace, I don't think this is such a good idea," he said.

"Don't be silly. We'll catch him by surprise."

I sprinted up the first two flights of stairs and used the handrail for the third. I guess a few more hours at the gym wouldn't hurt. Patrick managed all three flights effortlessly.

The hallway was dark and ominous, barely illuminated by the lone bulb that burned at the end of the corridor. I knocked on three G, and the door creaked open.

"Grace, wait a minute," Patrick growled. "You can't just barge in there—that's breaking and entering."

"Well, technically it's entering, not breaking."

I poked my head through the opening, and called out. "Mr. Kingman. Mr. Kingman, it's Grace Quinn from the IRS, and Patrick Fong. May we come in?"

I pushed the door open.

"GRACE!" Patrick was acting like an old lady, for heaven's sake.

"Silence is consent—check your English Common Law," I replied.

The interior was cluttered and dank. Bert Kingman's digs could use a maid, fumigation, or possibly both.

I fumbled for a light switch. This didn't look like the lair of a man who had just gotten a big payday. On what passed for a coffee table, there was a stack of mail. As I reached for it Patrick grabbed my arm.

"Tampering with mail is a Federal offense, Missy, or don't they teach you that at the IRS?"

"Okay, okay. Look for an address book, or something useful."

Kingman had fashioned a bedroom of sorts behind a tattered screen. As I approached the bed, I wrinkled my nose. Did this man ever change his sheets? On the other side of the bed, I spied something very interesting.

"Patrick, come here!"

I pointed to a half filled suitcase. "I think Kingman's planning a getaway," I said.

"Maybe he's just taking a vacation. People do that, you know, Grace."

"Maybe. But either way, you need money. Much more money than a minimum wage job pays."

Patrick grabbed my hand and pulled me away. "Let's get out of here. I for one value my job and my freedom."

As we headed toward the door, I tripped on a tattered book the size of a cigarette pack. I bent down, pretending to adjust my shoe and scooped it into my purse without Patrick noticing anything.

When we reached the street, he inspected his car carefully for dents or scratches, opened my door and sped away.

"You're really something, Ms. Quinn," Patrick said. "Do you realize how dangerous that situation could have been? I think you need a full-time body-guard."

"Really." My mouth felt dry. As I looked at Patrick Fong, parts of me started tingling. His arms gripping the steering wheel were so muscular. I imagined how his long, slim fingers would feel slowly exploring my.... Oh my God! I sounded worse than Therese! I bit my lip trying to regain control.

"Are you applying for the job, Mr. Fong?"

Patrick gazed at me with an enigmatic smile. "Perhaps I will, at least for tonight."

"I presume you have references." My voice cracked a tad but I forced myself to face him.

"Tons of them. All satisfied customers." His voice was soft and sultry now, matching the deep sounds of John Coltrane.

A warm glow suffused my entire being. It wasn't love—couldn't be. But I was lonely and lust would suffice tonight.

"My hotel isn't far away," I murmured. "Just a few miles."

"I'm a patient man, Grace. Most things worth having take a while."

I abandoned any trace of pretense.

"Let's go. Why waste any more time?"

CHAPTER NINE

Despite my misgivings, our first time together was magical, a dizzying blend of sensations I'd never felt before. My confidence had evaporated the instant we reached the hotel leaving me awkward and shy, wary of sharing intimacies with this perfect stranger. Even the key card confounded me, refusing to blink its green entry light despite several attempts. Patrick scooped it up, put his hands on my shoulders and gently kissed my forehead.

"We can wait, Grace. Maybe the time isn't right." He stroked my cheek as if I were precious porcelain more likely to break than bend. "I want everything to be special for you."

My insides quaked, melting from his touch. I was certainly no ingénue, a disastrous first marriage and subsequent relationships proved that. But Patrick Fong was different, a heady mix of danger and desire that swamped my senses. Pleasure deferred might well be denied forever. I refused to take that chance.

I stood on tiptoe, pulled his face down to mine and kissed him hard. "I don't want to wait, Patrick. Let's go inside."

We sat there sipping wine, listening to the sounds of Roberta Flack on his iPod, escalating the tension to unbearable levels; playing a sensual game of Truth or Dare. Patrick put down his drink and pulled me to my feet. He slowly undressed me, punctuating each touch with honeyed words and gentle kisses. I returned the favor, blinking twice when I saw his body. Was this an illusion? Outside of a museum, I'd never seen a male form so perfectly sculpted.

But he was no fantasy. Patrick led me to the bed and proved how real every part of him was. I was insatiable, hungry for more, unleashing a depth of passion that was foreign to me. I felt no shame even when he switched on the light to look at me.

All the while, he murmured my name, saying those sweet, sexy lies all women yearn to hear.

"You're beautiful, Grace. So lovely. Such soft, smooth skin." He brushed his lips along my neck sending chills up and down my spine. "I've wanted to do that ever since I met you."

"Really?"

He laughed. "Oh yes. You almost didn't make it out of my office, Ms. Quinn. Good thing I value my freedom. The law frowns on that kind of stuff."

It was probably a lie, a slick patent leather line that had thrilled a thousand women. No wonder he used it so freely. It worked.

"I thought you were laughing at me. You never really answered my questions."

Patrick's eyes gleamed with mischief. "Go ahead then. Interrogate me. At this point I'm too weak to resist."

I doused the lights and tried my best, even though it took all night.

It was dark outside when his cell phone rang. The ring tone was vaguely sensual and mysterious, just like him. I fumbled for the phone, turned on a lamp, and checked the clock. Good grief! 3:00 a.m.!

"Hullo," I mumbled.

"I'm looking for Patrick Fong," said a gruff male voice.

I reached across the bed and handed him the phone.

"Fong, here," he said without hesitation. Patrick sounded wide-awake despite the hour.

I closed my eyes and concentrated on his end of the conversation.

"Yes. Really? Right away."

By the time I opened my eyes, he was almost dressed. I grabbed my robe and struggled to my feet.

"What's going on?" I asked. "Who in the world was that?"

"The office," he replied. "There's been a development in the Abacus case."

I watched him as he calmly combed his hair and splashed water on his face.

"Well?" I said. "What happened? Must be something important for them to call at this hour."

Patrick laughed. "I have to be in contact, you know that."

"No, I don't know that. It's hard to believe that a cultural attaché is on duty twenty-four/seven."

He held up his hands. "Come on, Grace, give it a rest."

"What was this development? I need an answer."

Patrick Fong was a pragmatist. He knew that his only hope of leaving the room alive lay in candor, or a reasonable facsimile.

"There's been another murder," he said."

"What! Not Jonathon?"

"That's always your first thought isn't it—Jonathon Grey." He flung his comb into the sink. "No, it's *not* Jonathon Grey. They found the body of Bert Kingman in a trash bin behind the hotel. He'd been stabbed."

"Oh my God! We were just at his place! No wonder he wasn't there."

I couldn't stop babbling. All I could think of was the address book burning a hole in my purse. Patrick grabbed his car keys and headed for the door. "Grace, I ... " He stopped speaking and turned around. "Be careful. No more detective work. I don't want you to get hurt."

Before I responded, he bounded out the door leaving me to wonder if he would ever come back.

I couldn't sleep. Visions of Kingman's garbage-strewn corpse invaded my dreams, turning them into nightmares. Every time I closed my eyes, I thought of Patrick Fong. That was a dream of a very different kind. There were no regrets, no awkward moments last night. His lovemaking, a mixture of tenderness and strength left me weak in the knees and greedy for more. It felt comfortable, as if we had always been together. No man had ever known me better.

Today I had to face reality. My glorious mystery man was lying to me about his profession and probably everything else. A cultural attaché doesn't get midnight phone calls about murder but an intelligence operative might. Patrick may have used me to see just how much I knew. He must have been certain I'd succumb. Not many women could resist that man's charm offensive. I didn't want to believe it but in view of everything that had happened, it was a reasonable assumption. Trouble was, I just didn't *care*.

An even more sinister possibility occurred to me. Patrick might be involved in the aborted theft of the Abacus and Maude's murder. After all, what did I *really* know about him? A man with a handsome face, great body and agile mind could still be a killer. The way he made love ought to be a crime at the very least. A major felony, punishable by a life sentence. I'd never kissed a killer before let alone ....

I had another problem—Kingman's address book. Evidence in a murder investigation nestled in the zippered compartment of my Bottega bag. If Clarke found out he'd call it material evidence and probably arrest me. I felt queasy just thinking of his "accessory after the fact" speech. What had seemed like a good idea was now a time bomb waiting to ignite.

Think Grace, think! I flipped absently through the pages of the book: It hardly seemed worth the trouble.

Apparently Kingman had never heard of the Palmer method. His penmanship was dreadful, his organizational skills non-existent. Grimy fingerprints made several names illegible and jam or some substance too gross to consider stained several pages.

I recognized the names and addresses of Cyrus Worthington and Jie-ling Chow but since they were his clients that hardly screamed guilt—his or theirs. Then I noticed a lump in the seam of the book. It took awhile. I'm not the neatest person. Finally I used my tweezers to pluck a thin slip of paper from the binding. It was a deposit slip! Bert Kingman had deposited $50,000.00 into his savings account the day after Maude's murder. Kingman, one of life's losers had finally struck it rich. Too bad he never lived to spend it. My hand trembled as I stared at the deposit slip. Kingman probably got a payoff from the murderer—and that sealed his fate. Suddenly, the little book made me very nervous. I had to dispose of the evidence fast!

I shoved it into my purse. Before heading out the door, I pulled on jeans, an over-sized sweater and a battered cap. It wasn't much of a disguise but it would suffice. It was barely 6:00 a.m., so maybe no one would see me. An all night copy place was only three blocks away.

I'm not equipped for a life of crime. Guilt oozed out of every pore as I slunk into the hotel lobby. The front desk was deserted and the doorman looked half asleep. Fortunately, the convention-goers were still tucked in their beds with visions of balance sheets in their heads.

I walked swiftly, my head down, collar turned up. There was the usual assortment of morning joggers, dog-walkers and health nuts roaming the streets but no one that I recognized. Nevertheless, each shadow made me jump, every noise made me wince. Those three blocks felt like three miles.

I hate making copies and I'm totally inept at it. Every jerk with a tenth grade education can do it flawlessly. I managed to lose half the content and mutilate the pages. Finally, the attendant took pity on me.

"For fifty cents a page, I'll make your copies," he said.

It was highway robbery and the best idea I'd heard that morning. "Deal," I said.

In no time at all, the stumpy little fellow produced two copies of the address book. He pocketed his pay-off and gave me an insolent stare.

"Anything else you need, lady?" he asked, licking his lips lasciviously.

"Not from you, Bud." I retreated with as much dignity as possible. Had I degenerated to that point? Maybe I had SLUT painted on my chest or a scarlet letter visible only to perverts.

The next task was to get that address book and deposit slip to James Clarke without compromising my identity. I racked my brain for the ideal solution—one that would deliver the goods without delivering me to the pokey. As I stepped off the curb, I narrowly escaped death by bicycle. Of course! It was an omen. Washington D.C. depended on courier services to deliver the documents, business papers, and probable graft that fueled the city. They were the life's blood of the city and the perfect solution to my dilemma. I flagged down a cab.

"Take me to K Street, please," I said politely.

The Cabbie hadn't gone to courtesy school. He swiveled around and faced me. "Lady" he said, "that's a big street, can't you be more specific?"

"I'm looking for the courier service that the big Lobbying firms use. Just drop me near any of them."

He muttered something quite rude and zoomed off while I buckled my seatbelt and said a silent prayer. In five minutes we pulled up in front of Capitol Courier Service, a shopworn storefront that was sandwiched between a deli and a dry-cleaner. A swarm of bicyclists and sedans with the courier logo blanketed the front door. Apparently, business was booming. I carefully wiped my fingerprints off the book, slid out of the cab and slipped in the front door. A massive woman of about thirty, whose nametag read "Flo", dominated the desk.

"Yes," she said. "Do you want bicycle or sedan service?"

"What's the difference?" I asked.

"About twenty dollars, hon."

"Oh, in that case, I'll go economy class. I need this package delivered to police headquarters."

After studying me for a moment, Flo lowered her gaze and handed me an envelope.

"Okay. Address this for me, and make sure you get the right precinct. The Metropolitan Police have a couple of locations."

"Will this get there today? My boss'll kill me if it's late—it's evidence in a court case." I hung my head and made my lip tremble. It wasn't hard to project fear. Just thinking of James Clarke and his thirst for vengeance inspired angst.

Flo was a compassionate woman. "We've all had that kind of boss, honey, don't worry. It'll get there before noon."

I paid her twenty dollars, took my receipt and fled. In the return address section, I had printed the name and address of Cyrus Worthington. That should give Clarke something to chew on!

CHAPTER TEN

I rushed back to my room and hastily showered and dressed. Today I had to staff that damned IRS booth. Most of the CPAs who stopped by just wanted to chat but a few had another agenda. Brett Roberts was my first visitor. He pulled up a chair and handed me a steaming mug of coffee. I was more than willing to take that bribe.

"Ma'am, I need help. Can the IRS help me, please?" Brett deepened his Southern accent.

"Oh stop it, Brett. I feel like a fool sitting here."

Brett pushed his chair against the back of the booth and looked around. He lowered his voice to a whisper. "I've been hearing things, Grace. Watch your back."

"What kind of things?"

"About you and Therese snooping into other people's business—very serious business."

"I don't have any idea what you're talking about, Brett."

"This Tax Champions stuff is bad news, Grace. Those guys are pretty desperate."

I blew on my coffee and took a sip. "Are they desperate enough to murder Maude?"

"Murder! What's wrong with you?' Brett said.

"Frankly, I don't give a damn about Tax Champions and the fools who run it. The courts will deal with them. I do care about Jonathon Grey—and you should too, Brett. We both know that Jonathon did *not* kill Maude. If those bozos are involved, I intend to find out."

Brett didn't answer me for a while. Then he pulled out his chair and stood up.

"Face it, Grace. If Jonathon didn't do it, the most likely suspect is his son. You saw him in action yesterday. Chris Grey has a bad temper. Don't forget that some of those 'bozos' still have pull with the Service. Your executive career could be very short."

Brett picked up his things, and headed for the exit. In his haste, he forgot his coffee mug. When I picked it up I almost dropped it. The logo said "Tax Champions: Protecting the average Joe."

It had never occurred to me that Brett Roberts was involved in the tax shelter mess. Brett was so straight-laced, so honorable, so risk adverse. Maybe I didn't know him as well as I thought. I was gnawing on this problem when Mary Hagan appeared. As usual, she looked and smelled perfect—hair, nails, French scent, Armani suit. I thought about the hole I'd noticed in my stockings and abruptly sat down. Mary was sure to raise her sculpted brows at me if she saw that.

"Grace, you look down," she said. "What's the matter?"

"Ah, nothing. I was just wondering if someone I'd known for ten years could be a scoundrel."

"Who's the scoundrel in question?" Mary asked.

"Brett Roberts. We used to work together in Chicago, and I know he's a good guy."

Mary frowned. "Correction. You *knew* him ten years ago. People can change a lot in a decade."

"Maybe I'm making too much of it, but I think he might be involved in this Tax Champions mess. It doesn't make sense—why would he even risk it?"

Mary got that smug look again. She lowered her voice. "Well, I understand that Brett is in some financial difficulties."

"Brett! I can't believe it. He was always the soul of caution, for Christ's sake."

"Unfortunately, Brett crossed that new frontier they call 'male menopause'. I've heard rumors that he became very close to some young chippie at his office."

I looked at Mary in total amazement. "What in the hell is a 'chippie'?"

She smiled sweetly at me. "You know, a bimbo, slut, whatever you want to call it. Those treats can be expensive. Even a decent man might need an alternate source of funds."

I suddenly remembered something Brett had mentioned the night Maude died—how she'd been at his firm asking questions about Tax Champions. Stratton-Miles would dump him if he became a liability.

"Grace, are you in a trance? I asked you about this Bert Kingman person—the guy they found murdered last night." Mary never let me forget that she was my boss and a very well informed boss at that. I decided to give an expurgated account of my exploits last night.

"I only met him once on the night Maude died. He was incoherent—he'd been knocked out and he was bleeding. Of course, he could have been the inside man on the Abacus theft. Frankly, he seemed a bit dull-witted to me."

Mary began that toe-tapping routine of hers. "*Everyone* seems like a dullard to you. Start living in the real world for a change."

I shifted in my seat. I had the uncomfortable feeling that this lecture had just begun.

Fortunately, at that moment I received a text from Jonathon. I risked reading it under the piercing gaze of my boss.

"Mary, I'm sorry but I have to return this call. May I catch you later?"

I felt myself blushing despite the relentless blast of air-conditioning in the room. Now I knew how a bug feels when the can of Raid looms overhead.

Mary laughed. "Relax Grace, we've all been there. Besides it's lunch time anyway and I have a meeting." She grabbed her briefcase and smiled coyly. "You'll have to tell me all about him later."

Whew! I headed to the front desk searching for a private space to use my phone. Jonathon's message was concise. "*Call me, ASAP. Jonathon*"

He answered on the first ring. "Grace! Can you meet me at Kramerbooks in about thirty minutes? We have a lot to talk about."

You bet we do! That gave me just enough time to dash to my room, and freshen up. I hadn't seen a sign of Patrick but you never knew. In record time I was on my way up Connecticut Avenue to Kramerbooks, a café and bookstore for people who actually cherished the printed word. It was staffed by employees who were both literate and well read, a true rarity these days. Rumor had it that a former President had purchased *Leaves of Grass* from this very store for his young inamorata.

Jonathon wasn't in the bar area, but when I checked the small café he and Chris were both seated at a back table. He waved to me and being the gentleman that he was, rose and pulled out my chair. Chris didn't budge.

You'd never guess that Jonathon had spent any time under duress; he was as impeccably groomed as ever. His son was not so fortunate. Chris looked like a train-wreck—unshaven and rumpled. I took a bit of comfort from that.

"Oh Jonathon, I was so worried. Are you okay?" I saw Chris roll his eyes.

"Believe it or not, I'm just fine. I wasn't arrested, merely 'detained' for questioning. When my attorney showed up, Clarke had to release me."

Chris slammed his water glass on the table. "That doesn't mean you're out of the woods, Dad. They just didn't have enough evidence to make a charge stick. Yet."

For once, I had to agree with disagreeable Chris. Jonathon was still the prime suspect.

I leaned forward. "Clarke told me yesterday that you had Maude's blood on your suit, Jonathon. He thinks you stabbed her in a fit of passion ...."

"Passion—for that old cow. What a joke." Chris Grey's voice was bitter.

"It you'd let me finish my sentence, *Christopher,* I was going to say, that Clarke thinks Jonathon killed Maude to protect his son. *You,* Chris."

Chris blanched, and Jonathon grabbed his arm. "Of course I didn't kill Maude—for that or any other reason. I had an appointment with her but I never even talked to her. She was dead when I got there. You saw me, Grace."

Chris Grey stuck out his lip. My God, the man was pouting.

"There's more, I'm afraid." I ignored Chris, and turned toward Jonathon. "Last night, that rent-a-cop Kingman, was murdered. The cops think someone killed him because he saw something the night Maude was murdered."

Jonathon leaned forward. "What! The guy who called himself private police? That guy is dead!" He was dumbfounded, so distraught that for the first time, Jonathon actually looked his age. Chris on the other hand, seemed jubilant. "Dad, that's great!" he said.

Both Jonathon and I turned to Chris. "What are you saying?" Jonathon asked.

"It's simple, Dad. If this guy was murdered last night, you're off the hook. You have the best alibi of all—police custody."

I hated to burst his bubble, but of course I did. "We don't know when Kingman died. Jonathon might still be in danger. But I know, that is, I understand, that someone was bribing Kingman to keep him quiet. Someone with a good deal of money."

Chris Grey narrowed his eyes. "How do you know all this anyway? What business is it of yours?"

"Easy, Chris." Jonathon said. "Grace, maybe Kingman was part of the Abacus theft. After all, we only had his word that he was assaulted. He might have been faking."

I took a deep breath. "There are two possibilities. Either Kingman was part of the Abacus plot and was double-crossed, or Kingman saw Maude's murder and was blackmailing her killer."

Chris posited a third scenario. "It could have been a random murder. This city has plenty of those every week."

"Maybe," I agreed. "But how many victims are murdered on the day they deposit $50,000 in their savings account?"

Chris whistled. "That's a lot for a security guard."

"Or anyone else," Jonathon added. "Grace, are you sure about that?"

I looked at my shoes. It wasn't easy to deceive Jonathon Grey.

"I have it on the very best authority but don't quote me. And then there's the threatening phone call I got."

"What!" Both of the Greys exclaimed in unison.

After I summarized my situation, Jonathon looked at his watch and stood up. "That does it. Grace, stay out of this from now on. It's far too dangerous."

I ignored his very sound advice and continued speaking. "I think this whole mess is related either to the Abacus or to Maude's pursuit of her 'big story'. And that involves Tax Champions, Chris, I'm sorry. We've learned that there's some kind of recording that proves intent to defraud the government."

Chris Grey jabbed his finger at me. "Who is this 'we' you're talking about and how do you know about this alleged evidence?"

"Maybe you should ask your buddy Kelvin Cates about it, Chris. You two seem pretty tight." I grabbed the finger he was wagging at me, and twisted it.

"Ow!" he yelped. "You bitch!"

"Funny, that's what the person on the phone called me. Was it you, Chris?"

Jonathon pounded the table. "Stop it now—both of you."

Chris and I glared at each other. After a minute I swallowed hard and said, "I'm sorry Jonathon, you've got enough on your mind."

Chris Grey lowered his grey-green eyes. "I'm sorry Dad. And no, I didn't threaten her."

Jonathon patted his son's hand. "I know, son, I know. But we have to work together not tear each other apart. Grace, I meant what I said. No more heroics, do you hear me?"

I crossed my fingers and my ankles. "Of course, Jonathon," I said sweetly.

I raced back to the San Simone just in time to conduct my afternoon seminar. Today the topic was benign: *Navigating the IRS: how to help your client*. A large and enthusiastic group provided examples of power-mad IRS agents preying on their clients. I'd heard this song so many times before that I could sing every verse from memory. Most of them admitted privately that their clients might have run afoul of the law, unintentionally of course. It was all a big misunderstanding and they were paid quite handsomely to untangle the mess.

Two hours of conflict made me thirsty. I longed for the giant bottle of Pellegrino in my hotel room and thanks to an express elevator; it took only a minute to reach my floor.

The door to the room was ajar. Damn, that meant that the maid hadn't finished yet. I cautiously pushed it open and faced a disaster. Every sofa cushion, pillow, mattress and suitcase had been slashed, trashed, or upended. The pockets on my suit-jackets were ripped, my make-up defiled. Even the phonebook had been destroyed! Advice from one of those crime buster shows rang in my ears: don't enter a crime scene, leave immediately. I fled. Down the deserted hallway, past the ice machine and into the solid frame of Lt. James Clarke. He knew by my wild eyes and frantic hand gestures that something major had happened.

"Ms. Quinn, Grace—hold on! What's wrong?"

At first, I couldn't speak. My brain knew what to say but my lips wouldn't cooperate. Clarke guided me to a chair and picked up the house phone across from the elevator.

"Send hotel Security to the third floor right away. This is Clarke, Metro PD."

I refused to cry, it was just too stereotypical. Instead I grabbed my lace hanky and blew my nose. That actually helped. Clarke was watching me patiently waiting for me to regain my senses.

"Someone ransacked my room," I stammered. "He ruined my clothes! He destroyed my make-up!" I was gathering steam now incensed by such blatant brutality.

"How come you said 'he'? Do you know it was a man?"

"Of course I do! No sane woman would ruin a perfectly gorgeous Chanel jacket. Do you realize how much I paid for that—on sale of course."

Clarke was beginning to look bored. "Obviously, you have something someone wants very badly. Now, what could that be I wonder?"

"I don't know. Maybe there's a maniac on the loose, a murderer whose blood lust ...."

Clarke interrupted me in mid fantasy. "I get the picture, Ms. Quinn. But I think we both know that this is connected to Ms. Morrissey's murder and to that Museum stuff."

He hadn't mentioned Al Kingman. Was that a deliberate omission or a trap?

Clarke kept staring at me in the most maddening way.

"Funny thing," he said, "I was hoping to run into you. I got a parcel delivered to me this morning."

I managed a blank look. "So?" I said.

"It contained a piece of evidence in a murder investigation. You wouldn't know anything about that now would you, Ms. Quinn?"

"I didn't take anything from the Exhibit Hall where Maude died except my notes." That was one trap I'd avoided rather nicely. I hadn't even lied.

Clarke grinned. "Did I say it was from Ms. Morrissey? Never mind, I bet the courier service can identify the sender. If not, we may be able to find some fingerprints."

I breathed a silent prayer that big Flo believed in Girl Power. She might hate nosey cops too.

The elevator doors opened noisily disgorging an East Asian man wearing a San Simone Hotel blazer. He was no Patrick Fong but under the circumstances, he'd do nicely.

"I'm Rodney Patel," he said, "Hotel Security."

Rodney and Clarke spent a few minutes doing cop/former cop bonding, after which Rodney turned to me.

"I'm so sorry for the inconvenience, Ms. Quinn. Please allow us to move your things into a suite—no charge of course."

"My clothing is torn, I'll need a seamstress or something. I can't sew a stitch."

Mr. Patel handled that inconvenience as well. "Don't you worry. We have an expert tailor on staff. It will be our pleasure to repair everything."

Clarke muscled in immediately. "Not until we dust for prints—it is a crime scene, after all."

Patel nodded to him, and took my arm. "Let's stop by the front desk and get you settled."

I couldn't resist darting a glance at Clarke. He shook his head in disgust.

I was treated like visiting royalty by the hotel staff. The Concierge took me in hand and led me to a private office. "May I get you anything to drink while we make up your suite?" she asked.

"I would love a Pellegrino—no ice and a lime."

She whisked away and returned a few minutes later with a large bottle of Pellegrino, a crystal glass, and a plate of tea sandwiches with fruit. The San Simone knew how to treat crime victims.

When my suite was ready, the Concierge returned. She handed me a large manila envelope with my name on it. The handwriting looked very familiar.

"This was delivered yesterday," she said. "With all the disruption, I'm afraid we misplaced it."

She escorted me to my very plush accommodations and left me alone to tear open the envelope. I gasped when I saw read the message. It was from Maude!

"Grace, I'm sending you this for safekeeping. It's high tech stuff, fresh off the drawing board. Those Tax Champion idiots never even noticed it. We didn't always get along, but I know you have integrity. If something happens to me, make sure this gets to the right people.
Maude."

Something that looked like a flash drive tumbled from the envelope. It was tiny, no more than two-and-half inches. I had no idea in the world what it was. As usual, Maude had the last word.

I crossed my fingers and rang Therese's room extension, praying that she was there. She was. I gave her my new room number and told her to join me on the double. Her idea of on the double tuned out to be twenty minutes. I sat and seethed until she arrived.

"How do you rate a suite?" Therese asked. "It must be nice to be a government employee."

When Therese found out how I earned my new digs, she shut up fast. I handed her Maude's letter and watched her mouth fall open.

"Oh my God," she cried, "this is too much. Maude speaking from the grave, you getting burgled. Grace, I'm scared." She managed a sly grin. "Still, it is pretty cool of old Maudie, using that spy store stuff. I've read about it. Never seen it before though. These talking heads on television are yapping about the NSA. Huh! Joe six-pack, not to mention your nearest and dearest can record you any old day."

I decided to spill every secret I knew about the unsavory mess—the address book, the flash drive and Brett Roberts' warning. I didn't mention my interlude with Patrick Fong but that was private.

"Since Brett mentioned you, I felt you ought to know. You could be in danger, Therese. You have good reason to be scared."

Therese had that green eyeshade look on her face. She was obviously constructing a mental balance sheet weighing the pros and cons of our little project. I hadn't realized she was capable of that much silence. It worried me. Finally the veil lifted and Therese returned to planet earth.

"So what if there's some danger," she said. "This is the most fun I've had in years! Come on. Bring that baby out and let's start the party."

I had some trouble getting it to work. I'm not mechanical at the best of times and my hands were shaking. As I fumbled around, Therese grabbed the flash drive, inserted it into my laptop and made that machine sing. There was some static, but not much. We heard a conversation among three people, probably men. Only one voice rang out—the flat Mid-western vowels of Kelvin Cates.

"You know why we're here. The IRS has been snooping around Tax Champions and we need to be careful. Don't make it easy for them."

A muffled voice of indeterminate gender interrupted Cates. *"I'm worried about our latest advertising campaign. We're going to get caught."*

"You wimp. How are we going to reel in the suckers if we don't embellish a bit?"

A different male voice chimed in. *"No shit. Can you just see Joe Six-pack, taking the wife and kiddies to Disney World, and writing off all his expenses. We'll be long gone by the time he gets audited. It's beautiful."*

Cates again. *"You didn't complain when we split the profits last year. We got a legal opinion on our side."*

Laughter from all.

"Are you sure we can trust him? His father was a real straight arrow."

Voice number three again. *"Don't worry. That's why we have our source at the IRS helping us out."*

Cates chimed in. *"Watch out for that snoopy bitch Morrissey. She's been sniffing around."*

Speaker number two chuckled. *"We know how to deal with her too."*

We heard the sound of a door slamming. Maude Morrissey's hot scoop had ended.

Therese was elated. "That's it Grace, we've got it! Intent!"

I agreed but there was one big sticking point. Criminal tax fraud was one thing, murder was quite another. Maude's evidence wouldn't necessarily nail her killer.

"We have another problem, Therese. How do we get this thing to the cops without involving ourselves?"

"What do you mean, Grace? Just hand it to Clarke. After all, it's not your fault if Maude sent you something. Come on, I'll go with you. Grab your stuff."

I knew Therese's motive and it wasn't a thirst for justice. The sight of men in uniforms makes her weak and she has the traffic tickets to prove it.

As we passed the front desk, the helpful Concierge called my name.

"Oh Ms. Quinn, you've got a message I didn't want anyone to know you'd changed your room," she whispered.

She handed me one of those, 'while you were out' slips from Patrick Fong!

" *Meet me at the Panda Exhibit—National Zoo—4:00 p.m. Patrick*"

Patrick Fong was pretty conceited if he believed me to just drop everything and meet him. On the other hand, purely in the interests of justice, I should hear what he had to say.

I gave the envelope to Therese. "Could you go by yourself to the precinct? I've got ...."

Therese snatched the note and read it. "Are you kidding? Of course I can handle this myself. *You* go handle Patrick Fong."

CHAPTER ELEVEN

She trotted out the door and hailed a cab while I walked the two blocks to the Metro. Maybe I should check out Cyrus Worthington's place in Cleveland Park while I was in the vicinity.

I exited at the National Zoo amid an impossible throng of tourists, ill-mannered school children and office workers. The clock on the bank building blinked 101 ºF degrees. I felt hot, sticky and unattractive. The miserably humid air turned my hair into a mound of wilted lettuce that no amount of hairspray would revive. Oh well, maybe Patrick would get turned on by honest sweat.

Very few zoo-dwellers were visible. They fled to their air-conditioned enclosures proving again which species was superior. The pandas were invisible probably nestling on an indoor ice floe. I plopped on a bench as Patrick emerged looking cool and sexy. Not surprising—maybe the man lacked sweat glands. More likely he wasn't even human.

Without saying a word Patrick grabbed me and planted a big kiss on my lips. Heads turned, school-kids snickered and I didn't care. He might be using me, probably was, but that was one chance worth taking. *Baby, use me up!*

"I just had to do that," he said. "I couldn't stop thinking about last night. It was special." He looked at me and shook his head. "You're trouble, I knew it from that first day. I've never met a woman quite like you." Patrick laughed and held out his hand. "Come on, let's go inside and sit on a bench. It's getting hot out here."

He grabbed my satchel, and opened the door for me. "Hey, this is heavy. What in the world do women carry in these things? Your purse looks just as heavy."

I was not about to betray the secrets of the purse even to Patrick. Men appreciate a sense of mystery and most of them are too smart to even look in a woman's handbag. It's a gender thing inherited from our cave dwelling ancestors.

We shared the bench with a hunched old lady who was nose deep into the *Washington Post*. Patrick took my hand and smiled. "I missed you, Grace. Even though it's only been," he looked at his watch, "thirteen hours and ten seconds." He ducked his head. "Believe it or not, I'm usually not this foolish. There's just something about you ... " He grinned.

Who could resist a man like that? Patrick cleared his throat, and lowered his voice.

"There's something else you should know about Kingman. You were right. He was leaving town. The police found a bus ticket to Cleveland in his pocket. He was shot in the head, in the forehead, actually. They think he was sitting down at the time."

"I thought you said he was stabbed! Patrick, tell me the truth! You're not some desk-jockey for the State Department, are you? Please—I have to trust you."

He dropped my hand. Those eyes no longer sparkled. They were cold and obsidian. "You're right," he said, "trust has to be earned. I'm not an office worker. Not everyone is free to just blurt things out, Grace."

"Oh, like me, you mean." Things were definitely going downhill. "Kingman was being bribed by someone. Who was it?"

Patrick stood, his posture Marine stiff. "What are you talking about? You're not the only one who has trust issues." He loomed over me. "Where did you get that information? You're playing a very dangerous game, Grace. Now tell me the truth!"

"A confidential informant told me," I said primly. "Naturally, I'm not free to divulge the name."

We spent a moment exchanging glares. I cracked first by asking him about the Abacus.

"I saw the security guys moving the Abacus. Where were they taking it?"

Patrick bit his lip and practically spat out his reply. "It'll probably go to the Sackler. Jie-ling Chow knows the particulars." His smile verged on malicious as he said that name.

"Have they made any progress finding the thieves?"

"None that I've heard of," he said in clipped tones.

The strain between us was palpable. As I reached for his hand, Patrick looked at his watch.

"Oops, I'm late for an appointment," he said. "We'll talk later."

He practically sprinted across the floor and out the door. From the guilt that covered his face I suspected that the name of his urgent appointment was Jie-ling Chow.

I felt like the biggest fool in the Universe. That might be an exaggeration—just in the District of Columbia. After all, I hadn't committed a crime for him or lent him money. Yet.

I refused to brood. He was only a man, there were plenty of fish in the sea, and men were like busses, always another one around the corner. There. I'd repeated every cliché ever uttered by a despondent woman. The truth—Patrick was someone special. I seldom meet a man who is handsome, sexy and smart. Correction. I've *never* met a man with all those qualities, certainly not at the IRS. No matter. I would survive. I'd already had one husband, several lovers, and more than a few admirers. This wasn't the end of the world. It just seemed like it.

The best tonic for depression is hard work. I decided to forget Mr. Fong, and check out Cyrus Worthington's digs in Cleveland Park. His street number was on the copies I'd made of Kingman's address book.

Cleveland Park, scene of President Cleveland's summer home, has all the charm of a small village despite being nestled in the heart of Northwest Washington. I loved strolling down the tree-lined streets even though the risk of heatstroke loomed. Most of the mansions had been converted to commercial use, embassies, or schools but a few of the old homesteads remained. Cyrus lived on Newark Street, right in the middle of the historic district. His neighbors were an enchanting array of Victorian, Queen Ann and Mission style frame homes that had been lovingly restored and maintained. There had to be love involved to provide the upkeep for these beauties. It cost a mint! I wandered down the block searching for his home—3411 Newark Avenue. When I found it, I was shocked.

The Worthington Mansion was a large Classical Revival that had seen better days. It reminded me of a nobleman of reduced circumstances who now resided in genteel poverty. Despite its peeling paint and neglected grounds, it still looked like a mansion to me. Once a dwelling exceeds 10,000 feet, I call it a mansion. Where was all the Worthington family money? It certainly hadn't been squandered on their homestead.

I screwed up my courage, climbed the stairs to the graceful porch, and rang the bell. Perhaps a servant would answer, preferably one who didn't speak English.

The door opened slowly and a sweet -faced old lady emerged. Her smile was radiant and a bit too trusting in view of the times. Some kind of con artist could get in! I stepped forward, and stretched out my hand.

"Good afternoon, I'm Grace Quinn with ... the Government. I'm an acquaintance of Mr. Worthington." I decided that mentioning the IRS might not be the smartest move. Citizens tended to recoil at the very name.

"Oh. Cyrus isn't home yet," she said. "I'm his sister, Madelaine. Won't you come in?"

Madelaine's face was innocent of make-up, her light brown hair pinned to her head. Although I judged her to be in her seventies, there was a luminosity to her skin that gave her a radiant, almost ethereal look.

"I don't want to disturb you," I said mendaciously.

"Nonsense. I'd welcome the company. We could have tea." Madelaine tilted her head, and beamed. "I don't get many visitors these days."

Naturally I leapt at the chance. The entryway was papered in a faded flower print. I admired the elaborate dentil molding and molded archways that led to a small parlor.

The floors were beautiful walnut planks that needed a face-lift. Years of Washington sun had muted the Persian rugs and they were a bit threadbare. The patina of age was a permanent resident of this place.

Miss Worthington waved me to an antique sofa in her parlor. It was a lovely Louis XVI canapé with needlepoint upholstery. An ebony baby grand piano graced the opposite corner.

"I'll get us some tea, Dear. Will Earl Grey do?"

"Of course, of course. Please don't go to any trouble on my account."

Madelaine flicked her hand. "It's really a pleasure. Besides, I think Mrs. Day is still here. She's our char."

I got this eerie feeling that Miss Worthington had morphed into Miss Haversham. No doubt the tattered, moth-eaten wedding dress was packed away in the attic. She perched on the chair opposite me, her back ramrod straight. "Now. How do you know my brother?"

"We're both affiliated with the Abacus Exhibit. You probably know about it through Dr. Chow."

"Chow? Can't say I know him." Miss Worthington looked confused. "Was Cyrus expecting you, dear?"

Luckily, tea arrived, wheeled in on a cart by a stocky Irish woman in her mid-fifties. Madelaine insisted on pouring. Her hands were speckled claws but they were strong.

The elegant tea service was Herend, Rothschild Bird pattern. I'd priced some at auction and it was incredibly expensive. Several of the cups were chipped but the delicate saucers were wafer thin and beautiful.

"Your china is so lovely, Miss Worthington. Is it a family heirloom?"

"Yes. How kind of you to notice it. Almost everything in the house is a treasured memento. Cyrus says we'll be able to restore our home before long."

I felt something soft brush my leg. It was a Persian cat with a glorious coat of marmalade colored fur. He glared at me, daring me to touch him. "Meow" he said. Actually, it was more of a command that I scratch his back and admire him.

"Who is this?" I asked Madelaine. "He's gorgeous."

She flushed with pride. As a pet-owner myself, I could relate.

"This is Whistler," she said scooping up her pet, "and he can be a very naughty boy."

I stood and examined the oil painting above the sofa.

"How exquisite! Is this also a Whistler?"

She looked a bit nostalgic. "My mother loved his work. She collected it, you know."

"Really."

I was puzzled. I seemed to recall seeing an identical painting among the Freer's excellent Whistler collection. This was a superb copy.

"I remember when I was a girl," Madelaine mused, "I would pretend that I was the princess in the picture 'The Princess from the Land of Porcelain,' that's what it's called you know. Mother would open the old trunk in the attic and let me dress up in her long white gowns." She wiped her eyes. "I'm sorry, dear, it's just such a happy memory."

"What a responsibility to maintain a beautiful old home like this."

"Oh it is," she enthused. "But Cyrus says it's a sacred trust. That's why we've got to restore it. Wait, let me show you."

Miss Worthington scurried from the room and returned with a cardboard tube.

"See. This is the architect's drawing." She pulled a sheaf of papers from the container.

"Wow, that's quite a project," I said.

I was beginning to grow nervous. If Cyrus caught me snooping around his home, he might renovate me!

I rose and shook Madelaine's hand. "Thank you for being so gracious. Please tell Cyrus that I called."

Miss Worthington's eyes had a dazed look that suggested drugs or senility.

"Oh, so soon. Please come back again. Now what did you say your name is, Dear?"

"Mary Hagan."

CHAPTER TWELVE

I walked slowly toward the Cleveland Park Metro Station. The condition of Cyrus Worthington's home was shocking and needed an enormous amount of money to spruce up the old homestead. According to Madelaine, his ship was coming in. Wait a minute. He'd better hope it was an armada!

I arrived at the Metro entrance and grabbed the escalator handrail. Washington etiquette dictated that travelers who wanted to walk down the steps must be given right of way on the left. I'd cursed unwary tourists many times when they ignored the rules. Since I was engrossed in thought I stayed to the right. It was five-thirty, the rush hour peak. Government workers, school kids, tourists, and business people surged down the steel stairs. Audacious riders, mostly male, ran down the left hand side without holding the handrail. Let them try that in high heels with a purse!

The painting in Madelaine's parlor astounded me. It was either an exquisite copy or a true Whistler. I'd have to check the Freer just to be sure. A genuine masterpiece would be worth millions, but the rest of the house hardly suggested an abundance of cash. I shifted my satchel to my left arm, and kept my purse pressed against my chest. The Post had reported several tales of purse snatchings during tourist season. I wasn't going to make it easy for anyone ....

WACK! I felt two very strong hands in the small of my back. They gave me a push that propelled me down the remaining third of the steel stairs. It happened so fast I couldn't cry out. I had about three seconds to think "Oh my God!" before I went airborne. I lay crumpled on something soft and squishy, while shouts for help and "Shut down the stairs" rang out. I never lost consciousness but I could feel something sticky sliding down my face, and something smelled awful. I lifted up my head and tried to rise. Blood trickled into my ear. It was so dark, almost black.

"Don't move, honey," said a kindly voice. "You're going to be just fine."

I looked up into the face of the Station Master. People were stepping over me to exit the escalator and I could hear sirens."

"How did you trip?" he asked. His nameplate read, "Edward Duffy, Stationmaster."

I couldn't formulate sentences yet.

"What'd you mean fall—she was pushed! I saw someone with a backpack push her."

I couldn't tell if the speaker was a man or woman. I shifted my shoulder, and noticed that my purse was still on my arm. My right hand was twisted and swollen where I'd landed on it, and my left knee hurt. The squishy cushion below me started to seep some noxious liquid all over my skirt.

"My stuff, my stuff!" a scratchy voice complained.

"You—stand back and keep quiet," Edward Duffy commanded. "You may be a hero."

"WHAT!" said scratchy voice.

"Your garbage bag cushioned this young lady's fall. She could have broken her neck."

The wail of an ambulance filled the air. Soon two paramedics walked down the stairs and cordoned off the area.

"What have we got here, Ed?" asked the older guy.

"This young lady fell."

"She was pushed!" a voice interrupted. "I saw her."

Duffy turned to a worker. "Get a statement, and interview anyone else who saw something. Most of them are long gone—don't want to miss their trains."

"How are you feeling, Miss?" asked the other paramedic. "Let me check things out for you. What's your name? I'm Joanne." She was a slim black woman in her early twenties.

"Grace, my name is Grace. And I'm fine."

She chuckled. "I'll be the judge of that, Grace. You're going for a little ride in the ambulance."

I tried to protest.

"Sorry, Grace, those are the rules. You know about rules, don't you?"

"I work for the Federal Government," I croaked.

A big smile split her face. "Well then, you do know all about rules."

Her partner moved over and said. "Okay Miss, we going to get you on this board, and into the elevator. Do you have your things?"

My purse was still around my shoulder, but my satchel was missing.

"My tote bag!" I cried.

"What's it look like Grace," said Joanne.

"It's a black woven leather Bottega Venetta tote," I said.

"Well, it's not here. But it sounds to me like you still have your fashion sense at least. You know, that purse of yours absorbed a lot of the force." She turned it around. "Louis Vuitton, huh? I guess it pays to buy good leather."

Amen, Sister. I closed my eyes and slipped into the land of nod.

◇◇ ◇ ◇ ◇

Bright lights were shining in my face, and I couldn't move my hand. *Where was I?*

The last thing I remembered was the gentle pinch of a needle, as a doctor examined me. My head hurt. I tried to pull myself up but there were metal sides to the bed.

"Welcome back to the living, Grace." That syrupy voice was very familiar. It belonged to my boss.

"Couldn't you think of something less dramatic," Mary Hagan asked, "maybe a coma or amnesia? You've got the entire D.C. Metro system in an uproar."

"Let me out of here. This is so embarrassing."

"Who cares? You came this close to killing yourself or snapping your neck. You should be grateful. Anyhow they're going to release you as soon as the Doctor signs off."

"What time is it?" I gasped.

Mary flicked her wrist over and glanced at her watch. It was something dainty with diamonds—Swiss, I think. Expensive, I know.

"Let's see, it's now ten p.m. You've been here four hours.

"My tote bag! He stole my Bottega tote bag!

"What are you babbling about? You survive an accident and whine about a bag. Grow up!" Mary gave me that thousand-yard stare.

Remind me never to nominate her for the Florence Nightingale Award. Compassion was definitely not her thing.

"Besides, what were you doing over in Cleveland Park? That's a long way from the San Simone and the CPA convention."

"W-a-t-e-r," I gasped.

A knock on the door provided a welcome diversion. Maybe the doctor was here to spring me.

James Clarke poked his head in the doorway. "Well, well, Ms. Quinn. Do I smell a lawsuit against the District? You actually got a hospital room." He looked inordinately cheerful as he smiled at his little joke

Enough already! "What are *you* doing here?" I asked.

"We get copies of all incident reports on the Metro. When I saw your name, I got curious. This has been a bad week for you."

"You have a talent for understatement, Lieutenant," I said. "Now leave me alone."

Clarke pulled up a chair and sat backwards in it. "What *really* happened?"

Mary Hagan went on alert. I swear her ears pricked up like a terrier's.

Unfortunately, she had met her match. Clarke narrowed his eyes and beat her to the punch. "I'm sorry, Ms. Hagan but I'll need to interview Grace in private."

Mary bristled. "I am her supervisor, Lieutenant. Also and her friend and advisor."

Clarke was unimpressed. "Fine. You can advise her after our interview. Thanks for your cooperation." He opened the door and pointed.

Mary flounced out the door without a word of goodbye while Clarke pulled his chair next to my bed and took out his note pad.

"Now. I think we have some things to discuss," he said.

Maybe it was the near-death experience or my fear of penal servitude. I spilled almost every bit of information I'd gathered along with my suppositions and conclusions. Naturally, I saved the juicy parts about Patrick Fong and anything that might implicate Jonathon Grey and I didn't mention Maude's evidence.

Clarke spent at least an hour in my room. He tried to be pleasant but I detected that faint frat boy smirk in his every sentence. Despite the risk to life and liberty my detective work failed to impress him. Before he left, Clarke handed me the *Washington Post,* which he'd thoughtfully opened to the death notices. Maude had scored a home run. Her murder made page one and a flowery portrait of her life was featured in the obituary section. I'm sure the distinction had her beaming from her final resting place.

The *Post's* crime reporter partnered with their chief business correspondent to describe the CPA conference, Maude's position at Tax Chat and of course, the Abacus. Fortunately they referred to me only as "a participant at the conference," and Jonathon as a "prominent accountant." Tax Champions was not mentioned. The article concluded with a lengthy quote from Cyrus Worthington on the significance of the Abacus and it's importance to Sino-American relations. In death as in life, Bert Kingman had poor timing. His murder missed the late edition.

Clarke stared at me as I read. "Anything missing, Ms. Quinn?" he asked casually.

"I don't see any mention of Mr. Kingman—the security guard."

Clarke covered his mouth and yawned. "Not everyone has your attention to detail. Remember that package I told you about? Oddly enough, someone sent me some of Kingman's personal effects."

"Really. What did you get?"

Clarke started fiddling with his tie. "Oh this and that. It seems our Mr. Kingman was moving up in the world. He made a big savings deposit only yesterday."

"No kidding."

Clarke stood and headed for the door. "Kingman was well paid for whatever task he performed. I guess he fell short somehow. You know how hard it is to get good help these days." He gripped the doorknob and paused.

"At least you can't pin that on Jonathon Grey," I said. "You had him in custody."

Clarke wheeled around. "I never said when Kingman was killed, and besides, there are two members of the Grey family who might be involved in this."

Clarke knew how to make an exit.

◇ ◇ ◇ ◇ ◇

My doctor sauntered in just before midnight. He was a balding, angular fellow in his thirties who slouched against the wall as he reviewed my chart.

"I guess you're fit to leave us," he said. "Doesn't look like you have a concussion or any internal bleeding." He seemed disappointed with the mundane nature of my injuries.

A nurse appeared and handed me my discharge papers and a prescription for Valium to relax my muscles. Hot damn—at least I'd scored some good drugs. I struggled to put on my jacket, mindful of a sharp pain in my chest. A heart attack, I knew it! Before I pressed the call button, I remembered sticking Maude's flash drive in my bra. Against all odds, it was still there. No wonder I felt a twinge!

Mary opened the door before I removed it. She gathered up my things and helped me to her car. I was suspicious of this new, solicitous version of my boss. Knowing her, there had to be an angle somewhere.

"Grace, you never had a chance to tell me. What really happened?"

I just couldn't bear to discuss my brush with death. The Valium dispensed by Doctor Feel-good made me drowsy and ready for oblivion not a heart-to-heart chat.

"Mary, can we talk tomorrow?" I asked. "I feel wiped out."

She really had no choice. Although I'm sure Mary yearned to throttle me, her good manners and fine Southern upbringing won out.

"Naturally. Call me tomorrow." She dropped me off at my hotel and sped away.

CHAPTER THIRTEEN

As soon as I reached the suite, I inventoried my war wounds.
My hand really hurt, I had twelve staples in my head and a
steady ache. Miraculously nothing had broken although I
feared that a blood clot might be swimming through my
bloodstream, waiting to attack. I fell into bed exhausted,
praying I wouldn't die of a concussion before seeing Patrick
again.

After a sound sleep, I awakened feeling fragile but
motivated. My mission today was simple: attend the afternoon
session of the conference and avoid Mary Hagan if it was
humanly possible to do so. If time permitted, a visit the Freer
Museum would also be in order. That conversation with
Madelaine had piqued my curiosity about out that Whistler
painting.

It took awhile to get dressed. My shoulder ached and my
swollen hand refused to perform routine tasks. Luckily the
Jacuzzi in the suite was just what the doctor ordered. By 8:00
a.m., I looked almost normal. A bit of concealer hid most of my
bruises and my hair cooperated nicely. I stuck the flash drive in
my bra again.

A sharp rap on the door startled me. I'd had far too many
surprises of late.

"Grace, let me in!" It was Therese, armed with espresso and
croissants. She'd never looked more like an angel despite her
unorthodox garb. Today's ensemble was a rather strange outfit
reminiscent of a gypsy. She had paired layers of beads, and a
gauze cotton skirt with an orange peasant blouse.

"What do you think?" she asked, pirouetting. Luckily, no woman expects an honest answer to that question and no true friend provides it.

"You certainly look festive," I said. "Is this your ethnic wardrobe?"

Therese grinned. "I'm trying to work against type. How many CPAs could pull this off?"

That begged the broader question. How many CPAs would even try to pull it off?

Suddenly Therese turned and stared at me. "Oh my God, what happened to you?"

"I fell."

"Oh my God, you were attacked. It was Chris Grey, wasn't it?" Therese started hyperventilating. "Have you called the police? I told you he was dangerous!"

"You're such a drama queen. If you calm down, I'll tell you what happened."

I gave her a concise account of my adventures, romantic interludes included. Naturally, the sex angle derailed her concentration.

"You finally did it with Patrick. Was it wonderful? He looks so virile. I bet it was."

"Therese, we're not in high school. I refuse to discuss details."

She was unrepentant. "But you liked him. You're going to see him again, right?"

"Perhaps. I'm more concerned with the murders, and I need a favor from you."

Therese brightened. "Sure," she said.

I fished the flash drive out of my blouse and handed it to her. "Can you make a copy of this? You're pretty good with technical stuff."

She waved her hand. "Not a problem. What else can I do?"

"For one thing, keep your mouth shut about that information. I mean it, Therese, someone tried to hurt me and I think Maude's recording is the reason."

She looked thrilled. "Oh, this is so exciting. I've got it, I can check alibis—find out where Cates and Braddock were yesterday afternoon."

"Be subtle." A nasty thought popped into my mind. "And while you're at it, find out where Brett Roberts was, too."

Her mouth opened. "Brett? Whatever for?"

I repeated Mary Hagan's little tidbit about Brett and his menopausal fling.

"That's disgusting! I thought he was one of the good guys."

"He may be. Just be careful. And remember, Therese, don't trust *anyone*."

"Even Jonathon Grey?" she asked.

It pained me to say it. "Even Jonathon Grey."

◇ ◇ ◇ ◇ ◇

I took a cab to the Freer. It was cowardly and expensive but I couldn't face riding on the Metro. I had to know if Cyrus Worthington's painting was real or a brilliant forgery. The Freer had the definitive Whistler collection in America and was staffed with very helpful curators.

I perused the guidebook, looking for the painting. There it was: "Princess from the Land of Porcelain," salon thirteen. I followed the map to the spot but unfortunately the trail went cold. Instead of the elegant oil I'd expected, there was a plain white sign. "Princess from the Land of Porcelain"—on loan. I flagged down a curator and asked for help.

He was a sylph-like man dressed in black whose nametag said "Rob."

"Let me check my records," he said. "That's funny, we always note the location of the painting, even when it's on loan." He dialed a number and spoke urgently to someone.

"I'm sorry," he said frowning. "For some reason we don't have that information. I intend to get to the bottom of this." He trotted off with a very determined air.

Since I was at the Freer, I couldn't resist a quick visit to the Peacock room. It was a splendid example of Victoriana, full of gilt, priceless porcelain, and designer touches by James Whistler himself. According to legend, Whistler had quarreled with his client over the Peacock room and the client refused to pay him. Ultimately, it was disassembled, shipped to America, and reconstructed at the Freer.

I was so absorbed by this nineteenth century drama, that I collided head-on with Jie-ling Chow.

She summoned her rictus grin and greeted me.

"Oh Ms. Quinn, how nice to see you. I'm so glad your injuries were not serious."

I was puzzled. "Injuries?" I said.

"From your accident of course. Subways can be so dangerous."

I yearned to slap that insufferable smile off her face but curiosity won out.

"I'm surprised you would even know about that," I said. "It isn't common knowledge."

She made a little half-bow. "Oh. Patrick told me."

I could feel my blood pressure climb. "Patrick?" I asked.

"Patrick Fong, of course. We're old family friends. He was my classmate at Stanford before he came east to attend Georgetown Law."

That was a whole lot of information to absorb. I feigned disinterest. Unfortunately, I wasn't very successful at it. Jie-ling moved in for the kill.

"We have a kind of 'understanding' you see. Chinese people are strong believers in tradition. Men tend to choose a bride from their own kind."

I fought to maintain my composure. "Americans are less bound by the past," I murmured. "We value independence and intellect over homogeneity."

Jie-ling simpered. "Interesting. Would you like to join me for tea, Ms. Quinn?"

My real wish was to kick her ass but tea was a more civilized alternative. We walked to the Sackler, the museum adjoining the Freer and ordered tea. I decided to steer the conversation toward less volatile topics.

"Please accept my condolences about Mr. Kingman," I said.

"Who?" she asked.

"You know, your security guard. He was murdered on Tuesday."

Jie-ling looked distracted. "Oh yes. I heard about it. Very unfortunate."

Dr. Chow was one cold fish. Obviously, she cared very little about anyone or thing, not connected to her. I quizzed her about the Whistler collection in general, and the missing oil.

"Missing?" she said vaguely. "I'm afraid that's not my field of expertise."

"Yeah, it was housed in salon thirteen—maybe that was bad luck. On the other hand, my birthday is on the thirteenth, so I guess the number's not all bad."

Jie-ling stared rudely at me ignoring my little bon mot. I got the idea that she didn't like me much.

Our conversation had just about run its course when Cyrus Worthington joined us.

"Jie-ling, I've been looking all over for you," he said pulling up a chair. "It's about the Abacus."

She smiled through gritted teeth, and motioned to me. "You remember Miss Quinn, with the *IRS*, Cyrus."

He looked around wildly, as though I'd dropped in from outer space. "Oh yes, the woman from the other night," he said vaguely.

"We were just discussing Bert Kingman, Dr. Worthington. I'm so sorry for your loss."

Cyrus seemed surprised that I was capable of speech.

"Oh yes, terrible thing," he mumbled.

I decided to take a risk. Bending toward them, I lowered my voice. "I understand that Kingman may have been bribed," I whispered. "Maybe it had something to do with the Abacus."

Cyrus slumped down in his seat the victim of severe depression or a near fatal stroke. . Jie-ling Chow poured him a glass of water and said, "Here Cyrus, drink this." She turned toward me and spoke in a deliberate monotone. "The murders are no concern of ours, or the museum. They are a police matter. Your friend was probably too nosey for her own good. People get hurt when they pry, Ms. Quinn. You should think about that."

She pushed out her chair and rose. "I really must excuse myself. I have an engagement tonight with a special friend."

I had a good idea who that special friend was.

"So nice to see you again, Ms. Quinn."

This time, I was the one who bowed. "Likewise, Dr. Chow."

Without Jie-ling to muzzle him, Cyrus Worthington was all mine. I decided to quiz him about his home.

"I understand that you live in Cleveland Park, Dr. Worthington. You're really lucky! I just love the homes in that neighborhood."

Cyrus still looked preoccupied, but he perked up when his favorite topic was broached.

"Well, yes, you know my family has lived there since President Cleveland's time. They said he was a dreadful neighbor, always hosting noisy parties."

I decided to fawn. Men of his age expected it and they were generally harmless.

"It's an awesome responsibility, though, holding something in trust for the future."

For the first time, he actually looked at me. His eyes sparkled and he clasped my hand.

"I started the Cleveland Park Preservation Society, you know. We lobbied hard to prevent developers from putting up their nasty high-rises. It's a public trust!"

His voice trailed off, lost in thought.

"But it's so expensive to restore those old treasures," I said. "A lot of people say it's cheaper to bring in the bulldozers."

His head shot up and his face turned that alarming shade of puce I remembered from the night of the murder. "Heresy!" he shouted. "My dear girl, if you only knew. We must save our heritage. It's worth any sacrifice!"

Zealots make me uncomfortable. You're never sure how far they'll go to make a point.

I distracted him by mentioning his other great love—the Golden Abacus.

"What about the Abacus, Dr. Worthington? I understand you'll exhibit it here."

Cyrus ran his hand through his white mane and shook his head.

"We may not exhibit it at all, I'm afraid. Everyone's nervous after the break-in, and with insurance, and other concerns, the Chinese government may withdraw their sponsorship."

"And of course, there are the murders," I added helpfully. "They must complicate things."

Cyrus glared at me. "Don't be absurd. They have nothing to do with the Abacus." He gathered his papers, and pushed out his chair. "Kingman was a fool," he said. "Everyone knew that." Doctor Worthington stomped off without a backward glance.

Frugality trumped fear. I rode the Metro back to the hotel despite considering it a death trap. Since the car was deserted I slumped into a seat and indulged in a spirited interior monologue. Jie-ling Chow was a nasty hag who shouldn't be taken seriously. Still it annoyed me that Patrick had told her about my accident. I could just picture the two of them gossiping, probably in Mandarin. Patrick *must* have told her how else would she have known. Why didn't he contact me? Didn't he even care that I'd almost been killed! Typical. After getting what he wanted, he'd returned to his putative bride.

Arranged marriages were so embarrassingly third world. No wonder he omitted that piece of information. He never even mentioned that he was a lawyer, although that was certainly understandable. I couldn't complain. Patrick Fong had delivered incredible sex without complications. I'd been a fool to think he was special. He deserved the Dragon Lady.

I took the Metro elevator to the street level. The down escalator was just too daunting, with its nasty steel teeth grinning at me. Since the CPA conclave was in full swing, I ducked into a session on "How to Grow Your Practice: Twenty Strategies for Pleasing Clients." Most of the seats were occupied by eager accountants clutching tablets and making copious notes. I slid into the back row and focused on the speaker, a glib marketing professor from Georgetown, who was remarkably entertaining. Right before the break, two men climbed into the seats on either side of me. Kelvin Cates and Evan Braddock, whose concept of casual attire would set the fashion world back a decade, did their best to block my escape route. I didn't panic, at least not right away. After all we were in a room filled with people. At the break, I tried to climb over Cates, the human lump.

"Gracie, leaving so soon. We need to have a little chat."

"Excuse me, Kelvin, I have another appointment." I managed to whack his arm with my bulky purse.

"Ow! Don't get nasty, *Ms.* Quinn." Cates rubbed his elbow.

"I thought you'd be eager to talk to us, Grace. You've certainly been asking enough questions." Braddock sounded more pompous than menacing. That gave me courage.

"Okay, what do you want?"

Cates moved closer. His pungent cologne could clear any room. Obviously the man was unfamiliar with the 'less is more' philosophy.

"Let's go where we have more privacy," he said.

"No way, *Kelvin.* I know your idea of privacy. I'll stay right here."

Braddock tapped his knee. "For Christ sakes, just ask her. We don't have all day."

Cates was such a lummox! He never was any good at improvising. Finally, he pulled himself together and lowered his voice.

"You've been spreading rumors about us, Grace. That's libel. We could sue you for slander."

I laughed. "You never had a grasp of the English language, you ape. There's a difference between slander and libel. Look it up, if you own a dictionary."

Cates began to sputter so Braddock edged into the conversation.

"Look Grace, maybe we can come to a business arrangement here. Maude just didn't understand but you're a lot smarter. If you have something of interest to us perhaps we can make financial arrangements." Braddock's grin was so revolting I actually preferred his grimace.

"A deal like you made with Kingman—no thanks!"

Both of them seemed genuinely puzzled. "Who's Kingman?" they chimed in unison.

Braddock tried a veiled threat. "You know, Grace, the Commissioner and I are neighbors. We belong to the same golf club."

"How nice for you. When the indictment comes down he can hand it to you at the clubhouse."

Braddock's eyes narrowed. "Did Maude give you anything that concerns Tax Champions?"

"If she did, I wouldn't sell it to you. I'd give it to Lieutenant Clarke. After all, it's evidence in a murder case." I turned to face Cates. "Maybe two murders."

Both of them cringed at the word murder. Cates grabbed my arm and squeezed it hard.

Braddock intervened. "Our interest is civil, not criminal. We know nothing about any murders."

"Yeah, remember that," echoed the beefy Cates. "You're asking for trouble."

Participants in the next session started filling the room and I heard someone call my name. It was Jonathon Grey, GQ perfect in Ralph Lauren. He stood in the aisle and greeted the two stooges.

"Hey, guys. How are you doing?"

They murmured a greeting, and jumped up. "Excuse us, Jonathon, we have to go," said Braddock.

Jonathon watched them, and grabbed a seat. "Well, that looked interesting," he said. "Did I interrupt anything important?"

"Absolutely not. The Bobsey twins were trying to strong-arm me."

Jonathon frowned. "Something about Tax Champions, I gather. Grace, you really ...."

I interrupted him. "Face it, Jonathon. Tax Champions has to figure into Maude's murder. There's no other explanation."

Jonathon ducked his head. I know he found the subject painful but he was acting like a wimp! Maybe he wasn't the heroic figure I'd always fantasized about.

"Are you free right now, Jonathon? There are some things you need to know."

He nodded, resigned to the inevitable. "Why don't we go to my hotel room?" he asked.

At one time, my whole body would have quivered at that invitation. Now it was just another room.

I followed him up to the eighth floor in total silence. Jonathon fidgeted with his cell phone, seemingly oblivious to my presence. When we reached his room, he cleared a newspaper off the sofa, and sat rather self-consciously on the bed. Without Chris to run interference, the atmosphere was strained. That's a shocker.

"Grace, your face is bruised? Did you have an accident."

Gee, Jonathon thanks for noticing! I sipped the Pellegrino he'd poured for me, and launched into the tale of my adventures. When I finished, Jonathon's face was blank.

"What did you do with the flash drive, Grace? It could be dangerous to carry it around."

"Actually, I sent it to Clarke."

Maybe I was paranoid but Jonathon seemed awfully interested in that piece of evidence.

"Chris should be relieved. I think it exonerates him."

Jonathon nodded absently. "I wonder who this inside source is."

"An IRS rat! I have my suspicions, I think it's Cheap Suit."

Jonathon did a double take. "*Who?*"

"You know, the special agent—Devon somebody. You'd think he'd dress better, if he was taking bribes."

Now Jonathon looked thoroughly confused. "I don't get it," he said. "These guys had to know their scheme couldn't last."

This was no time to be delicate. "They did mention, an, um, *legal opinion* they thought would save them. I think they meant Chris, Jonathon. I'm sorry."

Jonathon's voice was steady and unemotional. "I know my son. He's got integrity."

He looked at me, daring me to challenge him. I glanced away.

"Jonathon, I have to ask. Did Chris know Albert Kingman?"

"I doubt it, Grace. Chris doesn't know many security guards."

Ouch! The caste system was alive and well. I decided to push my luck.

"Well, does Chris have an alibi both nights? You know Clarke will be asking that if we don't."

Jonathon looked crestfallen. "I don't know, Grace. That's the truth. Chris has become a stranger lately, ever since he joined Tax Champions. I'm the last person he confides in."

I felt like a heel. It didn't stop me from pressuring Jonathon, but it did induce a healthy measure of Catholic guilt.

"Jonathon, promise me you'll find out. Please."

He nodded curtly. "I'll find out," he said. "Besides, this Golden Abacus thing may still be the answer. Bert Kingman probably saw Maude's killer and blackmailed him. It has to be." Jonathon set his lips in a firm line.

"You said you'd ask around about Tax Champions. What'd your buddies have to say?"

Jonathon grimaced. "Most of the ex-IRS guys were stunned at the stupidity of the thing, and frankly envious of the money. But you know, I spoke with my friend Les who's a crackerjack tax lawyer. He thinks they're skating on the edge of the law, avoiding disaster. It's strange—almost like someone inside is calling the plays."

I jumped up. "See, I told you. Cheap Suit, I mean Devon Hall, is working on the criminal case. He's feeding them information. Cates is no mastermind, that's for sure."

Jonathon removed his glasses, and rubbed the bridge of his nose. "Don't forget, it might be a *former* IRS-er, someone who has contacts inside."

The name Brett Roberts popped into my head. I told Jonathon what Mary said.

"I'd hate to think that," he said.

"Better Brett than Chris. See what you can find out."

Jonathon stood up, and squared his shoulders. "I hate this cloak and dagger stuff. It's more your game than mine, Grace."

I'm not certain that was a compliment. Jonathon was no Lord Peter Wimsey that's for sure. He was so passive!

We left room 813 together. Neither of us worried about appearances anymore.

CHAPTER FOURTEEN

I felt sick—physically ill. My head throbbed, and my swollen knee hurt. I looked at my Rolex—three-thirty—plenty of time to find the IRS booth and exude tax worthiness.

I ducked into the lady's room to make some repairs, wincing as I viewed my bruised face, and red eyes. Then it hit me. This is where I'd last spoken to Maude just four days ago! I could almost hear her braying about her big scoop. It was spooky. When the door opened, I screamed. Not a piercing shriek, just a lady-like squeal.

"Oh for God's sake, Grace, get a grip!" It was Therese, the gypsy CPA.

"You scared the shit out of me! For crying out loud, be careful."

She was unabashed. "Well, if I did, this is the right place for it. Come on, I've been looking all over for you. I have news!"

Her high spirits annoyed me. "Later. I have to work."

"Don't worry, I'll go with you. Nobody's going to stop by that stupid booth, anyway."

"Gee, thanks for the vote of confidence."

"You are such a grouch," Therese said affectionately. "I'll bet Patrick Fong could kiss away those blues."

"Don't be obscene."

She linked arms with me, and trotted merrily to the exhibition room. Nothing could deter Therese when she was in one of her manic states.

My assistant was thrilled to escape. Business hadn't been brisk this afternoon.

Therese pulled her chair back toward the rear of the booth and whispered.

"Here's my report! First, I took the flash drive to Clarke. Well, he wasn't in but I gave it to the cutest detective ...."

Before she could enumerate his virtues, I interrupted. "Therese, just the facts, Ma'am."

"Oh, yes. Alibis—I've got some pretty solid information." She produced a leather notebook and flipped it open. "Okay, Cates, that 'hunk a hunk of burning love' has no alibi for the night of Maude's death. Remember, we saw him carousing earlier that evening. He does have a rock solid alibi for the time of your accident, though. Believe it or not, he was the guest of honor at a ceremony held by the public policy section of the AICPA. That's a laugh, isn't it?"

"Hysterical. Continue."

"He's also unaccounted for on the night Kingman bought it. Of course, we really don't know what time he died, do we?"

"Clarke was coy about that."

"Anyway, Braddock was with Devon and that other guy, according to Devon. That is actually his name." Therese dimpled. "Grace, you will love how I got the scoop!"

I was afraid to ask.

"I chatted up Devon during lunch. He didn't look bad at all in casual clothes. In fact, he has a damn good body."

"Therese, focus please," I begged.

"You're such a spoilsport! Don't worry—nothing happened. I sort of intimated that if he played his cards right, I would be his dessert. Pretty clever, huh?"

"Actually, it sounds appalling. You, er, didn't put out did you?"

"Of course not. He could be a murderer. Anyway, Devon said that Braddock was giving a deposition to the Justice Department yesterday afternoon. I think it covers the period of your brush with death."

Therese smiled sweetly. I considered strangling her but time was short.

"Go on."

"Okay. Now the guy you call 'clenched fist,' the real angry one—he's disappeared. At least Devon doesn't know where he is. By the way, his name is Tom Welker and he's a CPA. He's some kind of manager at Tax Champions."

I was impressed. Once again, Therese had done an amazing job. She might get promoted from Watson to Holmes before long.

"Oh, I almost forgot—I'm not sure that Devon is crooked after all. He told me the case against Tax Champions is almost complete. They need just one more piece of information."

Therese winked. "I guess *we* know what that information is, don't we Grace?"

"What else did you ask him?"

"Just one thing. I asked why he hung around felons all the time. He gave me this kind of sexy grin, and said I'd know very soon."

By 6:00 p.m., I'd had enough. I bypassed the madding crowd, caught the elevator and limped to my suite. I needed time to rest and try to piece together what had happened. Therese's snooping seemed to clear Cheap Suit/Devon of conspiracy, unless he was incredibly clever. I considered the possibility of a "Murder on the Orient Express" solution but it was hard to imagine Cates and Braddock orchestrating a sophisticated scheme. Chris Grey might be another matter.

The foyer of my room smelled wonderful. The temperature was frigid, just the way I liked it, and the maid had tidied up. A beautiful bouquet sat on the table, adding an elegant touch. There was a small card attached to it. I flung off my jacket, and dumped my purse on a chair. I was so tired. I considered sacking out on the couch, but the lure of fresh, soft sheets spurred me on. I took a few steps into the darkened bedroom, reading the card as I walked: it was from Jonathon.

"That's soooo sweet," a mocking voice said.

I whirled around, my heart thumping. Patrick Fong was lounging on the chaise with a martini in his hand! He leapt up, and put his arms around me.

"Patrick! What are you doing here? How'd you get in?"

"Oh Grace, my God! Are you okay?" He gently brushed my hair from my forehead. "I wish *I'd* been the one to send you flowers."

I had to admit his arms felt wonderful. I fought the urge to melt into them and stiffened my shoulders instead. Patrick pulled back, and examined my bruised face. I was glad I'd freshened up not too long ago. Sympathy was fine but bruises were over the top.

"What's wrong, Grace?"

"I could have used that hug last night." I tried for a tone of icy distain but unfortunately I sounded adenoidal and whiny. "Dr. Chow said you knew about my accident. No, let's call it what it was—an assault, attempted murder!" I stepped back toward the door.

Even I could hear the unattractive note of hysteria rising in my voice. I shut up.

Patrick looked stricken. "Believe me if I could have been with you I would. But I've been monitoring the situation. I knew you were okay."

"*Monitoring!* Is that what you call it—a *situation?*" I was losing control—fast.

Patrick must have sensed that I was close to breaking. He grabbed my shoulders, and spun me around. He face was solemn, his eyes impenetrable.

"Sit down, Grace. I have something to tell you."

Oh my God! A thousand thoughts raced through my mind: *he'll confess to murder, he'll say he's married, admit that he's using me, or slit my throat!* I was ready for anything. *Just don't say you're leaving—please.*

"I'm a cultural attaché, Grace, nothing more. I work for the State Department, and occasionally I get to work with the guys on the theft and smuggling beat." He reached for his martini and drained it in one swallow. "My assignment is to observe any activities surrounding the Golden Abacus and to assist the Smithsonian. I wish I could tell you that I have a dangerous and exciting job—I know that's what you'd like to hear. Face it, I'm just a desk jockey."

"How did you get involved in this," I asked.

Patrick didn't answer right away. He seemed to be weighing something in his mind.

"I shouldn't be telling you this. I could get in a lot of trouble. But you sound so cold that I want you to understand."

He seemed sincere and I believed him—sort of.

"My unit was tipped that someone might try to grab the Abacus. Someone who's trying to destabilize relations between China and the U.S. Losing a national treasure could do it."

I couldn't help it. I had to ask. "Where does Jie-ling Chow fit into this? Is she a cultural attaché too?"

Patrick ducked the question by offering me a drink. There was no need to die of thirst in aid of a good cause. Anyhow, he'd been drinking from the same pitcher. It couldn't be poison.

"You know that Cyrus Worthington is up to something, I presume. I took a trip out to Cleveland Park on Tuesday—the day I was attacked."

His eyes regained a bit of their sparkle. "I'm aware of your little excursion. Keep going."

I wanted to quiz him about that, but I couldn't digress.

"Cyrus has a money problem. Either that or he's very cheap. I had tea with his sister, and she gave me the grand tour. That place needs some serious rehab."

Patrick exhaled loudly. "How in the hell did you manage that? Madelaine is very wary—paranoid even. We've been trying to get into that place for months."

"Sisterhood is power."

Patrick shook his head. "Never mind, did you learn anything else?"

I toyed with the idea of misleading him but if he was really packing Federal heat, that was a very bad idea. "Actually, there was one really odd thing. Madelaine showed me a beautiful painting—a copy of a Whistler, I guess."

Patrick laced his long elegant fingers together. He said nothing but tension heightened his toned body. He seemed more feline than ever, coiled and ready to spring. Think lion, tiger or cougar—not house cat.

"Anyhow, according to Madelaine, her mother collected Whistler, and this painting 'Princess from the Land of Porcelain' looked identical to one I'd seen at the Freer."

"So what? It's probably an excellent copy." Patrick's features were impassive. He was definitely hiding something.

"Maybe," I said, "but I don't think so. I went over to the Freer yesterday and the Whistler wasn't there. It's supposedly out on loan."

He sat down on the chaise and crossed his legs, his smile indulgent and a trifle patronizing.

"That's hardly a scoop. Museums do that all the time."

"I'm *aware* of that Patrick but I spoke with one of the curators. He couldn't find a record of the loan. It was a serious breach of museum protocol."

Patrick stretched again. As a diversionary tactic it was very effective.

"Look, we both work for the Federal government. How many breaches of protocol do you see in one day at the IRS?"

He had a point but I was unwilling to concede the issue. "That would be a major blunder in any organization. I think you should investigate it."

"Oh you do. Are you finally admitting that investigations should be left to the professionals?"

"Only if the professionals are up to it. In this case, Therese and I seem to be doing your job."

"I *told* you that's not my job." Patrick wasn't smiling now. He fiddled with his glass and said nothing.

"By the way you don't seem surprised that I visited the Worthington house."

He hung his head. "I watched you," he said sheepishly. "Remember that appointment I told you about at the Zoo? I had to join my partner in the surveillance van. We were parked across from Worthington's house."

I paused to consider that. Come to think of it, there was a battered van parked on Newark Street. Could it be the one?

"Describe your van," I said.

Patrick laughed. It was a hearty male sound, nothing forced.

"You are *so* suspicious," he said. "Okay, Nancy Drew, I give up."

His description matched the vehicle I'd seen. I nodded and he continued to speak.

"I have to admit I was *stunned* when you came tripping up the street and waltzed right into Worthington's house. What were you doing there, anyway?" Patrick's expression belied his words: he was serious.

"That sounds like an interrogation," I said. "Should I get an attorney? After all, I'm being questioned by one."

Those almond eyes weren't dancing now.

"Think about it from my perspective, Grace. You might be involved in this crime. I'm obliged to ask you."

He put a finger to his lips, as I started to protest. "Let me continue, please. You were on the scene of the Abacus theft."

"Aborted theft," I corrected.

"Granted. *You* found the dead body and in the eyes of the police that automatically makes you a suspect. What's more, you knew the victim and you knew the other person in the room—intimately." His gaze grew flinty.

"You mean *Jonathon?*" I asked.

"The same. The one person you've been hell bent to protect from the minute this thing happened."

I started sputtering. "How *dare* you suggest something tawdry? I told you he's my friend, nothing more."

He gave me a curt nod. "Then there's the way you insinuated yourself into the investigation. That's very suspicious. You badgered Clarke, got your friend Therese involved, and sauntered into my office with a *very* transparent story about self-improvement. I never bought your act about learning Asian culture. Not for one minute."

I was steamed. "Well, you made a very unconvincing *volunteer* if I may say so!"

He pressed his lips into a mean, thin line. "I guess that's why you seduced me."

"WHAT! You bastard, you made all the moves."

Our cozy chat was now a battle but Patrick wasn't finished. "I admit I enjoyed it. You do very nice work. Besides I don't mind being used by a beautiful woman."

I raised my hand to slap his face but he caught it, slowly kissing my fingers one by one.

I twisted away and turned my back to him.

"What's the matter, Grace? Does the truth hurt?" Patrick was mocking me, daring me to lose my temper.

"I let it slide when you tricked Kingman's employer and lured me into illegally entering his apartment," he said.

"Lured you! You insisted on coming." I plopped down on the edge of the bed. The nerve of this guy!

"You removed evidence from a murder scene. That's a felony, Ms. Quinn."

"You're delusional, *Mr.* Fong. No wonder you have a boring job. Brush up on your criminal law. Kingman's apartment wasn't a murder scene at the time."

His laugh was sharp and hollow. "Oh that's very comforting. You're only guilty of a minor felony."

I tried to act cool but it was hard. That damn address book!

"Don't look so startled," Patrick said. "Clarke told me about the address book you sent him."

Now I got it—Clarke had been schmoozing with the Feds again. That rat!

"I don't know what you mean." Lying to Patrick was easier than I thought it would be.

He lowered his voice. Now he was Mr. Cool. "Perhaps *you* killed Kingman. Maybe he was blackmailing you, Grace. That address book might have contained something that incriminated you."

Patrick seemed almost bloodless now. I couldn't detect any emotion in his calm voice. "You took an immediate dislike to Jie-ling. Now you're trying to sully the reputation of Cyrus Worthington. Who knows what evidence you planted in his house." He opened the closet, and fingered my Chanel blazer. "We know how much you love nice things, Grace. How far would you go to get them?"

I was speechless but not for long. I clasped my arms behind my back and started pacing in tight circles.

"How about this scenario?" I said. "You admit you saw me at Cyrus's. You could have easily followed me to the Metro and pushed me down. After all, you're an excellent suspect too."

I faced Patrick and pointed an accusing finger at him. "You have an intimate knowledge of Asian Art and probably Jie-ling Chow as well. Who better to steal the Abacus?"

I wish I hadn't mentioned her but it felt so good.

Patrick was amused. He grabbed my index finger, brought it to his lips and gently sucked it. I wanted to throttle him but I didn't want him to stop. *Is it possible to be both angry and turned on at the same time?*

"There's more," I said, finally backing away from him. "You made sure to volunteer at the Smithsonian, giving yourself access and opportunity. You and your old family friend, Jie-ling could have conspired, leaving poor Cyrus holding the bag. You had access to the security arrangements. It would have been easy for you."

"You paint quite an exciting portrait of me," Patrick said with a smile. "I only wish it were true."

"Thank you," I said stiffly. "I'll bet you know how to use a weapon. Even I can handle a gun. I trained with our criminal investigators."

He stifled a laugh. "Maybe I should be afraid. I can't picture you armed and dangerous but it's an alluring thought."

I wasn't finished yet. I was just getting started.

"Don't forget. You love expensive things too. You treat that BMW of yours like your child. No federal salary covers that."

He rose and started walking toward me. "It's not a crime to love something beautiful," he whispered, staring at me.

I took a step backward. "You charmed your way into my life. You used me. I was a fool."

Patrick smiled. "I didn't hear you complain. I'm the one who can't get you out of my head."

My hand found the doorknob. With any luck I could run into the living room and be gone before he reached me. I *could* run away but I didn't want to. I kept talking.

"You even lied by omission. You never said you were a lawyer. Though of course, I can understand why you...."

He took slow, deliberate steps until he reached me. I caught my breath unsure of what would happen next. Patrick unclenched his fists and closed the bedroom door. He took my hand, kissed it, and pulled me to him.

"I *never* lied to you," he said softly. "And I never will."

He scooped me up and gently placed me on the bed.

CHAPTER FIFTEEN

It was a long languid night that left me feeling whole. Patrick gently kissed my bruises and every other place that ached. He knew more about pleasing a woman than any man has a right to know. He seduced each part of my body, electrified every nerve ending, leaving me weak but satiated. I fell asleep in his arms feeling safe for the first time in so long. When the morning sunlight streamed in I was alone. Patrick must have left while I was dozing. Maybe it had all been a dream. No matter—it was wonderful.

I was in serious danger with Patrick Fong, half in love with him already even though I'd just met him. How many ways can you spell disaster? He was unlike any man I'd ever met—smart, sexy and devious. We hadn't resolved anything about the murders and I didn't believe his cover story for one minute. He called himself a nerd but he picked locks and moved like a panther. For all I knew he might be involved in the Abacus plot—or worse.

It was impossible. All I stood to gain was a broken heart or a stretch in the Pen.

We hardly knew each other. Both of us had demanding careers that would tear us apart if nothing else did. Then there was the Jie-ling factor. She said they had an *understanding*, and Patrick ducked my questions about her. They were probably "betrothed" or some other quaint custom. Every sensible bone in my body screamed *caution,* but my treacherous heart kept thudding every time I thought of him. I had to let him go before it was too late—while I still could.

A knock on the door startled me. Oh God, maybe he was back!

"Just a minute," I called out as I raced for the bathroom mirror. By some freak chance my mascara had stayed put, and despite a serious case of bed-head, I was able to resurrect my hair. I tied my robe, applied a hint of lip-gloss, and opened the door.

"Grace, I was worried about you," said Jonathon Grey. "I called last night, but couldn't get you."

I hoped Jonathon didn't see the disappointment on my face. I pulled my robe tighter.

"I was really tired. I didn't even hear the phone. Thanks for the flowers—they're lovely."

Jonathon stole a glance at the undergarments strewn over the floor. He was far too discreet to mention it, of course.

"May I come in for a moment?" he asked.

"Oh, of course. Excuse my manners, I'm still a bit foggy."

A night with Patrick Fong could cloud any woman's mind.

Jonathon's face was drawn. He looked as if he hadn't been sleeping well.

"Look Grace, I have a big favor to ask you. Tell me if it's too much."

"You know I'd do anything for you. How can I help?"

"Well it's not for me, actually. It's for Chris."

Chris! Through sheer effort, I managed to keep a pleasant smile on my face.

"What is it? Tell me."

Jonathon looked down. "He's in trouble, Grace and he just needs somewhere to stay for a day or so."

"What kind of trouble?" I asked.

"Lieutenant Clarke found out about some quarrel Chris had with Maude on the night she died. He questioned me about it but I didn't know anything."

I forced myself to remain calm. "But if he's innocent ...."

For once in his well-bred life, Jonathon interrupted me. "Don't you see. Even if they don't charge him, it'll kill his legal career if he's a suspect. No firm wants an attorney with that stigma."

"He wants to stay *here*—with me?"

Jonathon actually laughed. "Of course not, that's why I thought of it. No one would ever suspect he'd be with *you*."

I'm not sure that was a compliment but it certainly rang true. Christopher Grey was the last person I wanted as a roommate. What if Patrick found him here? I don't think Mr. Fong was into ménage à trois.

"It wouldn't be for long. He'd sleep on the couch."

I hated to see Jonathon beg—it was so demeaning. He was my friend and mentor. I had no alternative.

I reached into my purse, and pulled out the room key. "Here, give him this. I'll get another one from the Concierge."

Jonathon's eyes glistened. "Thank you, Grace. Look, we need to talk. I found out some interesting information about Tax Champions."

He finally noticed that I was not quite ready for primetime. "You'll want to get dressed, of course. Let's meet in the breakfast room at eight. Will that give you enough time?"

I glanced at my watch, surprised to find that it was just six-thirty in the morning.

"Sure, I'll be there."

Jonathon kissed my forehead and left. It was a fatherly kiss that didn't affect me at all. I guess another chapter in my life had closed this week.

I raced to make myself presentable. At 10:00 a.m. I had to lead a seminar on the thrilling topic of "New IRS Compliance Initiatives." That demanded attire that was stylish, with just the hint of a dominatrix. I chose a severe navy suit with a discreet side slit and paired it with a red silk blouse that promised more than it delivered. As I rushed toward the door, my cell phone rang. I hesitated. This was not the time for a threatening call.

On the other hand, maybe *he* was calling. I picked it up and heard the dulcet tones of my boss.

"Grace, I was beginning to think you'd gone AWOL."

Mary Hagen had a peculiar sense of humor. The smart move was to ignore it.

"I was just on my way to a meeting, Mary. What's up?"

"I'm going to sit in on your seminar. You know, learn from a pro."

Mary was obviously annoyed. My tactic was to embrace the positive.

"Wow, that's a compliment. Do you have time for lunch afterward?"

"Sounds like fun. See you soon. Bye bye."

There's something unsettling about a grown woman who says "bye bye," but if any one could get away with it, it was Mary. I fled before there were any more surprises.

Jonathon had commandeered a booth in the back of the restaurant. Judging from the gleam in his eyes, he must have ingested plenty of caffeine. I noticed he had also shaved and changed into a handsome gray suit with chalk stripes. The guy had such class. How'd he ever hatch Chris, the devil's spawn? He waved me over, and pulled out my chair.

"You look remarkable, Grace. Every man in here envies me."

For a minute, I had to shake myself. Remember, Grace, Jonathon is a friend with a cranky wife and an odious son. I scanned the room looking for Patrick. Unfortunately, he wasn't there to see us together. His jealousy of Jonathon was so obvious that it lifted my spirits.

"What did you find out?" I asked. "It's been driving me crazy."

"Believe it or not," he said, "Tax Champions seems to have dodged the bullet—at least for now."

I was shocked. "Are you serious?"

He hunched over the table. "Yeah. A friend at Justice told me that these guys lead a charmed life. They altered their promotional activities just enough to pass the legal smell test."

"But how did they know the right moves to make?"

Jonathon grimaced. "That's the big question. They always relied on extravagant promises to rope in the suckers. Now they've added some fine print that could save them."

I couldn't say what I was really thinking. Maybe that great advice came straight from Jonathon's son.

"My friend says there has to be a traitor at IRS, or the US Attorney's office. You know how that process works, Grace. It's strictly need to know."

"Do they have any leads?"

"Not yet. They're considering polygraph tests. And get this— *they've* got a mole in Tax Champions. A highly placed mole." Jonathon leaned back in his chair. His face lost all animation.

"Well, who is it?"

He removed his glasses, and polished them. "I don't know. He wouldn't tell me. I guess they're afraid of compromising their guy—if it is a guy."

Then something dawned on me. "Therese found out that one of the Tax Champions managers has disappeared. Some guy named Welker. I saw him a couple of times, and he was always scowling. Not a nice guy."

"So?"

Must I spell everything out? Maybe Jonathon could use more caffeine.

"What if he's the government mole, and he's gone underground? Maybe the bad guy routine was just an act."

Jonathon crumpled his napkin into a ball. "If that's the case, he didn't do a very thorough job. Besides, with the kind of money flowing through Tax Champions, anyone could be tempted."

I didn't have the heart to ask if Chris would be susceptible.

"But what about the flash drive?" I asked. "Surely that was enough."

"What flash drive?" Jonathon looked mystified.

Where was that big brain I'd always admired? Chris must have stolen a few IQ points from his dad.

"You know, the one Maude sent me. It proves intent to defraud, I'm sure of it."

Finally, Jonathon perked up. "Did Clarke send it to the US Attorney's office? You know the criminal and civil sides sometimes ignore each other. Maybe I'll just drop a word to my buddy at Justice."

I had to address the big question. "Jonathon, what about Chris's alibi for the murders? Remember, you said you'd ask him."

"He wouldn't tell me. Said he had an important meeting both nights but wouldn't specify. The funny thing is, Chris doesn't seem particularly worried. I'd be traumatized by the thought of prison, but not Chris."

I gulped. I might as well just come out and tell him. "Jonathon, Therese and I saw the argument between Chris and Maude. That is, Therese actually saw it and I would have if I'd had my glasses."

He caught his breath. "You mean, *Therese* reported Chris?"

"Nah, but they were standing out on the street. Anyone could have seen them and three hours later Maude was dead." I gave a little shrug. "Jonathon, you've got to convince him to come clean. It's the only way."

"I guess," he said glumly. "Listen, I know you have to run. I'll call your cell later. Maybe we can reconnoiter in your room."

"Okay." If one more man went in or out of my suite, they'd call the vice squad. The maid was already giving me fishy looks.

He picked up the check and left while I spent a few minutes inhaling caffeine and dreaming about last night. I relived every glorious minute, each touch and sensation.

"Hey!" Therese plopped down next to me. "Aren't you doing a seminar soon?"

I glanced at my Rolex. "Yep, in exactly twenty six minutes. Why?"

"Are you free for lunch?" she asked.

"Not really. I'm lunching with your favorite person, Mary Hagan. Want to joint us?"

Therese cackled. "Are you kidding? I'd rather kiss Kelvin Cates. What I really wanted to tell you is, there's a big poster on the wall saying that the grand opening of the Abacus exhibit is tonight at the Freer."

I felt like a lab rat—Therese was watching my every move.

"Sounds like something we should see. Meet me in the lobby at seven."

I should have known she wouldn't let me escape that easily. "What's going on with Patrick?" she asked. "Have you seen him lately?"

"Why?"

"Oh nothing. I thought I saw him hanging around here today."

I tried to act casual. Therese lowered her gaze and tried to act nonchalant.

I jabbed a fork at her. "And ...?"

Therese was a rotten liar. "Nothing", she said guiltily, "I better go. See you tonight."

She sped off, leaving me to my imagination.

My seminar was lively. I'd arranged it as a debate and had plenty of volunteers eager to argue *against* the IRS position. Only a few stalwarts advocated for the Government. I noticed Mary Hagan at the back of the room hunched over her notebook. Maybe she really was interested. More likely, she was evaluating my performance.

The only surprise was Harry Hawkins. He was the picture of gloom as he sat in the first row holding his head. When he raised his face, I caught him scowling. This was not the Harry I'd worked with so many years.

After ninety minutes of spirited debate our session concluded. Most of the crowd vaporized eager to find a good luncheon spot. Harry Hawkins didn't move. In fact, I don't think he even knew that the seminar was over. He stayed in the front row, shoulders slumped, head bowed. That was a-typical behavior for sociable Harry and it worried me. I left the podium and sat down next to him.

"Hey Harry, what's going on?"

He raised his head, his expression blank. "Oh Grace—I didn't see you."

Whoa—who did he think was in front of him for the past ninety minutes? I'm not one to pry but Harry needed help.

"Harry, what's wrong? Can I help?"

He shook his head hopelessly. "I wish you could. Grace, I thought I was so smart. I was a fool!"

This looked like an opportunity—no Cates or Braddock to interfere.

"It's about Tax Champions, isn't it Harry? I thought you guys had gotten good news."

Harry's smile held no mirth. "I believed in those guys. Grace, you know me. They said we were completely legit. We even had IRS support."

I leaned closer. "Who was your inside source, Harry?"

He intended to confide in me. I was sure of that. Unfortunately company arrived.

"Grace, are we still on for lunch?" Mary Hagan swirled in on a cloud of Creed and promptly put both Manolos right in her mouth. "Hi Harry. How are you doing? Want to join us?"

Harry gave a guilty start, and gathered up his things. He grabbed his handkerchief just in time to catch two honking sneezes. "No, I ... thanks anyway Mary." He nodded to me, "Grace, good to see you." Harry rabbited down the aisle like a much younger man.

"What is *wrong* with that guy?" Mary asked. "You'd think he saw a ghost. Well, let's get going, we're on the clock."

For a woman obsessed with perfection, Mary could be incredibly dense about issues other than style. A perfect bob didn't necessarily make one empathetic.

"Let's try Robert's," Mary said naming the hotel's most elegant restaurant. It was an edict not a suggestion.

"Fine with me."

We easily found a table overlooking the well-tended grounds. The CPA crowd was notoriously tight with a buck so they flocked to fast food emporiums not fine dining places. The menu was just right for calorie counting: Caesar salad with ice tea for Mary, and Pellegrino for me. She always called it "Sweet Tea", a Southern expression I think.

Mary came straight to the point. "Okay Grace, now what's going on about the murder? Why didn't they indict the Tax Champions boys today?"

"Wait a minute, that's two different issues."

Mary snorted. "Okay, make it easy on yourself. Start with the murder or shall I say, murders."

"I'm not sure what's going on. Clarke hasn't been badgering me lately."

She cocked her head, and narrowed her eyes. "Come on, I know you too well. You're not the type to back off."

I tried to look offended and failed. "I have heard a few things," I said cautiously. "But none of it's official."

Mary leaned forward. "Spit it out," she commanded.

I outlined my theories to Mary, including the bribe to Kingman, and the link between Maude and Tax Champions."

She stared me down. "I understand there was a recording. Something incriminating?"

Damn, this woman was hard to fool. "I thought I already mentioned that. Maude sent me some gizmo that I'd never seen before. A flash drive recorder—that's what they call it. The Tax Champion crowd would call it dynamite."

Mary took the practical CPA approach. "Could you actually identify the voices?"

"Only Cates, that loudmouth. But he kept blabbing about some secret weapon—an IRS quisling who would keep them out of jail."

"That's outrageous! Who is it?" Mary was ready to jump out of her seat and tackle the miscreant.

"We don't know. I think it might be that special agent but Jonathon pointed out that it could be a *former* employee with good connections."

"Like Brett Roberts?" Mary asked. "He still keeps in touch with most of us but I thought it was fairly innocuous." She daintily dabbed her lips with the linen napkin. "I just hate to think IRS guys past or present would be that corrupt."

"Or stupid" I offered. "Of course there's a lot of money involved and that's a temptation."

We took a moment to munch our salad. I eyed the breadbasket, but remained strong. Patrick Fong wasn't going to see me bloated by carbs. The Dragon Lady was rail thin.

I screwed up my courage. After all, Mary was my boss, and I hated to involve her in anything personal.

"There is one thing," I said. "Do you have any contacts at the State Department?"

Mary gave me a look of pity. "I once was *close* to the Deputy Secretary. Is that enough of a contact?"

"Could you inquire about two people? They're both involved with the Abacus and maybe the murders."

Mary looked at me. "Is this a personal or professional inquiry?"

I gulped. "A little bit of both. But there is something going on and I think it would help solve Maude's murder if we could rule out some people."

Mary extracted a red Gucci notepad from her bag. "Okay. Give me their names."

"Patrick Fong and Dr. Jie-ling Chow. He's a lawyer, she's a bitch."

Mary started choking on her lettuce. "I get it. Let's see what I can find out. Some of this stuff is probably on the Internet, you realize. Brush up on those computer skills, Grace. You're living in the past. Never mind, leave it to me. *You* focus on finding this IRS insider. Maybe I better have a little chat with that Lieutenant Clarke."

She signaled for the check and paid it. "It's my treat," she said. "You did a great job at the seminar today."

CHAPTER SIXTEEN

Spying on Patrick was a nasty trick. On the other hand, he really left me no choice. He promised never to lie but he had. If "trust but verify" was good enough for a President, it would serve my needs perfectly.

I dreaded the evening's gala. I could just picture the icy distain of Jie-ling Chow, or Cyrus's rage if he found out about my visit. I was so distracted that I almost collided with Evan Braddock. His lip curled with distaste but he managed a halfway civil greeting.

"Watch out!" He caught his briefcase before it fell and reached out to steady me. "You know you really should be more careful," he said. "It would be so easy to get hurt."

I'm no hypocrite. I wouldn't pretend to like this creep.

"I guess it pays to have insurance—doesn't it Evan?" I smiled with total insincerity showing my pretty teeth.

He gave me a curt nod, and rushed off.

I spent the next three hours at several exciting seminars. "Pathological Partnership Debt," and "Partnership Disguised Sales." were both crowd-pleasers. Unfortunately, I had to miss "Tax Aspects of Real Estate." My mind was numbed by the profusion of facts, figures, and humorless chat.

I hoped my new roommate was on another planet, and not lounging on the couch. I wanted plenty of time to compose myself before tonight's festivities. Fortunately, the room was empty—no Christopher Grey. I barricaded myself in the bathroom, and began a few simple beauty rituals. I had to look cool and confident tonight no matter what happened.

Yellow is my favorite color so I chose a lemon silk sundress and strappy sandals. If Patrick saw me, I would radiate confidence and smoldering sexuality—at least that was the plan.

Therese must have read my mind. She wore a sheath of coral linen and a big grin.

"Let's do it, Grace," she said as she flagged down a cab. "You'll show up that snooty Chow woman."

I was so nervous the butterflies in my stomach metastasized. A large crowd was hovering around the Freer, waiting for the doors to open. I didn't see anyone from our conference but I did recognize Rob the helpful curator. Opportunity was knocking!

"Hi Rob," I said, "We met yesterday. I'm Grace and this is my friend Therese."

Therese and Rob exchanged nods. He glanced appreciatively at our outfits, although it was obvious that he had no carnal interest in us.

"Quite a turnout," I observed. "Is Dr. Worthington here?"

"Of course," Rob said. "And I suppose his *friend* Jie-ling will take center stage."

I recognized a kindred spirit in Rob as we exchanged knowing looks. When the doors opened he excused himself and helped direct the crowd.

"Come on, Grace, let's go see the Abacus," Therese said. Since she was a member of the Freer, we had tickets to the reception. We signed our names at the desk and headed for the bar. A gaggle of upscale art lovers hovered over the canapés.

"That poor bartender looks lonely," Therese said.

"Behave yourself. He also looks young."

"So what, I'm young—in spirit. I'll get you something to drink." Therese sprinted for the bar managing to out-maneuver a determined matron in basic black with pearls. She immediately chatted up the server.

I wandered toward the Peacock Room searching for the missing Whistler.

The gallery was deserted or so I thought. While I was marveling at the exquisite porcelain I heard the murmur of voices, and a girlish laugh coming from behind a jade screen. I could see the silhouettes of a couple on the screen.

"I missed you, little one," said a faint male voice. "Where were you last night?"

A kiss muffled her reply. She pulled away, and said something about a "tease."

A more discreet person would have stepped away. I leaned into the conversation.

"Don't worry, that's only work." The voice sounded familiar. "She means nothing to me."

I suddenly felt faint, as if a vengeful spirit had slapped me. It would have amused me if it wasn't so damn tragic.

As I edged out of the room, Cyrus Worthington burst in. He didn't even see me.

"Jie-ling" he called. "Where are you? The ceremony's starting."

She stepped from behind the jade screen, her cheeks slightly pink from exertion, holding the hand of Patrick Fong.

He looked beyond Cyrus and glimpsed me. I quickly pivoted and lurched out of the Peacock Room feeling sick and ashamed. I had to find some privacy—fast. There was no need to cry. It wasn't the first time I'd made a fool of myself over a man. After all he didn't owe me anything. I'd been stupid to fall for his line of bull. I saw the Ladies room sign and cannonballed into the nearest stall. The slamming door told me I had company.

"Grace, are you okay?" Therese called out. "I saw you run in here. What's the matter?"

"Nothing, I'm fine. I guess that drink made me a bit woozy."

"What drink? I still have yours. Oh well, come on then. The ceremony's going to begin."

I combed my hair, and applied fresh lipstick. Never underestimate the power of beauty rituals.

I joined Therese with my head held high. She wasn't fooled.

"Okay, tell me."

"What are you talking about?" I asked.

"It has to be something about Patrick. You were cooler when you found Maude's corpse."

I pushed the door open. "You're crazy."

The Abacus was in Salon thirteen, encased in an even thicker shell of Plexiglas. It might be impregnable but it wasn't beautiful. The Chinese government must have put its billion-person foot down hard. Cyrus, Jie-ling and Patrick Fong formed a protective circle around the Abacus. Jie-ling wore a traditional Chinese dress of white silk that complimented her figure. I tried and failed to find some flaw in her appearance.

Cyrus and Patrick both wore tuxedos but the similarity ended there.

Patrick's beauty easily eclipsed the Abacus. I tried not to stare but it was impossible. He looked like every fantasy I'd ever had right down to his slicked back ponytail. I focused on Cyrus instead.

"He's gorgeous, absolutely gorgeous," Therese said as she gawked at Patrick.

"Cyrus? Don't tell me you're going for old men these days."

She shook her head, and smiled. "You know who I'm talking about. If I were you, I'd claw her eyes out."

"Exactly what did you see this morning?" I asked Therese. "You'd better tell the truth."

Therese hung her head. "Ah Grace, what's the use." She fumbled with a button. "I saw Patrick with *her* early this morning."

Even when the news was bad, I loved hearing his name. "So what? Maybe they had a business meeting."

"Maybe." The doubt in her voice was palpable.

The microphone burped. Cyrus tapped it and launched his opening salvo. I have to admit I missed most of it. By wedging myself between Therese and a particularly tall man, I could see Patrick without being obvious. His expression was bland, his smile fixed. Those beautiful almond eyes were glued to Jie-ling Chow. It's astounding how much that hurt.

Jie-ling took the microphone. "Thank you so much. We're thrilled to present this great national treasure of China. As you know, it was almost taken from us. We must therefore use the most stringent security measures to safeguard the Abacus. Unfortunately, the distinguished scholars who planned to examine it will be handicapped." She turned to Patrick and clasped his arm. "Thanks to the dedication of my dear friend Patrick Fong and the State Department, we will complete this important cultural mission."

Patrick stepped forward and bowed. I caught him staring straight at me before he quickly turned away. Bastard!

Cyrus took command again. "Please feel free to circulate throughout the museum and see all our treasures. Enjoy your evening."

"Let's go!" I grabbed Therese's arm and tugged her toward the exit.

"Not so fast," she said. "This could get interesting."

"I'm out of here. Do whatever you want."

Therese rolled her eyes and grabbed her purse. "Okay, okay." Suddenly she pinched my arm. "Grace—he's coming over here." She pointed to Patrick, who was making a beeline for us.

I pivoted and moved swiftly through the crowd. It was juvenile. I should have faced him. He almost caught us, until a distinguished man with his trophy wife intercepted him. I saw them shaking hands and making small talk while we made a clean getaway.

I couldn't bear the thought of sharing my suite with Chris Grey. Not tonight. Therese offered me the extra bed in her room and I gratefully accepted. Neither one of us said much on the way to the hotel. We took turns in the shower, switched off the lights, and tried to sleep. I kept replaying the look of adoration in his eyes as he gazed at Jie-ling. I'd paid a big price for eavesdropping. Patrick considered me "business" not pleasure. His words burned into my brain: "She means nothing to me." It was a long, restless night. In two days, the official part of the conference would end and everyone would scatter. The weekend was reserved for specialty meetings, sub-committee functions, and the conference gala. My involvement ended on Sunday as did any hope I had of finding Maude's killer. Bummer!

The next morning Therese performed an act of mercy by surfing the Lobby buffet for provisions. She returned juggling coffee, croissants and fruit. Her generosity made me suspicious—she was hiding something.

"Here Grace, you need this more than I do," she said as she handed me a steaming mug of coffee.

"Thanks." I grabbed the mug and sipped it greedily. Even weak coffee was a godsend.

"Hey, where's the *Post*?" I asked.

Therese turned away. She could never face me when she was hiding something.

"Oh, I already skimmed it. It's over here." She pointed to the basket.

"Okay, what are you hiding?"

I stalked across the room and grabbed the newspaper. The front page was filled with the usual accounts of international mayhem and political treachery. I tossed it aside and searched for the Style Section. That always contained wry accounts of society foibles and my favorite column, "The Reliable Source."

Tidbits about the rich and politically connected made us nobodies feel informed and slightly contemptuous.

"You don't want to look at it—not before breakfast." Therese held something behind her back.

"*Give* me the Style section," I said, holding out my hand.

It wasn't hard to find: the featured item was an account of the Abacus reception at the Freer. The caption under center photograph said it all: *"Dr Jie-ling Chow and fiancé Patrick Fong celebrate a successful evening."*

Suddenly the coffee was bitter, the croissant dry as dust.

My voice was a bit shaky. "Jie-ling takes a nice picture, doesn't she?" I asked. "Apparently the exhibit was a big hit."

Therese came over to me and hugged me. "I'm sorry Grace. Who knew he was such a cad!"

In spite of everything, I whooped with laughter. "Cad—I love that word and I think we're the only ones under ninety who even use it." I grinned at Therese. "Thanks, my friend. This too shall pass."

Brave talk. I guess it wasn't a total shock. Jie-ling said they had an "understanding." It was my own fault for letting down my guard.

I checked my watch. "Oops, I have a seminar in ninety minutes. Time to get the show on the road."

I stepped into my dispirited lemon sundress and grabbed my purse. Somehow, my strappy sandals weren't quite as festive as they had been. I needed to get the notes from my suite, change clothes, and face Christopher Grey. I squared my shoulders and marched to the elevator. Young Mr. Grey don't mess with me today!

The chain was on my hotel door so I knocked loudly. "Let me in, it's Grace."

A sleepy male voice asked. "W-h-o-?"

"You know who—*Grace Quinn,* the authorized occupant of this room. You have about three seconds before I kick the damn door in! And, you'd better have clothes on, too."

"Okay, okay." Chris Grey cautiously opened the door, peering out. "Where were you last night?"

"None of your business. Let me in."

He swung open the door wearing a rumpled sweat suit. A pillow and blanket decorated the couch, but his suit hung neatly on a hanger. We both stared at each other.

"I really appreciate this ...."

"Forget it. I did it for your father not you."

Chris plopped down on the couch. "You really don't like me, do you?"

"Have you ever given me any reason to?" I asked. "How long will you be here? I have to check out on Monday."

"Don't worry. I won't bother you for long." Chris jumped to his feet. "Hey, some guy came knocking on your door last night about two a.m." He turned, his eyes bright with malice. "Said he was your boyfriend."

Patrick! It had to be.

"You *opened* the door?"

"Nah, I just told him you were busy."

My throat felt dry. "Did he leave a message?" I asked.

"Just said to tell you he didn't lie—whatever that means. Sounds like an excuse to me."

CHAPTER SEVENTEEN

I turned away from Chris Grey and brushed some lint from his suit jacket. The inside pocket sagged. I felt a hard, heavy object in it.

My heart beat like a pair of castanets. *Oh my God—it's a gun! I have to get out of here before he uses it again.*

"Why does Clarke want you?" Chris blocked the door so I slowly edged away.

"He wants to ask me some questions that I can't answer," Chris said. "Questions about the murders."

I ran to the bedroom and slammed the door. Where the hell was my phone?

Chris popped the door with one kick, and leapt across the room.

He grabbed my hand before I could dial a number. He was breathing hard, and cursing.

"What the hell is wrong with you, woman?" he asked. "Are you crazy?"

"I'm not the one with a gun!" My heart was beating so fast I thought I would faint. *Great! He wouldn't have to kill me .I'd die right here of a heart attack."*

He loosened his grip. "Don't scream. Please."

I stiffened but didn't scream.

"Okay, come into the living room and we'll talk." He rolled his eyes, "I knew this was a mistake. You're too damn nosey."

He walked in front of me while I looked unsuccessfully for a weapon. If only I could remove my shoe.

Chris Grey reached into his other suit pocket. "I've got something to show you," he said.

Oh my God, he's got a knife! I'd rather be shot—it's quicker.

It wasn't a weapon in his pocket. Chris Grey pulled out a badge—a federal badge. He turned around and held it up. "Are you satisfied now?" he asked. "I'm an undercover agent for the Justice Department."

I couldn't believe it. "Does Jonathon know?" I asked.

Chris shook his head. "I'm so far undercover my own family doesn't know. And it has to stay that way, at least for a little while longer."

"Why don't you just tell Clarke?"

He looked exasperated, like he wanted to gag me. "We don't know how far down the corruption goes," he said. "There's a lot of money involved."

I was still processing everything. "So you're the mole they were talking about?"

Chris tensed. "Who was talking about a mole?"

"You know on the flash drive thingy. Cates and his buddies."

"Oh yeah. I know all about that. The big problem is the IRS mole. Someone is feeding these crooks inside information. When I find that out, we'll arrest the whole bunch of them."

I had to ask him. "How did you end up doing this anyway?"

He didn't want to tell me. In fact, I think he would have happily used that gun to slug me.

"They came to me when I was working at Stratton," he said.

"They?" I asked.

"Justice. They needed someone to infiltrate Tax Champions, gain their trust."

I still didn't like him, but for Jonathon's sake I was glad.

"You know your father never doubted you."

Chris Grey folded his hands. "But I doubted *him*—especially when it came to you."

"Me? Nothing ever went on between us. We're friends."

"Well my mother didn't think so and it hurt her. I'll always hate you for that."

We exchanged glares.

"He had no business fooling around with a white girl," Chris said bitterly. "I heard him saying 'Grace this,' and 'Grace that'. It made me sick!" He got up. "It still does."

I wanted to kick him. Hadn't Jimmy Carter shown that lust in your heart isn't wrong?

"Where do we go from here? I promised your father you could stay here, and you can."

"Just keep your mouth shut. Don't tell anyone and I mean anyone about this. It could blow everything—not to mention endanger my life." Chris Grey spat out the words.

"You mean you still don't know who the traitor inside the IRS is?"

"Not yet, but we will. I think it's a former executive—someone with good contacts."

"What about Maude? How did she fit into the whole mess?"

Chris sighed. "She really didn't. She just puttered around asking questions. Like you."

I took the high road. "You quarreled with her that night. Remember, we were there."

"You're really pushing it. Maude wanted to blow my cover. Somehow she found out or thought she did. That bitch would have destroyed two years of work."

I really didn't like Chris Grey. "You love to call women bitches, don't you?"

He wasn't fazed at all. "When the name fits ... " he said, looking at the clock. "Don't you have someplace to go?"

"Yikes!" I ran to the bedroom, got my things, and headed for the shower.

Time was running out. My window of opportunity was closing, and I had nothing to show for it. Mary Hagan expected results and a disappointed Mary meant a devastated Grace. I had to question these guys before the conference ended and they scattered. The hell with Patrick Fong! He and the Dragon Lady deserved each other!

The weakest link was Harry Hawkins so it made sense to start with him. By lurking near the front desk, I was able to see most of the participants as they scurried to their sessions. Harry was hard to miss. He shuffled across the lobby like a dying crab. I popped into the classroom and parked myself next to him.

"Hi Harry, what's going on?" I said brightly. "This should be a great session."

Harry jerked his head up. "Uh, Grace, how are you." He looked around for reinforcements and found none. "I'm just getting settled."

Harry was too polite to snub me, too agitated to fake it.

I saw Brett Roberts across the room, and waved. Brett gave me a wry salute. Apparently he too was intrigued by the topic: "Resolving Problems with the IRS." None of the other suspects joined the group.

After a half hour of lecture, we broke into pairs. I couldn't have planned it better.

"Harry—its just you and me baby! Pull your chair over."

He gave a half smile and joined me. Even though the room was icy cold, Harry was sweating. I pulled my sweater tight and touched his arm. "Are you *okay* Harry? Here, use my handkerchief."

"No, Grace, I've got one somewhere." He fumbled in his pocket, produced a sodden lump of linen, and began mopping his brow. "I'm really not feeling very well."

"Harry, get a grip! You can save yourself, make a deal."

He kept his head down. "I don't know what you mean, Grace."

Harry was an unconvincing liar. He'd suck at poker.

"Harry—think! You have a family. You're a decent guy. You can live to audit again."

"I'm not a rat. Besides, I can't help you." He pointed to the blackboard. "We should do the exercise."

"Screw the exercise, Harry, we're talking about a murder rap."

His face was ashen. "Murder? You mean Maude?"

"And Al Kingman, the security guard. Harry, this is serious."

Harry looked miserable. I think he was close to tears. "I don't *know* anything—at least about murder."

When a man is down, a kick can work wonders.

"What they really want is the IRS traitor. Who is it, Harry?"

"I keep telling you, I DON'T KNOW!"

"What about Chris Grey—he's connected, isn't he?"

Harry laughed. "He has no contacts at the IRS. They all hate him. Now Jonathon Grey is another matter."

I got a sudden jolt. "Are you implying ...?"

"No, No, I didn't mean anything. Jonathon's solid. Look Grace, maybe I can find something out. But not now. Meet me at the arboretum after lunch."

"Harry, it's really hot out there. Maybe we should wait 'til tonight."

"Just be there, Grace." Harry jumped up and hustled out the door.

Brett Roberts scrutinized every step that Harry took.

I actually welcomed the mind-numbing sessions that day. I hardly thought of Patrick Fong or his bride to be. Therese floated by at mid-day, with a quizzical smile on her face.

"How are ya doing, Grace? Can I get you anything?"

Yes, Patrick Fong's head on a plate. "No, I'm fine. Thanks for asking."

I stopped at the Concierge station, in case I had any messages. How pathetic!

Why would he even bother? I did get one note—Call Mary Hagan." Had that woman ever heard of cell phones?

I marched toward my suite with leaden steps. What now? Mary's secretary, Shirley answered on the first ring.

"Hi Grace! Mary said she'd meet you at noon, by the bar." She giggled. "She said she's got some hot news for you!"

I wasn't sure I could take any more of Mary's hot news. At least Chris Grey had gone somewhere. Straight to hell, I hoped. As I gathered up my purse and keys, I noticed a vellum envelope on the floor. Someone must have slipped it under the door. My hands trembled as I tore it open. The message was simple: *Grace, trust me. I love you. Patrick*

My first reaction was sheer joy—*he loves me, he loves me!* A tsunami flooded my brain, sweeping away every painful memory. As soon as the waves subsided, I felt an anger that torched every twig of sentiment. How *dare* him! Did he think I was one of these simpletons who excused anything just to hear—*I love you?* Patrick was obviously one of those vile men who had to keep at least one woman on a string—a serial philanderer. Not this woman. I tore up his note, and trashed it. I considered flushing it down the toilet, but why damage the plumbing? I love grand gestures but it was heavy vellum.

I had to focus on solving the case. Maude's murder would be avenged no matter what. I hustled down to meet Mary Hagan and get the lowdown. I didn't dare keep her waiting: tardiness was one of her many pet peeves. Shit! There she was standing outside the wine bar tapping that foot again. Black was the color of the day. Mary reminded me of a particularly stylish grim reaper.

"It's about time. Where have you been?" she asked.

"Well I was ...."

"Never mind. Let's grab a seat at the bar."

We sat at the end of the bar, ordered a salad, and played with our napkins. Mary was leading up to something unpleasant. She chattered about inconsequential things— promotions, fashion, and politics—for what seemed like an eternity. Finally, she daintily dabbed her mouth with a napkin and reached in her briefcase. She adjusted her reading glasses, and paused theatrically.

"My contact at State came through, as I knew he would." She gave a dimpled smile. "I can't *show* you this but I'll read you the highlights. Hmm ... " Mary enjoyed prolonging agony— mine.

"Okay, here it is: Dr. Jie-ling Chow—PhD, Asian Studies, Stanford; post-doc work at the University of Beijing. Very impressive. She's thirty-four years old, an only child of an American mother and Chinese father—never married." Mary showed that dimple again. "Of course, after today's *Post,* we know that will soon change, don't we? Let's see—she was raised in affluent circumstances but her father lost most of his money playing the Asian markets. Has a condo in San Francisco and an apartment in Beijing. No police record, no children, no pets." Mary paused. "Nothing too suspicious. Was that what you were interested in, Grace?"

I managed a weak smile. She enjoyed toying with me.

"Now the next one is *really* interesting," she said. "Patrick Fong—also a PhD in Asian Studies from Stanford. Got his JD at Georgetown and joined the State Department four years ago. He's thirty-three years old, has a twin brother who's a shrink, and a shit-load of family money! The Fong Family Trust has its own entry in *Wikipedia* if you can believe it. No wonder Jie-ling latched on to him! If he looks anything like his photo he's also one hot guy! Has a black-belt in Tae-kwon-do and a townhouse in Georgetown, never married, no children, two dogs."

I turned aside as the blood rose to my cheeks. Okay, maybe it would take awhile to forget him but I could do it. *Patrick has a twin, and two dogs! My God! Forget the fact that he's rich ...*

"Did you hear me, Grace? What have you got for me? I did my part, now deliver."

"I don't have the answer—yet. But I did have a heart-to-heart with Harry Hawkins today and he may have some info on the mole this afternoon."

Mary wasn't buying it. "*When* this afternoon?"

"We're meeting around five."

Mary's lips pressed into a thin line of disapproval.

"Let's get something straight, Grace. I don't care who murdered that harpy Maude or the rent-a-cop. Do you hear me? I want to find this viper in the IRS who is screwing with the tax system. I want to personally deliver his head on a platter to Justice."

I'd never seen Mary quite this agitated. Her mascara even started to streak. Not a pretty picture. She threw her napkin on her plate and jumped down from the stool.

"I better go with you to talk to Harry. Where are you meeting him?"

"Mary, please, I don't think that's such a good idea. He's scared of you or something."

She preened a bit at that. Fear can be a potent weapon.

"You better turn the heat on him then. By the way, I had a little chat with Clarke and he wants to see you again. Today."

"Why?" I asked.

Mary freshened her lipstick. "Something about harboring a fugitive."

CHAPTER EIGHTEEN

James Clarke bothered me. Maybe it was his cynicism or the way he doubted anything I said. He met me in the lobby lounge dressed like a preppy with a mean streak.

"Thanks for coming, Ms. Quinn," he said. "Maybe you can clear something up for me."

"Glad to help in any way, Lieutenant." I tried the innocent look that charmed the nuns in grade school.

Clark kept patting his pocket, seeking the elusive smokes. "Two words—Christopher Grey."

A long, pregnant pause ensued. This was Clarke's game after all, not a quiz show.

"Where is he, Ms. Quinn? A little bird told me that you might know. Apparently your suite sees more action than a hot sheet motel."

"I hope you're not suggesting any kind of romance between us!" No need to manufacture fake indignation when it came to Christopher Grey. I glowered at Clarke. "I have no idea where he is and I resent the hot sheet remark."

That was technically true since Chris could be almost anywhere, and the hot sheet remark was over the top even for Clark.

He focused the baby blues on me. "Chris Grey may have murdered your friend."

"I very much doubt that. Everyone yelled at Maude. She was a most annoying woman."

"I suppose you have a *theory* about this." Contempt dripped from each syllable.

"I don't know why I even bother. I keep telling you that the murders are linked to the Abacus. It makes sense and it explains why Kingman was snuffed."

Clarke snorted. "*Snuffed!* You've been watching too much TV. Do you have any viable suspects?"

I longed to shout out "Jie-ling Chow" but I knew better. There was no proof.

"You have a lot of Federal contacts," I said. "Ask your buddies." I rose. "If that's all Lieutenant, I really must go."

Clarke blocked my path. His clenched fists told me that he was really steamed. "I know what I'm doing, Ms. Quinn. I know for instance that private collectors want the Abacus and they're willing to pay for it. I know that Dr. Chow and Dr. Worthington could use the money." Clarke grinned maliciously. "I also know that they wouldn't have the $50,000 to buy Kingman's silence but one of *your* friends would."

I tried not to react. I had to deprive Clarke of that satisfaction.

"You know who I mean, don't you Ms. Quinn?"

"If you're accusing Jonathon again … "

"Oh no. This is someone much wealthier, much better connected."

"Stop it! Say what you mean."

Clarke moved away from me. "Fine. I mean Patrick Fong."

"You're crazy! Why would Patrick get involved in a crime?"

Another tight smile from Clarke. "Well let's see: maybe he wanted some excitement or maybe he wanted even more money. Then there's the oldest motive in the book. Maybe he did it for love."

He flung the Style section of the *Washington Post* at me and smirked. I blinked for just a second as Patrick and his fiancée stared out at me.

"You should write fiction, Lieutenant," I said reaching for my sunglasses. My hand trembled.

"Maybe so but if you hear from Christopher Grey let me know. I can find Mr. Fong myself."

"Of course. Are we done here?"

Clarke waved his hand in dismissal. "A pleasure as always, Ms. Quinn."

He was a most annoying man!

◇ ◇ ◇ ◇ ◇

I had just enough time to scoot over to the Pavilion and meet Harry Hawkins. Every time Patrick's name came up my heart plummeted. Maybe it was his twin brother I saw romancing Jie-ling Chow. I cursed my own capacity for self-delusion.

The humidity outside was unbelievable. The forecast had predicted a heat index of 110 °F an indicator that felt like a modest understatement. The Pavilion area was deserted except for a solitary figure. Poor Harry—he was drenched in sweat and making a mostly futile effort to mop his brow. I almost felt guilty for trapping him this way. Then I thought of Mary Hagan.

"Hi Harry. Thanks for coming."

He turned bloodshot eyes toward me. "You know Grace, its funny. The Brits call this kind of do-dad a "Folly"—kind of apropos, don't you think?"

I slapped him on the leg. "That's the Harry Hawkins I know and love. I've been thinking—what about this Welker guy? The few times I've seen him he seemed to have a vile temper."

Harry shook his head. "Aw, I don't think so, Grace. Tom is too low level to be the mole. Plus, he was kept kind of out of the loop."

I leaned forward. "Harry, I've seen this guy in action. He's nasty!"

Harry shrugged. "You told me the guard was bribed. Where would Welker get that kind of money? I don't think he's the one, Grace. Besides, Maude really didn't talk much with him."

"Where is he? I heard he's disappeared."

"Probably hiding in the Cayman Islands or maybe Brazil." Harry made little dirt piles with his shoe.

"Was the money that good?" I asked.

Harry chuckled. "Big bucks, Gracie, big bucks. Of course most of it went in a three-way split—Cates, Braddock, and the Mole. Millions."

I swallowed hard. "Weren't they concerned about tax evasion? Remember Al Capone!"

"Hey, these guys weren't that stupid. I know for a fact that Cates and Braddock claimed it and paid taxes on the whole enchilada."

"I wonder if the mole did that? After all, any IRS executive has to file that pesky financial disclosure statement. A stray million or so is bound to raise eyebrows. Maybe it is an ex- IRS guy."

Harry relaxed a bit. "I won't lie—we all did pretty damn well. Most years, I got half a mil. Naturally I've got a big mortgage and college expenses but it was so tempting."

"What about Pam, Harry?"

"Oh, I didn't want my wife to work. Women shouldn't have to."

I gave him a murderous glare.

"Oops. Sorry, Grace. You know I respect career women. Pam's not like that. She's so soft and feminine."

I reminded myself that Harry wasn't feeling well. It would be unseemly to break his arm.

"Okay then, who do you think killed Maude?"

Harry started to sweat again. He twisted his handkerchief into big knots.

"I really don't know. She had this recording. That I know. Kelvin said it could sink all of us. They offered Maude money but she laughed in their faces. I think she enjoyed having that kind of power."

I interrupted. "I know all about the recording, Harry. I gave it to the cops on Wednesday."

He gasped, growing even more pale.

"Don't worry. I listened to it and you can't hear anyone but Cates. His big mouth is always the loudest." I grabbed Harry's arm. "What about Kingman? Do you remember anything about him?"

"Grace, I have no idea who this Kingman is. I was with Kelvin and Evan for almost the whole night that Maude died. I don't think they had anything to do with it."

Harry looked so miserable I almost took pity on him—almost.

"We're talking double murder here, Harry."

His breathing was labored. "What can I do?" he cried.

"I'm no criminal attorney but I think if you bring them the IRS snitch you can cut a deal. Save yourself, Harry. Snoop around. I'll help you if you do."

Poor Harry. If we'd been on a cliff, he would have jumped. He hung his head, and mumbled. "Okay, I'll check around. I think Kelvin knows who the mole is. He's dropped a few hints."

"Find out soon before Cates cuts the deal. You know he'd rat out anyone."

We both jumped up as we heard someone approaching. It was Brett Roberts.

"Rumors are flying, you two. Is three a crowd?" Brett slapped Harry on the back and winked at me. Harry gave a nervous laugh, and made his excuses.

"What was that all about?" Brett asked. "Harry looks like a beached carp."

"Ah, you know our Harry, always a worry-wart." I sat down next to Brett. He was studying my bruises.

"When are you going to stop playing detective, Grace? Just look at you. You're a mess."

"Gee thanks, Brett. You're a real pal."

Brett touched my shoulder. "You know I care about you. Next time you may not be so lucky. I've been talking to Therese, and she says ...."

"Stop right there! *You're* the one I'm worried about. Are you in trouble, Brett?"

He swallowed hard. "Depends on what you call trouble."

"You're not involved with Tax Champions, are you?"

"Hell no! It might be easier if I were." Brett reached in his pocket and pulled out his checkbook.

"You know what my savings account balance is?" he asked. "Twelve dollars and thirty-four cents. Great. Isn't that just great? I'm a big success, Grace, and I'm broke."

It seemed unlikely that Brett was the Mole. He was just too poor.

"What happened?" I asked. I'd heard some variation of this from him before. Brett always had a zipper problem.

He smiled, that sweet, lazy smile. "The same thing that always happens with me. I got caught up with a cute little twist who thought I hung the moon. Must of thought I owned it, too."

"Does Marie know?" I asked.

He shook his head. "Not officially, no. But when she looks for the kids' college fund, she'll figure it out."

I'd known both Brett and Marie for a long time. "You could always confess. Tell her you have a gambling problem." I looked up at him and grinned. After all, he had gambled with his marriage.

"You think that would work?" he asked.

"Trust me, a woman would rather have a reformed gambler than a confirmed cheat."

Patrick Fong, you louse

Brett's face brightened. "You may be a genius," he said, ruffling my hair. "Come on, let me buy you a drink."

We headed for the bar in companionable silence.

The happy hour crowd was still going full steam. That meant dancing, singing and imbibing lots of liquor. Even accountants can get rowdy with the right beverage. I joined Brett and several old friends and began to "party hearty." It was a relief to just have fun—no romantic complications, intrigue, or sleuthing. None of the usual suspects showed their face. Therese trotted in and treated us to her rendition of "Please Release Me."

That fueled a spirited Karaoke competition, which proved definitively that very few of us could sing. One surprise came from Brett Roberts. He did an amazing version of "the Gambler," which prompted chants of "more, more." I danced every dance, and drank far more than I should have. I admit it. I was tipsy. Maude, Kingman, the Abacus and Patrick Fong were far from my thoughts—at least for the moment. By ten o'clock I had enough. Therese, a true party animal, was leading a conga line when I slipped away. I took a deep breath to steady myself. Like most drunks, I pasted a silly smile on my face and walked very carefully past the front desk.

"Oh Ms. Quinn, I have something for you." It was my pal the concierge.

"This just came in for you," she said, as she handed me a note. "I'm glad I caught you."

It must be from Harry. Maybe he found the mole!

The message was succinct. *Exhibition Hall—ten thirty tonight—Come alone—Patrick.*

Suddenly, the fog of alcohol lifted. *He was here!* I checked my watch—10:01, I had just enough time to run upstairs, and freshen up.

Fortunately, my suite was vacant. Chris Grey was playing his best role—absent. A few touches to my makeup, and a fresh outfit took almost no time. Then I started thinking—why the Exhibit Hall? It was macabre. Maude's murder, the Abacus Caper, and my own involvement in this nightmare were all linked to that room. How did I know that Patrick left the message. It could be a trap. After all, he could have called my cell phone. Not as romantic but twice as effective.

A wiser person would have remained locked up nice and tight in her room. I'm not wise. If he was there nothing could stop me. I had to see him. I stuffed a pair of sharp tweezers into my purse. It wasn't much of a weapon but it was something.

I sped down the corridor to the conference center. It was deserted, and kind of spooky. If someone clobbered me no one would even know.

The door creaked when I tried the knob but it slowly swung open. The room was dark, illuminated only by the exit signs. I tripped over a box of folders, and gingerly picked my way along the perimeter of the room. Suddenly, an arm snaked out and grabbed me.

CHAPTER NINETEEN

We didn't have to say a word. Patrick gathered me in his arms, and kissed me so passionately that I gasped for breath. As he leaned down I put both arms around his neck and flattened myself against him. This was no time to be rational. I couldn't stop myself. It was foolish, insane—I didn't care. The only thing that mattered was being with him. I couldn't stop myself.

Patrick kissed my hair, and murmured. "I thought you wouldn't come. I missed you. I had to see you."

I raised my head and looked up at him.

"That stuff at the Museum—don't believe it," he said. "It's business."

I stiffened and pulled away. "That's what you told Jie-ling about me. Congratulations on your engagement."

Patrick pulled me close to him. "No, Baby, no. It's all part of the cover story don't you see. You'll know soon enough. It'll all be over." He looked into my eyes, "I love you. That's the only thing that counts. I'll never let you go. Never."

He pressed me against the wall. "Ouch!" he yelped." What *is* that?"

I looked down. "Oh, it's just my purse."

Patrick started laughing. "Grace, oh Grace." He shook his head. "I loved you from the moment you stumbled into my office. I can't explain it. I can't even keep my hands off you. I'm ... I'm not impulsive. I never get involved. You're a drug— beautiful, feisty. I worry about you."

"Why?"

"There's all this bad stuff happening, and you just plunge into things."

I didn't speak. Feeling him next to me was enough. He was right. Nothing else mattered.

"Look at me," he said, holding my face between his hands. "This Abacus mess will be over soon. Until then, we can't be seen together."

I pulled away, and watched him in the dim light. He was dressed in black, with his hair slicked back into a ponytail. I'm a sucker for a man with a ponytail.

"Just trust me," he said. "I love you. I won't ever hurt you."

Patrick kissed me again, and slid the strap of my sundress down. He slowly ran his lips from my neck to my shoulder and worked his fingers down the bodice of my dress. I closed my eyes, and clung to him as he gently massaged my breasts. I lost track of time and place, giving myself up to pure sensation. I forgot those reasons I should give him up. Realized that I couldn't do it.

Suddenly, we heard a noise. Patrick put a finger to his lips and moved back into the shadows.

"Grace! Is that you?" Jonathon Grey's voice rang out. Patrick grimaced and balled up his fists. He melted into the darkness, as I rearranged my clothes.

I stepped into the light. "What are *you* doing here?" I asked.

"Are you crazy? There's a murderer on the loose, and you're prowling around dark places by yourself. What in hell are *you* up to?"

I had to think fast. Fortunately, I'm very creative.

"Looking for inspiration," I lied. "You know, hoping Maude will point the way."

"You're going to break your neck! Hold on while I turn on the hall lights."

When Jonathon flicked the switch, I blinked in the sudden glare of the overhead. The room was empty and Patrick Fong was gone.

Did it really happen? Maybe the whole thing was a hallucination. I didn't care. I might be deranged but I was happy.

"Grace, are you okay?" Jonathon looked worried. "I ran into Harry and he was asking for you. Said he'd meet you a midnight."

"Harry—where?"

"At the hotel pool and before you say anything I'm going with you." Jonathon folded his arms, daring me to disagree. "It's simply not safe for you to traipse around by yourself."

"Okay," I said meekly.

"Come on. Let's grab a drink at the bar and catch each other up." Jonathon put his hand in the small of my back and escorted me into the corridor.

The wine bar was deserted except for a few courting couples. Therese was one of them. She had commandeered a back booth and was cuddled up with none other than Cheap Suit. I could only see the back of her head but by the sighs and giggles that wafted from their table, I assumed she was having a very good time.

Jonathon pointed to the bar. "Is this okay?"

"Absolutely." I was feeling so mellow I'd agree to sit anywhere.

He ordered a scotch straight up. I began my own abstinence regimen, by ordering Pellegrino.

"Chris and I had a long talk," Jonathon said. "He told me all about the undercover assignment."

I looked closely at my old friend. His face radiated both joy and relief. Fatherhood must be hell at times.

"I understand I have you to thank, Grace. Thanks for clearing things up with him." He sipped his Scotch pensively. Neither one of us needed to elaborate about that comment.

"Chris has always been quiet—even as a boy."

I would have substituted sullen, disagreeable, and sneaky to describe Christopher Grey.

"But I knew, I just *knew* he'd never be dishonest. He's like his mother—shy and easily hurt."

I didn't dare respond to that one. Jonathon was ambling down a twisty path.

"He's really grateful that you took him in." When he saw my look of disbelief, Jonathon amended his statement. "*I'm* really grateful that you helped my son. I won't forget it."

I touched Jonathon's hand. "I owe you so much. That was the least I could do."

The look in his eyes made me wary. *Oh no, not another declaration of love.*

"We've known each other a long time, Grace, and I've always cared for you. If my situation had been different, who knows? As it is, I value your friendship."

What was it with these guys tonight? Had I bathed in catnip?

He cleared his throat. "That's why I have to say, I'm worried about you and this State Department guy."

I leaned back. "Huh?"

"You know, this Patrick Fong. He's always hanging around and I think he might be involved in the murders."

"Why?"

"I don't know. There's just something funny about him. The night of Maude's murder, I saw him talking with that Kingman guy—you know, the one who got shot. Chris said this Fong came knocking on your door one night. I don't want you to get hurt."

It was unanimous. They cared for me and didn't want me hurt. Hurrah!

"Don't worry, I'm pretty tough. And Jonathon, thanks for caring."

He looked at the gilt clock on the wall, and jumped up. "Hey, we better get going. It's almost midnight."

"Do you know which way the pool is?" I asked. "I've never been there."

"Let me ask," Jonathon said. He dropped a twenty on the bar and spoke with the bartender.

"Okay, I've got it. Take a left turn, and the first door to your right."

We carefully followed the instructions. Jonathon is a CPA, after all. The hotel grounds were deserted, and it took us at least ten minutes to reach the pool. The beach chairs and chaise were empty and a towel was on the grass. I got a funny feeling.

"Jonathon, look!" I grabbed his arm and squeezed hard. Something was floating in the pool. It was Harry.

"Go get help, Grace, he may still be alive!" Jonathon dove into the pool and started towing Harry toward the stairs. I helped him drag the body out of the pool. Harry gave new meaning to "dead weight."

"He's still breathing!" Jonathon cried. He started CPR. "Grace! Get going! Harry needs help now!"

I stumbled toward the hotel, looking frantically for the front entrance. After one wrong turn I found it and ran straight for my friend, the Concierge.

"HELP! There's an accident by the pool. Ambulance!"

She was soothing and professional. Before I could even sputter a full sentence, the Concierge dialed 911. I headed back to help Jonathon and Harry, praying all the while that another death had been averted.

Jonathon, assisted by a jogger, performed CPR. We heard the wail of the siren and stepped out of the way.

"Harry … is he …?"

"He's alive—barely."

I handed Jonathon a towel. "It must have been a heart attack. He looked bad this afternoon."

He wiped his face, and took off his shoes. "I don't know, Grace. The back of his head is bashed in. Could have happened when he fell but maybe it's the reason he fell."

"I'm calling Clarke," I said. "This is just too convenient."

The Paramedics arrived and loaded Harry into the Ambulance.

"We have to go with him. He shouldn't be alone."

I couldn't help feeling responsible for Harry's condition. "How's he doing?" I asked one of the men, an older Hispanic looking guy. His tag read "Raul."

"He's still with us." Raul threw Jonathon a dry t-shirt. "You'll be next if you don't get into something dry."

We hopped into the back of the ambulance, watching Harry's grey complexion, hearing the steady beep beep of some medical contraption.

"Do you think this has anything to do with the Mole?" I whispered to Jonathon.

He shook his head, and shrugged. When we arrived, I called Clarke, and left a message. He was on duty but away from his desk.

We sat outside the curtained room, listening to Harry's labored breathing. At least he *was* breathing, and that was a tribute to Jonathon.

"You saved his life," I said. "I panicked but you saved him."

Jonathon shivered. "You would have thought of something if I wasn't there."

I handed him a container of coffee.

"I think Harry found out something—about the Mole, or maybe the murders. We must be getting pretty close."

SLAM! Jonathon pounded the side table, spilling coffee on his shirt and my sandals.

"Stop it! Right now! Don't you see what you're doing? You'll be the next one fished out of a pool, or a garbage bin."

I mopped coffee off him and my new shoes with a paper napkin. An orderly threw me a towel, and kept moving.

"Leave it alone, Grace! Let the police handle it!" Jonathon grabbed my wrist. "It's not some mystery book. You could die!"

"Yes, Grace. Let the police handle it."

I turned and saw James Clarke. He had his usual sardonic grin in place but his eyes weren't smiling. He made no apology for eavesdropping.

"I got your message." He ignored me and focused on Jonathon. "It's time you both told me everything. Come on, let's find someplace quiet."

"Harry," I said. "We can't leave Harry alone."

"Don't worry, Officer Chase will take good care of Harry." Clarke pointed to a beefy young patrolman with bulging biceps.

"I know the perfect place for our chat." Clarke nodded toward a small sign with an arrow pointing left. "Maybe if we sit in the Chapel, you two will finally tell the truth."

I cracked like a day old egg. Within ten minutes, Clarke knew everything we knew about the Mole. He still wasn't convinced that the murders were linked to Tax Champions.

"So far, all we have is supposition," he said. "I've checked the bank records of everyone involved with Tax Champions—none of them withdrew $50,000. Or anywhere near it."

"But Lieutenant, the Mole wouldn't stash that kind of money in a bank account. It's too easily traced. The Mole probably had it in a safety deposit box."

"Maybe he had it under the mattress. Either way, that doesn't help me. I can't get a search warrant without probable cause." Clarke twirled his pencil in precise little circles.

"Ms. Quinn, I think you've constructed some sort of fantasy about this Mole. He may not even exist."

Jonathon hung his head. He was either agreeing with Clarke or collapsing from fatigue. Either way he was no help to me at all.

Clarke turned to him. "I presume your son can verify this undercover assignment?"

Jonathon nodded.

"It's true," I said. "I saw his badge and gun, Lieutenant." Clarke dismissed my contribution with a wave.

"I'm sure you did, Ms. Quinn. You seem to be everywhere in this investigation. Now take Mr. Grey's advice. Stay out of it."

He pushed out his chair and got up. "Surely the IRS has some tax delinquent to punish or some innocent citizen to harass? That should keep you busy."

We headed back to Harry's room. Officer Muscles was still on guard and the prognosis remained unchanged.

"Go home, you two," Clarke commanded. "We've got this under control."

"What about Pam?" I asked. "What about his wife?"

Clarke had enough of my help. "Believe it or not, Ms. Quinn, we've done this before, although I'm not sure how we ever accomplished anything without your assistance."

Jonathon grabbed my arm and pulled me toward the exit. "Grace," he said through gritted teeth. "It's time to leave."

We didn't speak on the cab ride to the hotel. Jonathon said goodnight and headed up to his room. I knocked on Therese's door, hoping for company.

"Grace? What happened to you?" she asked, poking her head out the door.

"It's a long story. Let me in."

"Well ... I'm not alone." Therese said.

"Never mind, I get it."

I dragged myself to my suite, bolted the door, and fell into bed fully clothed. I didn't even check for bad guys.

CHAPTER TWENTY

I dreamed I was in a construction site. Workmen were pounding, pounding. Then I heard my name and awoke with a start.

"Grace Quinn, open this door immediately!"

Oh, God, it was my boss. What was she doing here today? I stumbled to the door and let her in.

"What happened to you? You look a mess!" Mary Hagan's dulcet tones belied her message. She was pissed!

She wore her business casual look—silk blouse, tailored slacks and Ferragamos. Naturally, her hair and makeup were perfect and she smelled divine. She perched on the bed and made herself comfortable.

"Sit down and tell me everything," she said. "What happened to Harry? Who's the Mole?"

"Harry's in the hospital, I haven't checked his condition in the last six hours." I checked my watch—it was 9:35 a.m.

"Well I have," Mary said. "His condition is 'unchanged' whatever that means." She straightened her blouse and gave me the eye. "Did you find the Mole or not?"

I know she's my boss but I got testy. "Gee Mary, since Harry was doing the dead man's float, he wasn't up to talking."

Mary blanched. "You mean, he couldn't even talk? I thought he had a heart attack or something."

I went over to wash my hands. "He had an attack alright. Someone tried to murder him. If it hadn't been for Jonathon, Harry would be dead."

Mary puffed out her lip. When she does that she's plotting and it portends trouble for someone—usually me.

"Well, we'll just have to think of something else. There must be a clue we've missed."

I had to give Mary credit; she wasn't as wimpy as the men. Of course, it was *my* hide on the line, but still ....

"Okay, here's the plan. I'll go downstairs and chat up some of the guys. We have only two more days to nail this thing. You keep working on the Museum angle." She gave me that dimpled smile. "Your contacts in that area seem pretty strong."

I ignored that comment and hauled myself up from the couch. "I'll get right on it."

My plucky can do attitude and sunny smile came in handy.

"Great! Check in later." Mary whisked out the door without a goodbye, leaving me to ponder my next move. I decided to visit Madelaine again. Cleveland Park was beautiful in the morning.

It took an entire hour to pull myself together. Hair, face and clothes had to be perfect for what I was planning. I stopped by a florist shop, and purchased a large mixed bouquet for my unwitting hostess. Now if I could only devise some pretext for this surprise visit.

Public transportation didn't appeal to me today. The weather was clammy and I wanted to avoid a return engagement with the Cleveland Park metro. The cab deposited me a block away from Newark Street. I wanted to make sure that Patrick's surveillance van wasn't around, before I made my move.

I summoned my courage and knocked on the door. Madelaine opened it, looking flustered and surprised.

"Miss err, Hagan wasn't it?" she said politely. "What a surprise."

"Actually, my name is Grace Quinn. I need your help if you have some time."

I handed the bouquet to her, and tried to look innocent. "You said I could come back if I needed more information about your house."

Sixty years of good breeding kicked in. Madelaine opened the door, and invited me inside with a gracious nod.

Suddenly, Cyrus charged down the stairs. He was dressed quite formally in long sleeved shirt, suspenders and dress slacks.

"What is *she* doing here?" he shouted. "I told you not to let strangers inside."

"Cyrus! Manners!" Madelaine put a hand on her brother's shoulder. "Ms. Quinn is our guest."

He stood glaring at me but he didn't forcibly evict me. After taking a deep breath, Cyrus turned to me.

"What is this all about? I understood that you were an accountant. Do we have a tax problem?"

"Certainly not and I'm not an accountant. I'm here to discuss art—James Whistler in particular."

The blood drained from his face. His sister didn't even flinch.

"Take our guest into the parlor, Cyrus. I'll get us some tea." She bustled off leaving us in awkward silence.

"I don't know what your game is, young woman but I have nothing to hide." Cyrus tried using bluster to intimidate me. "Perhaps you'd like to explain yourself."

I walked into the parlor. The wall that had housed the Whistler was empty.

"Where is it?" I cried. "You know the one 'Princess from the Land of Porcelain.'"

Cyrus raised a brow. "In the Freer of course. That's where it's always been."

He didn't scare me one bit. "Not quite. I went looking for it two days ago. No one knew exactly where it was."

"I think I should call the authorities," Cyrus said. "You're obviously demented. Jie-ling warned me about you."

His words were calm but his hand was shaking.

"You're right, Professor. Call the police. Ask for James Clarke—Homicide."

"Homicide! What are you talking about?"

"In case you've forgotten, two people have been murdered. I think it's related to your precious Abacus and the museum."

He began sputtering. "I assure you, young lady you're wrong. Why I know ...."

His tirade was interrupted by Madelaine, who pushed a tea trolley laden with goodies.

She'd used the Herend again.

"Now isn't this nice, Cyrus, a guest for tea. Let's sit down and take our places."

Madelaine pointed to a round table with four fauteuils. Her eyes were bright, and her cheeks had two spots of color. "Will you pour, Miss Quinn?"

I was glad to do the honors. I filled each cup, and took my seat. Miss Worthington passed trays of biscuits, and dainty sandwiches.

"Here Miss Quinn, I know you like milk and sugar with your tea. Cyrus and I take it plain."

I tried to be polite but my exploits last night had upset my stomach. To be honest, I was hung-over and milk was the last thing I needed. I bit into a scone and smiled. "Excellent, Miss Worthington. Did you make these yourself?"

Madelaine's voice rose several octaves. The woman was losing it.

"Please enjoy your tea. Cyrus, pass the sandwiches ...."

Suddenly, Whistler her ginger cat leapt up on the table, and tried to lap the cream.

Madelaine lunged for the pitcher, throwing it across the room. Milk splattered over the sofa, and pieces of fine porcelain scattered. Cyrus and I sat in stunned silence.

Madelaine clutched her pet and wailed, "I tried to stop her, Cyrus, but she wouldn't die. I pushed her at the Metro. I was so sure ... but she wasn't hurt. Now the milk—she won't drink the milk and I fixed it. Whistler, Whistler my baby."

She began to rock back and forth, crooning to Whistler. Like all felines, he resented assaults on his dignity and the lost cream enraged him. He strained to escape and yowled angrily.

Cyrus, his mouth wide open, sat glued to his chair. I wasn't thrilled myself. I toyed with asking Madelaine for my Bottega bag but decided against it. *Noblesse oblige* and all that.

Finally, Cyrus went to his sister, put his arms around her, and held her like a baby. He spoke to her in low, comforting sounds and guided her toward the stairs. I grabbed Whistler, locked him in the kitchen, and started mopping up the remains of the milk.

At least one mystery had been solved: Madelaine was my assailant!

When he returned, Cyrus was ashen.

"I've called her doctor," he said, "and made her take her medicine. She's really harmless."

"You couldn't prove that by me!" I said. "Cyrus, your sister needs professional help. Psychiatric care."

He cringed like a beaten man. "Please don't call the police," he begged. "She'd die in an institution. I'll tell you whatever you want."

I eased on to a chair and faced him. "Okay, tell me about the Whistler."

"I didn't steal them, if that's what you mean. I only *borrowed* a few to make Madelaine happy. She loves art, especially Whistler. You see, those paintings were family heirlooms at one time." He stared off in the distance. "When we were growing up ... before the money ran out."

It was a pathetic situation but I couldn't afford sympathy. "How long has this been going on?" I asked.

"For about four years. Madelaine lives in her own little world and those paintings were the only thing keeping her ... stabilized." He pulled out his handkerchief and blew his nose lustily.

"Your visit must have upset her. She just told me she was afraid you'd take the paintings. That's why she slipped out of the house, and ... " he paused.

"Tried to kill me, you mean?"

"She didn't mean it. She's not responsible." Cyrus started babbling excuses for his lunatic sibling.

"How do you handle it during the day? I mean she's not exactly compos mentis."

"Mrs. Day, her caretaker, is a trained nurse. Madelaine slipped away from her."

Now I understood. "Your sister described her as your 'Char.'"

Cyrus nodded fondly. "Oh yes, that's a comforting little fiction she made up. Makes her think it's like the old days."

I wanted to leave this madhouse but Cyrus and I had to finish our chat.

"Okay, Cyrus, who else knows about your little lend-lease act?"

He hung his head. "No one," he lied.

"Are you sure?" I persisted.

"Jie-ling. She caught me leaving the museum one day."

"Did you help her try to steal the Abacus?"

"Certainly not! She just pressured me for more authority. She wanted to be in charge of the Abacus exhibit." Cyrus swallowed several times. I handed him his tea and his drained his cup. I decided to skip any further refreshment at the Worthington house.

I leaned over and looked him in the eye. "This is important, Cyrus. What do you know about the deaths of Maude Morrissey, and Albert Kingman?"

Color rose to his cheeks. Cyrus was not quite tomato red—more of a strawberry hue.

"Nothing! I know nothing about any murder or theft. Ask Jie-ling. Ask anyone."

"Who do you think her partner is, Cyrus?"

He scratched his head and gave it some thought. "I can think of only one person," he said. "Patrick Fong."

My mind was reeling. Could I be that wrong about Patrick? I stumbled to the door, ignoring the stream of words from Cyrus. Finally, he grabbed my arm, and shouted.

"What about it? Are you going to the Police?"

I shook him off and turned around. "Not as long as you get her some real help."

He heaved a sigh of relief and asked, "Is there *anything* else I can do for you, dear girl?"

Several uncharitable replies came to mind, however, my better nature asserted itself.

"Keep our conversation to yourself. Don't tell anyone—especially Jie-ling."

"No, no, of course."

He opened the front door wide. "Just one thing, Dr. Worthington."

"Yes," he said warily.

"Did you happen to notice a black leather tote bag among your sister's possessions? A recent acquisition?"

Cyrus was mystified. "I'll look, but I doubt it. Madelaine is afraid of crowds. She never goes shopping without me."

I shrugged, grabbed the handrail, and walked cautiously down his front steps.

CHAPTER TWENTY-ONE

I was in a funk. Despite all my efforts, I was no closer to finding Maude's murderer than I had been a week ago. Who did I think I was, anyway? I had no authority, access or real connection to the crimes. The whole thing was only a mild diversion from my real life. Playing detective was fun—up to a point. I had to face facts: The Mole was still at large and Patrick's role in the Abacus caper was a mystery. I was sure of only one thing. My feelings for Patrick were strong. I might be in love with him.

Maybe it was time to go back to basics. Maude and Kingman's murder had to be related. The assault on Harry was probably another link in that chain. If only I could find the Mole, at least the Tax Champions angle would be resolved.

I decided to find Therese. Maybe we could pry a sliver of information from Cates and Braddock. Brett Roberts was out of it. His problems were anatomical not homicidal.

The Abacus caper would just have to wait. I longed to pin the whole thing on the villainous Dr. Chow, but unfortunately there were problems. If Jie-ling was involved in the murders, she had to have help. No way could she overpower so many people. She was certainly ruthless enough but she lacked physical strength. There was only one helper who fit: her dear friend and putative fiancé, Patrick Fong. Patrick said everything would soon be over. That could mean that he was headed on a non-stop flight to Rio with his playmate in tow. My head began to throb.

I cabbed it back to the hotel and marched up to Therese's room. Despite the "do not disturb" sign, I rapped loudly for a few seconds.

"Let me in, Therese. We have to talk."

It was 11:00 a.m. Surely she was awake by now. I heard faint signs of life and the door slowly creaked open. Therese wore an oversized T-shirt with a Treasury logo. Emblazoned on the back was the word, *Police*. Devon had obviously left a souvenir or two.

Her smile was as sunny as ever. "Grace! Come on in, I'm alone."

The room was a disaster area—clothing, pillows, newspapers and cigarette butts were scattered about. I was in no position to judge anyone.

"We have to talk. Do you know about Harry?"

"Harry?" she said. "What about him?"

I gave her the condensed version after which her mouth hung open in disbelief.

"What the *Hell* is going on here, Grace? The world's gone mad."

"Never mind that, we've got work to do."

"Huh?"

I wanted to shake her but I settled for clapping my hands.

"Therese—focus. Did Devon give you any useful information about Tax Champions?"

She beamed. "Actually, he did. The US Attorney offered plea agreements to the small fry, you know, Welker and several others but it wasn't enough so he got really tough with Cates and his boys. Jail terms—and not in some cushy Federal space. Hard time, places with drug dealers and Mafiosos."

Therese grinned thinking about it. "Cates shit a brick but Braddock was tougher. They didn't give up the Mole though. The funniest thing—Devon clammed up when I mentioned Chris Grey and the Mole. What do you make of that?"

"I think Chris Grey's out of it. He's on our side."

Her eyes narrowed. "Do you know that for a fact, or do you just want it to be true—for Jonathon."

Now I really wanted to shake her. "It's the truth! And stop harping about Jonathon."

"Well geez, Grace, how many men do you want? I mean you already have Jonathon and the gorgeous Mr. Fong. Leave some for the rest of us."

"Oh shut up! Let's focus on the murders. What about Maude's recording?"

161

"Devon thought that was great stuff. He thinks it might nail Cates if IRS can get its hands on it."

"What do you mean? Clarke must have sent them that disc."

"Nope. You know how the locals and the Feds screw around with each other."

Fortunately I still had my copy. To hell with James Clarke!

"I'll just give it to Cheap Suit, er, Devon," I said. Then I got a better idea.

"On second thought, I'll let Mary Hagan handle it. She's hot to nail that bunch and it may win me some brownie points."

Therese curled her lip. "I wouldn't give her the time of day. That woman is a menace."

I snorted. "Yeah, but she's my menace. Remember, she'll be recommending me for a permanent executive post. I need her good will."

"She's still a bitch, Grace. Don't trust her farther than you can throw her perfect little heels."

"You guys never liked each other. I don't know why."

Therese growled and started picking up her lingerie. "Oh, I almost forgot to tell you. IRS is using phone taps to trap the Mole. They're reading mail too. So far, no luck."

"You know how inept those clowns are, Therese. The Mole can rest easy."

I threw some pillows off the sofa and plopped down. "Remember Maude's *Big Story*? It had to be linked to Tax Champions. She wouldn't have known anything about the Abacus."

Therese shook her head. "Not necessarily. Maude still could have blundered into the theft attempt. The thief probably panicked and killed her. If Maude started yelling—well you know her loud she was. That woman could have doubled as an air-raid siren."

I tried not to agree but Therese made a valid point.

"Don't forget that Kingman guy," she said. "Someone might have paid him to knock off Maude or anyone else who got in the way. Remember that $50,000 bribe."

"Do I have to remind you that Kingman's dead too?"

"So what? Someone decided to terminate his employment. Happens all the time."

My stomach reminded me that breakfast was a memory and lunch was long gone.

"Hey. Let's order room service, and check on Harry. I suppose Pam is with him by now. Meanwhile, I'll get Jonathon and Chris Grey to meet me. Chris must know something about the Mole."

"What about me?" asked Therese.

"Your assignment is to question Devon about Cates and Braddock. Find out if they're hanging tough or copping a plea."

"Cates is more likely to cop a feel than a plea," Therese said, "but I'll try to find out."

"You really like him, don't you?" I asked Therese. "Devon, I mean, not Cates."

She got that goofy look that I'd seen on my own face recently.

"Yeah, I do. How do you feel about Patrick?"

I turned away hoping to distract her. I should have known better.

"You're blushing! Grace Quinn, you're in love with him!"

"Don't be silly, I hardly know him."

She smiled. "Sometimes it just happens. Why fight it?"

I sniffled. That's all she needed.

"You're crying! I can't believe it, you of all people."

This was no time to quote Shylock, besides CPA's rarely read Shakespeare. I shrugged my shoulders. "For your information, it's my seasonal allergies at work."

Therese was a bloodhound on the scent of trouble. "Bullshit!" she said. "Tell the truth."

"There's nothing to tell. Come on, let's get serious."

She didn't hear a word. "What'd he do? Oh no, he's married—the bastard! Men are all bastards!"

"Hold on, wait a minute. Patrick's not married. It's just complicated, that's all."

Therese was suspicious. "Are you sure?" she asked.

I exhaled loudly. "As sure as a security check from the State Department can be."

"That sounds like the work of your dear boss. I heard she was involved with some cabinet level guy." Therese was a firm believer in nourishing grudges. "Let me check up on him. I'll bet Devon knows all about Patrick Fong. I'll ask him."

She calmed down until she thought of Mary once more. "I told you not to believe that woman, Grace. Mary Hagan isn't happy unless she's fucking with someone."

I gave Therese a hug. "I know you're just trying to watch out for me but don't worry. Focus on questioning Devon about Tax Champions."

I started gathering up my things from her messy floor. "Therese—in the interests of time, limit the foreplay. You can screw his brains out after this mess is over."

We ordered coffee and sandwiches and called the hospital. No one would give us any information about Harry other than the usual "resting comfortably" malarkey. I suppose it beat "rest in peace."

I was too antsy to wait for room service. Instead I went to room 813, and rapped on the door.

"Jonathon, it's Grace."

I knocked more loudly this time. I knew I'd heard the television. Someone was definitely in that room. After five minutes, the door opened. Christopher Grey appeared wearing mismatched pajamas and a frown.

"Yeah? What do you want?" he grunted.

Maybe this bozo had been switched at birth with Jonathon's real son. He bore no resemblance to his elegant father.

"We need to talk." I wedged my foot in the doorway and refused to budge.

"Beat it, bitch." Young Mr. Grey had quite a vocabulary.

"I'm not leaving, so deal with it. Where's Jonathon?"

"None of your business. Leave my father alone."

We exchanged glares, having reached a conversational impasse. Fortunately, Jonathon appeared in the hallway.

"Grace! What are you doing standing out here? Let her in, Chris."

His son hesitated. "I said let her in." Jonathon's tone left no room for discussion.

Chris swung open the door and stomped off. Jonathon hid his embarrassment with a cough. "Excuse his manners, Grace. This entire undercover assignment has taken its toll on Chris."

I smiled at my friend. Despite the excitement last night, Jonathon was as dapper as ever.

I don't think I'd ever seen him in jeans before. Wearing a crisp blue shirt and deck shoes, he was a sight worth seeing.

"I'm so sorry to impose but I have to speak with both of you."

Jonathon narrowed his eyes. "Grace—I asked you to stop investigating."

"You mean snooping, don't you Dad?" Chris was a master at repartee.

"It's important, Jonathon. I think we can find the answers to Maude's murder if we pool our information."

I could see that he was weakening.

"We owe it to Maude, you know," I said softly.

Jonathon looked at his watch. "Look, we haven't had lunch. Why don't we meet at Tomate's at two-thirty? Both of us will be there." He looked at his son. "Okay, Chris?"

"Okay, Dad." Chris said sullenly.

I quickly left, and went to the lobby to check on Harry. This time, my call was more productive. I spoke with Harry's wife Pam, who had just seen his doctor.

"He's still unconscious," she said, "But the doctor is optimistic. Harry's arteries are clogged, he needs heart surgery."

"So it was a heart attack." I asked.

"Grace, that's the scary thing. Dr. Hoffman thinks someone bashed Harry on the head! Now who would want to hurt Harry?"

"He's a great guy, Pam. Is the policeman still there?"

"Yes, poor thing. He looks terribly bored."

"Tough." I said coldly. "I'll call you later."

I had to check my messages—I couldn't help myself. I hoped for something from Patrick, but I got a surprise instead. Cyrus Worthington left a message marked urgent

"Call me at work, please," it read.

I 'd left my cell phone in the room so I used the phone bank near the rest rooms. Cyrus answered immediately, sounding agitated and near hysteria.

"Thank you for calling, Ms. Quinn. I ... I want to repay you for your kindness to Madelaine. Something is amiss here at the Freer."

"What?"

"You said ... that is I thought ...."

This man could test the patience of a saint! He dithered for another few seconds before I intervened.

"Cyrus, is this about the Abacus? What's going on?"

The old man gulped. "I heard her today, talking about an exchange."

"Who? Jie-ling? What about her?"

"She said the antiquities market was primed for a big transaction. Ms. Quinn, I think it's happening tonight."

"Have you told the authorities?"

"No, well I was going to but I'm not certain."

I hated to ask this, but I had to. "Who was Jie-ling speaking with?"

Cyrus lowered his voice to a whisper. "Patrick Fong. She told him to meet her at eight fifteen."

He began to whimper. "What should I do? If I'm wrong, I'll lose everything but if she steals the Abacus ...."

"I'll help you." I said.

I could hear his sigh of relief. "Oh would you, Ms. Quinn! Dear Lord, that's such a comfort. Maybe it's nothing. After all, I'm an old man ...."

That went on for a while. Finally I interrupted. "Where and when, Dr. Worthington?"

"Meet me in back of the Freer at eight. I'll let you in the staff entrance. That is if it's all right with you or I could meet you at the front ...."

"No problem! I'll be there at eight, in the rear of the building."

Cyrus paused. "Please don't tell anyone. If I'm wrong, I'll be fired."

"You have my word," I lied.

I was tempted to tell Jonathon about the call from Cyrus but I knew what would happen. He'd give me a well-intentioned lecture about personal safety and my own recklessness. Worse still, he might insist on joining me. I'd deal with Cyrus myself. Senior citizens were still a safe demographic. If I really wanted company I could ask Therese, or even Mary.

La Tomate was crowded with affluent Washingtonians enjoying a lazy lunch. It wasn't hard to spot Jonathon's table—he was easily the hottest man in the room. Even Chris looked presentable. I suppose his father gave him some tips on personal grooming and deportment. Both gentlemen stood when I arrived and Jonathon held my chair. Chris narrowed his eyes and looked tempted to trip me. They ordered lunch, I asked for herb tea.

"Would somebody tell me what we're doing here?" asked charming Chris. "I'm not at liberty to discuss the tax case."

"That's funny," I said. "You spilled your guts about it the other night, as I recall."

Before war erupted, Jonathon intervened. "This is not helpful," he warned staring at both of us. "Grace, what did you have in mind?"

I took a deep breath. "I'm not interested in the legal issues. I just hoped that working together, the three of us could figure out who the IRS Mole is."

Blessed are the peacemakers. Jonathon mediated the discussion with courtesy and professionalism. "Give us some examples, Grace," he said."

"Okay, what's the profile of this person? Someone with knowledge of the tax process, and investigative practices for example."

"Someone who is part of the system—not likely to arouse suspicion." For once Chris Grey made sense. "I mean, we'd all notice if a total stranger was sniffing around."

Jonathon pointed his finger. "Maude might have known this guy, or gal," he hastily amended. "That should narrow the field a bit."

"Harry told me this Mole made millions from Tax Champions. That means it's someone who seems affluent."

Jonathon shook his head. "Maybe. But consider this. An intelligent person would never flash his wealth around especially in a paranoid organization like IRS. We can't assume the Mole would live or dress better than anyone else."

"Wait a minute!" Chris Grey interjected. "Let's go back to Harry Hawkins. Are you telling me that he actually discussed the Mole with you?" Chris balled his hands into tight fists. "He wouldn't tell anyone else anything. Claimed not to know about it."

"Harry and I are old friends," I said primly. "He trusts me."

Jonathon leaned across the table. "People, we're getting off track. Let's stick to our profile of the Mole."

"Okay, he's somebody smart. That advice he gave was very clever." Chris sounded almost wistful.

"That's interesting. Somebody clever ... " There was something—I just couldn't put my finger on it.

"And manipulative," Jonathon added. "I think this Mole engineered the whole scheme. It might have worked even better if Cates and Braddock hadn't gotten carried away. Let's face it, there's an enormous appetite for beating the government."

Chris snarled. "Just look at Cates. You can tell he has an enormous appetite."

"Chris, did they ever give any hint about the Mole—name, any detail they let slip?"

"Nah, they were cagey." Chris paused a minute. "Wait a minute! One time, Cates let slip that they were protected all the way up to the cabinet level. Something like that."

"Treasury!" Jonathon and I were aghast. "That would explain how they stayed one step ahead."

"Not so fast," Chris said. "It could be any Department—Justice, even State."

Jonathon turned to me. "What about Brett Roberts? You mentioned a financial motive."

I shook my head. "No, I spoke with him. He's clean."

Chris balled up his napkin, and threw it on his plate. "We're spinning our wheels here. What does all this have to do with the murder of Maude Morrissey?"

"Wait a minute. Tell us everything you and Maude discussed the night she died."

He pushed out his chair, prepared to leave, when Jonathon put his hand on his arm.

"Please, son. It's important."

"Okay!" Chris was not happy. He turned his body so that he faced his father. I had to crane my neck to see anything. Charming.

"Maude insisted that we meet. You know how pushy she was. Then she told me she knew I was working undercover for the government and she wanted to break the story."

"That's all? You mean that *you* were her Big Story?"

I tried to hide my disappointment but it was hard. "Are you *sure* she didn't say anything else? Think Chris!"

Jonathon put his hand on his son's arm again. "You said you were arguing, Chris. Did Maude mention the Mole?"

A light flashed in the dark space Chris called a mind.

"You know, she kept blabbing about the Mole, how she was going to break the story, and it would shock the tax community. I just ignored it, cause I figured she was talking about me. She made some comment about how self righteous IRS was about its executives—then she laughed."

"Maude always resented executives," I said. "She couldn't pass the program. If she'd nailed one, she'd have been ecstatic."

"Maude might have fingered the IRS Mole, the bad guy." Chris looked shaken. "If I'd listened, she might not have died." His voice trailed off.

"Unlikely." I said. "Knowing Maude, she would have enjoyed taunting the Mole, letting him suffer. She was always that way."

Jonathon nodded. "So where do we go from here? We still aren't sure that Maude's murder had anything to do with the Mole."

"I know. It could still be the Abacus thief but somehow I just ...."

Something flashed in my mind. "Chris, do either Cates or Braddock actually know the identity of the Mole?"

"If they do, they never admitted it."

As we started to leave, Jonathon gave me one quick look. "Remember Grace, no sleuthing. Chris, I think we should mention this to Lieutenant Clarke. Who knows, it may help him."

"Oh, you two are speaking to Clarke these days?" I said.

Chris curled his lip and said nothing. He *really* didn't like me.

"Treasury straightened everything out for Chris, thank goodness. He won't need your couch anymore, Grace."

"When are you guys going home?"

"Probably on Monday morning. I guess you'll have to keep us up on everything."

Jonathon kissed me on the cheek. "Take care of yourself, my friend."

Chris hissed. "Yeah, take care."

I think I was beginning to grow on him.

CHAPTER TWENTY-TWO

I ran into Therese in the lobby. She'd found Devon, I could tell by the stars in her eyes.

"Devon thinks Braddock may know something. Of course, you and I both know that the guy is a total blowhard who always *pretends* to know things. Anyhow Devon wants to talk with him again."

I shook my head and patted her on the back. "Sounds like you have a busy Friday night lined up."

"You bet!" Therese looked closely at me. "Okay, what are you up to? Come on, give."

I tried my innocent act. "Nothing. I just had lunch with Jonathon and ...."

"Was dreadful Chris there?" she interrupted. "Or was this a tête-à-tête?"

"Grow up. It was a strategy session, and yes, Chris was there in all his glory."

"What are *you* doing tonight, Grace?"

I know Therese. She wouldn't budge until I told her. The woman had a built in truth detector that rivaled sodium pentothal.

"I got a phone call."

"Oh my God, it was Patrick wasn't it. When are you meeting him?"

"Relax, Therese. The call was from Cyrus Worthington, your geriatric squeeze."

"Ugh! What did he want?"

I gave her the short form.

"Anyhow, I'm meeting him at the Freer at eight 8:00 p.m."

Therese crossed her arms. "Not alone, you're not."

"Don't be silly. You have some work to do while I go and hold Cyrus's hand."

Therese snorted in disgust. "And what happens if he's right? You could get between the Dragon Lady and a lot of loot. I think she'd enjoy killing you."

"Quite the watch dog, aren't you? Okay, let us compromise. If I don't get back here by ten, send in the Marines or whatever."

"By ten, you could be pushing up daisies. I'll call Clarke, I really will!"

I walked over to her. "Therese, listen to me. Clarke would just laugh at you. You know he thinks I'm a meddler."

"Duh!" Therese said with a nasty look on her face. "Clarke's right!"

Then she asked the question I dreaded.

"Where's Patrick in all this anyway?"

I opted for truth. "Cyrus thinks he's part of the conspiracy"

"*What!* You believe that old crackpot! Grace, that's bizarre, even for you."

"I don't know what to believe."

Therese grabbed her brush. "Well I do." she said as she vigorously brushed her hair. "I'm pretty good at judging men and Patrick is a keeper. I watched him look at you. He's crazy about you. Cyrus Worthington is just plain crazy."

I wanted to believe her. "Just go find Cates and Braddock and be subtle. Cates may look like the Pillsbury Dough Boy but he's got a mean streak. Braddock has always been a prick."

"Yeah, yeah, I know. But you better call me as soon as you meet with Cyrus."

"I will. Don't worry."

How do you dress for a spy caper? My solution was black—silk tank, shirt, cargo pants and running shoes, with some discreet gold jewelry. I felt invincible. Jie-ling Chow—watch out bitch!

I arrived at the Freer precisely at eight and walked casually toward the rear entrance. I would have whistled if I knew how. I didn't see any guards but why take chances?

Cyrus Worthington's head poked out of the door like an anxious turtle. He waved his hand feverishly.

"Ms. Quinn! This way—hurry."

A discreet sign said, "Freer Employees Only." Cyrus motioned me in, and locked the door.

"I've disabled the alarm on that door—only temporarily of course. Who knows which way Jie-ling will come in."

I checked my Rolex. "She doesn't have much time. It's already after eight."

Cyrus nodded, and led the way to a small office. "We can wait here. Jie-ling can't see us."

"That makes no sense, Cyrus. We can't see her either. We can't just hide in the back room. If we want to nail her, we'll have to show some spunk!" I jumped up, and started out the door.

"Wait! Wait! You'll ruin everything!" Cyrus was hopping around like Rumpelstiltskin. Maybe Therese was right—his battery pack wasn't fully charged.

I decided that coming here was a very bad idea. Cyrus imagined the whole business about Jie-ling. Both of us would probably be arrested.

"Please, Ms. Quinn," he begged. "You said you'd help me." He clutched my arm, and tugged. It was a pathetic spectacle but since I was already there, I decided to stay.

"Okay, but first, let's take a peek at the Abacus. Where are the Museum guards, anyway?"

Cyrus was all smiles. "They patrol every thirty minutes on the hour and half-hour. Come on, I'll show you."

He led the way through a labyrinth of twisty corridors. Ultimately, he opened a door that led directly to Salon thirteen. The Abacus was still there slumbering unaware in its Plexiglas tomb. There was no sign of anyone else. I checked my watch again. Eight-twenty.

"They're late!" I said. "Are you sure about the time?"

Cyrus started dithering again. "Absolutely! That is, I'm almost positive she said eight fifteen, though she may have said eight forty-five." He locked his fingers together, looking old and fragile. Then he staggered and placed his hand on his chest.

"Oh my God! Cyrus, er, Dr. Worthington, don't worry, I'll get help!"

I had to get my bearings. The Museum was a silent crypt. In view of Cyrus's condition, there was a certain irony in that. I bent over Cyrus, trying to remember CPR procedures. I hadn't excelled at the Red Cross course they'd forced me to take. He reached up and clutched my arm. His hand looked like a claw, but it had surprising strength.

"Pills!" he gasped. "Office."

I remembered that vial of nitroglycerin I'd seen Cyrus use before. He leaned on my shoulder and pulled himself up.

"Help me to my office," he said.

"But Cyrus, Dr. Worthington, shouldn't I get help? An ambulance?"

"NO!" he said, his eyes blazing. "They mustn't see me."

His color was returning, and he seemed to be doing better. I steadied Cyrus, and guided him toward the back of the Freer. He motioned toward a nicely proportioned anteroom that led to his office suite. A simple brass nameplate read: "Dr. Cyrus Worthington, Director."

The office lights were on. I helped Cyrus to a couch, and found his pills on the desk. He slipped one under his tongue, leaned back and closed his eyes.

I watched him closely. *How did I get into this mess? If he croaks, they'll say I killed him.*

Finally, he opened his eyes, and smiled. "Ah, Ms. Quinn, thank you for helping. Don't worry; I sometimes get these little attacks. They're nothing to bother with."

Right. It's perfectly normal to pass out.

I grabbed my purse, and took out a mirror and comb, just in case. If Patrick and the Dragon Lady appeared, I had to be ready.

"Look, Cyrus, it's getting late. I doubt that Jie-ling will pull anything tonight. I'm going to call a cab for you, and leave ...."

He moved so fast, I didn't even see him. When I looked up, the ailing septuagenarian had been replaced by a reasonably spry man with a big knife. Even his features looked different—sharp and sinister.

"I'm afraid that won't be possible, my dear." He grasped the knife, or sword, or whatever it was, and moved toward me. "I thought you'd fall for that little charade," he chuckled. He actually chuckled!

"But Dr. Worthington—Jie-ling—the Abacus?"

"I'm afraid that was an act also. I made it up." Cyrus preened like an actor accepting an award. I think he expected applause.

"Don't move Ms. Quinn. You're not going anywhere."

"You mean she didn't try to steal the Abacus?" I asked, still in denial.

"Of course not. I doubt Jie-ling has ever done anything dishonest in her life. I used her name to lure you here, Ms. Quinn. I knew you'd come."

"But why me?"

"To kill you, of course. You've become an irritant." Cyrus sounded peevish, annoyed that I had upset his routine.

"Is this about the Whistlers? Because I told you I wouldn't say anything."

"No no, Ms. Quinn. It's much more important. It's about the Abacus. It's always been about the Abacus."

I measured the distance between my chair and the door. After all, he was an old man, I could certainly out run him, or beat him in a fair fight. That thing in his hand changed the odds. It was heavy and ominous looking.

Cyrus walked to the door and bolted it. Then he reached into his pocket and pulled out a silk scarf. It was a lovely Asian print. He tossed it to me, and said, "Please tie that around your mouth, my dear. I can't take any chances."

"No way, you old coot. I'm going to scream my head off." I glanced at my watch. The guard should come buy any time now.

I felt something sharp flick my shoulder. Then Cyrus pointed the knife at my throat.

"Oh, I wouldn't advise it. I'm quite an accomplished swordsman, you know. This is a Dao—a type of antique Chinese saber used primarily for slashing and chopping. Ha ha—slashing and chopping." He tilted his head to one side, and smiled at me with paternal pride. "You have lovely skin, Ms. Quinn. I'd hate to see it disfigured. Of course, if you leave me no choice ...."

I grabbed the gag, and tied it around my mouth.

"That's better," said the Mad Hatter. "I know you love to talk but I want you to listen for a change. You've been so keen about the Abacus."

He stood over me with the Dao pointed right at my throat. Suddenly I heard the jingle of keys. The Guard!

Cyrus put his finger to his lips. "Not a sound now," he whispered, "or else I'll kill him."

The guard tapped on the door. "Everything okay, Dr. Worthington?"

"Fine, fine." Cyrus called out to him." Have a good evening Randal. I'll be leaving soon."

He waited until Randal's footsteps faded down the hall. Then he motioned me to the sofa. An appalling thought flitted through my brain. Cyrus must have understood.

"Please don't worry, Ms. Quinn. I have no designs on your person—at least none of a carnal nature." He smiled at me like a favorite uncle.

"Now, I'll tell you the real story of the Abacus." He moved toward me with the Dao tickling my throat. "I know you want to ask questions, that's natural. If you promise not to scream, I'll remove the scarf. Will you be good?"

I nodded. Don't all those cop shows tell you to ingratiate yourself with your captor?

He untied the gag, and prattled on. "I've devoted my entire life to beautiful things. Through study and restoration, I've managed to preserve our heritage."

Now I knew how it would end. This fiend would bore me to death.

Cyrus was in his own world, a world of culture and refinement. He caressed each syllable as he spoke. "The piece d'resistance was the Abacus. I can't tell you, Ms. Quinn, how it made me feel, just to be in its presence."

I didn't dare speak. Maybe the guard would come back in time.

Cyrus frowned. "Do you think they appreciated all my sacrifices? NO! I was paid a pittance, not enough to restore my own home."

He turned to me and took my hand. That left the knife balanced precariously in his other hand.

"My own dear sister, well you've met Madelaine, Ms. Quinn, was forced to endure a life of penury while others had so much. It wasn't fair."

She should be in the booby hatch with her lunatic brother.

Cyrus dropped my hand and steadied the Dao. I hoped his rug could absorb bloodstains—it looked like an antique Sultanabad.

"But Dr. Worthington, how can you expect to steal the Abacus from the Freer?"

He didn't like the interruption. I was supposed to listen not talk.

"I'm not going to steal it, you stupid girl."

I was puzzled. Cyrus tsk tsked, and grabbed my hair. "Don't you see?"

"Ouch!" I couldn't help it, that hurt. "I don't know what you're talking about," I said.

"I don't have to *steal* the Abacus from the Freer, you nitwit. It's already gone!"

"Huh?" My lips formed a perfect O. "Wait a minute! We just saw it."

His smile made every fright mask look tame. "What we just saw, Ms. Quinn was an excellent copy. The genuine Abacus was taken that first night at the hotel."

"How?" I wasn't capable of forming a complete sentence.

"Have you no imagination? I thought you were intelligent." He crossed his legs and adjusted the crease of his trousers. "Well no matter, I might as well tell you."

I stole a glance at the clock: 9:12. Another patrol in twenty minutes, another chance to do something.

"You mean you took it the night Maude was killed?"

Cyrus gave a petulant shake of his head. "I believe I just said that. Who is this Maude?"

"The woman you murdered."

"Murdered?" Cyrus stared at me as if *I* were the crazy. He gave one of those annoying titters of his, and said, "Where are my manners? Let me get you some brandy, my dear. You must be thirsty."

He got up and bustled about a lovely fruitwood commode. I saw my chance and eased off the couch, ready to spring. Cyrus wheeled around, still pointing the Dao at me.

"Don't think me a poor host but you'll have to pour," he said. "Madelaine often chides me about my manners. I forget the amenities when I discuss my work."

"I'm really not thirsty."

"Drink. I insist." Cyrus pointed the Dao at the decanter. I thanked him and poured brandy into two Baccarat snifters.

"Shall we toast the Abacus?" he said. His cheeks were flushed, his manner sprightly.

Dare I hope that this old fool will keel over?

We clinked glasses as Cyrus proposed the toast: To the Abacus!

I considered beaning him with the brandy snifter. The heavy crystal might do the trick. Unfortunately, by the time I heaved it, Cyrus would have slit my throat.

I recalled the advice one of those right-wing marriage manuals had given. *"To be a* TOTAL WOMAN, *focus on his interests, celebrate his victories."*

"How did you get the Abacus out of its case, Dr. Worthington? That couldn't be easy."

Cyrus seemed pleased. "I'm a lot stronger than I look. I spent years on archeological digs, after all. The Abacus isn't that large although it is heavy. I substituted the copy when the Abacus first arrived. All I had to do was stage an attempted robbery."

"That was very clever." Actually, it was damn near brilliant.

Cyrus was all smiles now. "I planned it very carefully, Ms. Quinn. I just didn't count on your meddling."

I didn't like the sound of that. The *Total Woman* to the rescue.

"How did you fool the experts who examined the Abacus?" I asked.

Cyrus puffed out his chest, and laughed. "Child's play. The experts examined the real Abacus *before* the switch. Afterwards, they didn't get a second chance."

Light finally dawned on me. *"You're* the one who insisted on that extra thick Plexiglas not the Chinese government. That way, no one could get too close to the Abacus."

Cyrus nodded modestly.

"You're very clever, Dr. Worthington," I simpered. "No wonder you've been so successful. But what will happen when the exhibit returns to China? They'll spot it in a minute."

"That's where Jie-ling comes in. *She's* the one taking the Abacus back to China. I fear that the Chinese will blame her for the mishap."

"Where is the Abacus?" I asked.

He playfully shook his finger at me. "I'll never tell. Let's just say it is safely in the hands of a prominent Chinese-American collector."

For once, I didn't know what to say. "Was it really worth two lives, Cyrus?" I asked.

His face darkened. "What are you blathering about?"

"The murders. Maude Morrissey and Bert Kingman."

Cyrus hit the floor hard with the Dao. "Nonsense! I never murdered anyone—until tonight, that is."

My heart took the express lane to my toes. I was running out of options.

"Stand up!" he squawked. "We're going on a field trip."

I felt the tip of the Dao in my back. A silk blouse was light armor against a sword. My one hope was to distract Cyrus, and bolt for freedom.

"Walk in front of me and no tricks," Cyrus barked. He jabbed the point of the Dao into my back. I felt a thin trickle of blood drip down.

If only I had my purse or even spike heels. I was paying the price for wearing sensible shoes!

"Where are you taking me," I asked, trying to remain calm. It wasn't easy.

"Move!" he responded.

An exit sign was the only light in the corridor. Cyrus motioned toward the freight elevator.

"We're going to the basement. You'd be surprised at all the paraphernalia they have there. It will be quite awhile before your corpse is found."

On the wall to the left I saw my salvation. It was an old-fashioned red fire alarm with a pull down lever.

I inched my way to the left, feeling the tip of the Dao all the while. I needed a diversion to throw Cyrus off his game.

I started coughing, convulsions wracking my body.

Cyrus blanched. "What's happening?" he shrieked. "Stop that!"

I clutched my throat, and rasped, "Asthma."

He shifted the Dao to his other arm. That gave me my chance. I lurched to the left, pulled the fire alarm, and raced toward the exit door, with Cyrus in hot pursuit.

I hit the crash bar and stumbled out the door into Patrick's arms.

CHAPTER TWENTY-THREE

Patrick pushed me out of the way, closed the exit door and stepped inside with Cyrus. In the stairwell I saw Devon Hall and Therese. Devon looked fantastic, cheap suit and all. He carried the ultimate fashion accessory—a nine-millimeter Glock. Therese had somehow acquired an aluminum baseball bat.

"Patrick!" I yelled. I could hear him speaking calmly to Cyrus Worthington. I opened the door a crack.

"Cyrus, what's all this about?" Patrick asked. "You don't look well."

Truer words were never spoken. Spittle dripped down Worthington's chin and his hair stuck straight out. His cheeks were mottled with red veins.

"Oh Patrick, you have to help me. She'll ruin everything."

"Who Cyrus?" Patrick's tone was almost gentle.

"That meddlesome girl. You know, your friend."

"Ms. Quinn—don't worry about her." He pointed to the knife. "That's some Dao, Cyrus. Let me take a look at it."

Patrick deftly spun the Dao out of the old man's hands before he could protest.

"Here, let me get you to a chair. Drink your brandy, Cyrus."

The sirens were growing closer. Patrick's voice was soothing. "You need medical attention. I'm going to get you an ambulance. Don't worry about Madelaine, I'll make sure she's taken care of."

Cyrus clutched his arm. "Thank you, my boy," he murmured.

Devon swept me aside and joined Patrick on the other side of the door. Therese ran up and flung her arms around me.

"Oh my God, Grace are you okay? You're bleeding!

I'd forgotten about the jab to my back. "It's nothing," I lied. "I thought you weren't going to tell anyone about this."

"Are you CRAZY? I called Patrick immediately and Devon too. They tried to keep me from coming but that didn't work."

I felt a little woozy. "I need to sit down for a minute." Therese stayed by the door, ready to swing the bat. "Where the hell did you get that thing?" I asked her.

"Little League convention," she said proudly. "They'll never miss it."

We could hear the sounds of fire trucks, and footsteps racing up the stairs toward us.

"I have to see Patrick," I said. I pulled myself up, and headed for the door. It opened and Patrick and Devon walked out. I could see paramedics bending over Cyrus Worthington, applying oxygen.

Patrick grabbed me, and held me tight.

"Jesus, Grace. I can't leave you alone for even a day." He turned his hand over and looked at the blood staining its surface. "You're hurt!" He spun me around and gently touched my wound. "It's not too bad. Come on, we're going to the hospital," he said.

"No o-o" I protested. "The bleeding's stopped."

"Tetanus, Baby, tetanus. That Dao's 200 years old!"

"Where's Cyrus? He stole the Abacus."

Therese did a double take. Patrick frowned.

"Cyrus is on his way to the hospital too. He had a real heart attack this time. You can tell us all about it on the way."

We exited to the street where Patrick had stashed his BMW.

"The upholstery—it'll get stained." I said.

Patrick threw Devon the keys, closed his eyes, and wrapped his arms around me. "I'll think of some way you can repay me," he said.

◇ ◇ ◇ ◇ ◇

I don't remember much about that ride or the hospital visit that followed. They welcomed me like a regular at the emergency room, and quickly tended to my wounds. In short order I was swabbed, medicated, and given a tetanus shot.

The doctor decided not to stitch the stab wound. "I don't see any need for that," he said, "it might leave a tiny scar but it can be your souvenir." It was Dr. Feelgood, the same exuberant resident I'd seen Wednesday night.

"You must lead an exciting life, Ms. Quinn. Two emergency room visits in two days is somewhat of a record." He beamed at me with inordinate good cheer.

"I'm an over-achiever." I would have added something rude but Therese dug her nails into my hand until it was numb.

"Behave yourself," she muttered.

"We're going to let you go back to your hotel," said Dr. Feelgood. He shook his finger playfully at me. "But remember, no more rough-housing."

A distinguished trio waited for me in the Lobby—Patrick, Devon and James Clarke.

I glared at Therese, who hung her head guiltily. "Oh yeah, I forgot to tell you. I called Clarke too. It took him awhile to get here."

For once, Clarke wasn't smirking. In fact, he seemed genuinely concerned. He nodded at me and said, "The Smithsonian's federal property. A crime there isn't my jurisdiction but I couldn't refuse Ms. Harding's invitation."

Patrick put his arm around me. I winced when he squeezed a little too much.

"Grace needs to rest. We can hear what happened tomorrow." Patrick arranged his jacket over my shoulders and hovered nearby.

"No, Patrick, it's okay." I glanced up at him, trying to look brave. He was so handsome I almost swooned. I wondered how long I could remain an invalid. The perks were great!

"Let's go back to her suite and hear everything," Therese suggested. "We could have a party—celebrate just being alive."

"Good thinking," Patrick said, "but Grace won't get any rest at the hotel once the press hears about this. My townhouse isn't far from here. We can go there." He gave Devon directions, and tenderly placed me in his BMW. Therese and Devon piled into Clarke's unmarked patrol car. I considered calling Mary and Jonathon but even the thought of it exhausted me. Tomorrow was soon enough.

Patrick used his iPhone to call someone—a housekeeper I guessed. He spoke in Mandarin, so I had no idea what he said. I prayed she was a toothless crone with bunions who had no designs on him.

He reached over and touched my shoulder.

"Excuse me for speaking Mandarin," he said. "Chen Lee still doesn't have a great command of English." He hesitated. "Grace, I have to tell you something."

Great! Now comes the stirring tale about family obligations, and Jie-ling Chow. I knew it was too good to last.

"I didn't want you to hear this with everyone around." Patrick massaged my shoulder.

Shit! Just blurt it out and get it over with. My God! Maybe he was married!

"It's about Cyrus. He didn't make it."

"Huh?" Relief flooded my body.

"He died on the way to the hospital. In view of what happened maybe it's for the best."

Patrick obviously considered me more tenderhearted than I really was. That old fossil deserved to die!

"How sad!" I said. I hoped the throb of compassion in my voice sounded genuine.

Patrick raised an eyebrow and stared at me. His eyes had that cynical look again.

"At least the murders are solved," he said. "Funny, I never figured Cyrus for a killer."

Something clicked in my mind. "Patrick, I'm not sure he was the killer. In fact, he denied any part in the murders." I shivered as I remembered the exact words.

"Cyrus made of point of saying I'd be his first victim. What an honor!"

He patted my knee. "Don't think about it. You'll have nightmares."

I closed my eyes and leaned back in the seat. If I slept with Patrick's arms around me, I wouldn't worry about nightmares— only sweet dreams.

We crossed into Georgetown, one of my favorite haunts. I loved the stately brownstones, and historic row houses. Patrick turned on "P" street, and pulled up in front of a lovely two story colonial. The draperies in the front room were pulled back, exposing a beautiful room with intricate dentil moldings. A brilliant crystal chandelier illuminated the area. He rushed over to my side of the car, opened the door, and carefully helped me get out.

"Are you sure you're up to this?" he asked. "If not I'll send them all home."

"I'm fine," I said bravely. "Besides you'd have to pry Therese away with a crow bar. I've got to tell my story sooner or later."

Patrick hesitated. "I just want to prepare you—Jie-ling's here."

My eyes widened but I said nothing. Invalids shouldn't curse. I think he got the message anyway. Patrick put his hands on my shoulders and murmured: "Don't forget, there's nothing between me and Jie-ling. We're like brother and sister—always have been. She's played a major part in this caper from the beginning. She has a right to know."

He took out his keys and opened the door. An older Chinese man clad in white greeted us.

"This is Chen, my friend and teacher," Patrick said. "He's taken care of me since I was a little boy." He smiled at the old man with the affection one would show a beloved relative.

"Chen, this is my guest Ms. Quinn. Please make her comfortable. She'll be with us … " he looked into my eyes, "for a long time."

Chen bowed, and took Patrick's jacket. If he was curious about me, it didn't show.

"Your other guests have arrived, Patrick," said Chen. Then he said something in Mandarin to which Patrick responded.

We joined Therese, Devon and Lt. Clarke in the living room. It was a large, beautifully proportioned space with gleaming walnut floors covered by an elegant Sarouk. I was surprised that the furniture was primarily French, not Asian. A fire burned in the massive marble fireplace. Chen had arranged a buffet, and was serving drinks. It sure beat the chips and dip we would have gotten from the hotel.

Patrick settled me on a red velvet sofa and fluffed a cashmere throw over my legs. Frankly, it was a little too warm but I didn't complain.

Therese, Devon and Clarke sat around the fireplace. Therese was chattering nonstop, from a surfeit of nervous energy.

"Don't you wonder how we beat you guys here?" she asked.

Without waiting for our answer, she blurted out,

"We used the siren—it was so cool Grace. I've always wanted to do that."

She turned to Clarke who flushed to the roots of his hair.

"In view of everything that happened … " He held out both hands palms up.

Finally, they stopped talking and looked expectantly at me. I heard the door chime and saw Jie-ling Chow stride into the room. Her manner hadn't thawed one degree. Maybe she didn't like strangers in her "brother's" house. Patrick leapt up to greet her.

"Come on in, Jie-ling. We were just getting ready to start. Would you like a drink or anything?"

She gave a little half-smile. "Chen, make me a martini— straight up."

"Of course, Miss Jie-ling," Chen replied.

He dropped a notch in my estimation. The bitch could have made her own drink!

Therese started moving from side to side. She always does that when she's impatient. If I'd been sitting next to her, she would have pinched me.

"You already know that Cyrus intended to kill me," I said. "What you may not know is the real story behind the Abacus theft."

"Theft! Wait a minute, Ms. Quinn," said Jie-ling. "The Abacus is still at the Freer. I checked."

I flashed a snarky grin at her. Patrick intervened, no doubt hoping to avert a catfight.

"You know, perhaps Jie-ling and I should start this story," he said. "It'll fill in the whole picture."

Jie-ling sat on the edge of the straight-backed chair she had chosen. She seemed to relish being the star of the show.

"I knew something odd was going on with Cyrus," she said. "Paintings and other acquisitions were going out on loan much too often."

"He said you caught him borrowing the Whistlers," I said. "That you blackmailed him into expanding your authority."

"Cyrus wasn't always truthful," she said. "But I'm sure you've found that out now, Ms. Quinn." Her smile was poisonous.

"Ladies! I think we're getting off track," Patrick said. "Let's stick to Jie-ling's story."

He put his arm around me drawing me closer. Jie-ling frowned.

"I called Patrick for help. The safety of the Abacus was very important to me." She nodded at him. "I knew I could trust him."

"Exactly what is your job, Patrick?" Therese trained her baby blues on his face.

His reply was no more informative than the one he'd given me.

"I work for the State Department, you know, cultural attaché."

Therese didn't let him off the hook. "No, I'm not sure I know what that position entails."

Devon was embarrassed, Clarke looked intrigued. Patrick neatly evaded her question.

"This and that—mostly boring stuff."

Therese wasn't finished. She pointed to Jie-ling. "How do you two know each other, anyway?"

Jie-ling and Patrick exchanged amused looks. "We're old friends, more like siblings actually. Our families have known each other for decades. I pretended to be Jie-ling's fiancé as a way of hanging around the Freer all the time." He exchanged smiles with Jie-ling again. "Cyrus thought I was a very jealous man."

Clarke bit into a shrimp puff. It beat the donut patrol by a mile. "Was State in on this officially," he asked.

Patrick nodded. "My job was to ingratiate myself with Cyrus, and run interference. We have a squad that deals with illegal marketing of antiquities."

I had a hundred questions but I didn't ask them. Fortunately, Therese did.

"So you didn't realize that the real Abacus was gone until Grace just told you?"

Jie-ling tightened her lips. "It was a very clever scheme," she said. "Cyrus controlled access to the Abacus."

Therese had never liked Jie-ling. She stared her down and forged ahead. "I'll bet the shit will really hit the fan now." She smiled sweetly at Jie-ling.

Patrick intervened again. "Maybe we should let Grace pick it up, here."

Clarke jumped in. "Just a minute. If anything was stolen at the San Simone that is *my* business, especially if it involves two murders!"

Jie-ling stiffened. "I assure you, Lieutenant, I know nothing of murder."

"I may be able to help, Lieutenant." It was time to tell my story.

Clarke shook his head, and laughed. "How come I'm not surprised."

I took a breath, and worked hard to produce a calm steady voice.

"Cyrus explained everything to me, right before he tried to murder me."

Therese shivered and even Jie-ling blanched. I had the full attention of everyone in the room.

"He waited until the experts authenticated the Abacus, then switched it with a copy. He did it on the same night he faked the botched robbery."

"Pretty slick," said Devon, a man of few words. "Maude must have caught him switching the Abacus. Kingman probably blackmailed him."

I glanced at Patrick. He hadn't dropped my hand the entire time we'd been in the room, but he was watching his guests with an intensity that frightened me. He squeezed my arm, encouraging me to continue.

"I don't think Cyrus murdered either of them. When I accused him, he seemed genuinely surprised. He was consumed by the Abacus, felt his efforts were ignored. His motive was purely financial."

Jie-ling stared at me and her expression was far from benevolent. "Where *is* the Abacus, Ms. Quinn? It's a matter of international importance!"

Clarke chimed in. "Grace, if you know anything, let's hear it. No more playing detective. There could be criminal sanctions involved for withholding evidence."

Patrick stood up, blocking Clarke's view of me. "Lieutenant, as Ms. Quinn's legal representative, I suggest you back down or I'll advise her to remain silent."

"Grace—silent? That'll be the day!" Therese whispered. "You're an attorney, Patrick?"

He nodded. "Now, she'd like to finish her story." He glanced at his watch. "It's almost one o'clock, and Grace must be exhausted. Can we *please* hear the rest of it?"

"There's not much more to tell," I said. "According to Cyrus, the Abacus was transferred to some well-heeled Chinese-American collector. He wouldn't specify who or where."

Jie-ling's face fell. "Oh no," she cried.

Patrick went over to her, and spoke. "Don't worry, my guys are already combing our records for a list of suspects. We'll find it, Jie-ling. I promise."

She put her head in her hands. "How did he expect to get away with it?" she asked.

I knew the answer. "He planned to let *you* take the blame, Jie-ling. The Chinese government might have considered you a traitor. Cyrus would have just walked away."

Clarke was deep in thought. He appeared to be calculating which approach would better serve his needs. Access to information meant survival in the nation's capital.

"Will you keep me in the loop, Patrick?" he asked. "This is a political hot potato."

"I'll contact you tomorrow if you're at work," Patrick said. He looked at his watch again. "I'm sorry to break this up, but it's really late."

Chen appeared and escorted the group to the door. Therese grabbed me and gave me a hug. "I'll bring you some clothes and your makeup tomorrow."

"Don't tell anyone where I'm staying. I'd like to have a peaceful weekend. What's left of it anyway. My cell phone will be turned off until further notice."

She turned her head, searching for Patrick, "Not even Jonathon Grey?"

"I'll handle all that," I said.

When they left, Chen bolted the door, and turned out the exterior lights.

"Anything else, Patrick?" he asked.

"No thanks. I want to get Ms. Quinn settled."

Patrick helped me up the curving staircase to a beautiful guest room done in shades of red and gold. The bed was turned down, fresh towels were in the adjoining bath and a bottle of Pellegrino rested on the nightstand. I was so exhausted I could have slept anywhere—the master bedroom preferably. Patrick grinned and handed me a delicate red silk nightgown and robe. I stared at it speculatively.

"Relax, it belongs to my mother," he said laughing. "She keeps a few things here. Let me help you peel off that blouse."

He gently removed the blood soaked blouse and put the robe over my shoulders.

I shuddered even though the temperature was far from cold. Patrick kissed me gently, pressing his lips up and down my neck and shoulder. I didn't want him to stop—each kiss sent shivers through my body. I struggled with the gown, trying to adjust the bodice. Patrick slid his hands over the red silk, running his fingers lightly down my arm and over the silky garment. I tingled in places I'd never thought of before. Funny, I didn't feel tired now.

"Here, let me help you," he said, sliding the straps off my shoulders and loosening the top. "Is there anything else I can get you?"

I pulled his face down to mine and whispered, "Stay with me—don't leave."

He closed the door, and doused the lights.

CHAPTER TWENTY-FOUR

I was alone when I awakened. The blinding sunlight streaming through the drapes told me I'd slept far too long. A glance at the French carriage clock on the dresser confirmed it—almost noon! How embarrassing! I forced my aching muscles to behave and sat upright. The red nightgown and robe were a crumpled heap at the foot of the bed. Mrs. Fong wouldn't like that, I bet. A knock on the paneled door shot an electric current through my body. Good Lord! What if Patrick sees me like this!

"Grace! Let me in. It's Therese."

I'd never been happier to see her.

Therese bounded in and rapidly sized up the situation. She grinned as I clutched a sheet to cover myself and sputtered a greeting.

"Hmmm—I guess you've recovered from your injuries," she said. "You should be glad I'm not Patrick. You look awful!"

She threw me the nightgown as I hobbled to the bathroom mirror to assess the damage. Unfortunately she was right. Mascara decorated my chin and my hair looked like it had fornicated with an eggbeater. My "souvenir" from Cyrus throbbed. In short, I was a mess.

"Here," Therese said, "I've got just the remedy." She carried in my make-up bag and purse. "Chen will bring up all your other paraphernalia," she said.

"How did you get this stuff?"

"Simple. Patrick was at the Hotel—bright and early. He asked me to pack your belongings and take them to you. Guess he was too shy to touch your unmentionables. Anyhow, Chen appeared in this humongous Mercedes and picked me up."

I was overwhelmed. "But the hotel—I didn't check out."

"Not to worry," she said. "I did it for you. Patrick's orders."

To my chagrin, I started crying. Therese was so mystified that she raised her arms in surrender. "What the hell's wrong with you? Did I do something to hurt your feelings?"

"No," I sniffled. "It's all so sudden. I've always taken care of myself. I'm not used to this."

"Honey, relax and enjoy it. Let me draw you a picture: a gorgeous, brilliant, sexy, rich guy is crazy about you and you feel sad? Are you sure Cyrus didn't knock you on the head?"

"It's just that," I couldn't stop crying, "I don't want to get used to it—to depend on it. In case it all vanishes."

I could always count on Therese for good sense. "Look Grace, do your beauty ritual. You know how that calms you. Then we'll talk." She walked over to the nightstand. "By the way, did you see this note?"

"What note?" I wailed.

For once, Therese didn't grab the paper and read it. She handed me the small envelope and folded her arms while I read it. I recognized the heavy vellum—Patrick must have written it before he left.

"I have to do a few things this morning. Sleep well and rest up. Remember that I love you. DON'T GET IN ANY MORE TROUBLE! Please ...." Patrick

Now I really couldn't control myself. Big heaving sobs breached the dam, and flooded my eyes.

"It's too much."

Therese came over, and pushed me toward the bathroom. "Trust me, you'll feel better after a nice hot shower," she said.

I noticed her reading Patrick's note and shaking her head. "You silly twit! All our lives we dream about Prince Charming. Now that he's here, you want a rain check. Buck up, Grace!"

She was right. The pounding water, bracing spray and fragrant soap rejuvenated me. Patrick's mother used a very high end line of bath and hair products.

I stepped into a luxurious spa robe from the Four Seasons and followed the enticing aroma of freshly brewed coffee.

Therese opened the balcony door and placed a tray of croissants and espresso on the table. For once I welcomed the humid air. Patrick's home had a beautiful Georgetown courtyard with exquisite landscaping and scores of flowering plants.

"You better put on your makeup, Grace. Patrick could be here any minute."

That did it! I grabbed some coffee and ran to my cosmetics bag. I could only hope that he left under cover of darkness this morning.

Therese chattered on while I made repairs.

"Oh, I ran into Jonathon Gray this morning. He was asking for you. That article in the Post aroused his curiosity especially since he knew about Cyrus. He left you a message on your cell."

"What did you tell him?" I asked.

She answered with wounded dignity. "Nothing."

I was skeptical. "Really, Therese?"

She became less adamant. "Well, I did say that you were okay—you wouldn't want him to worry, would you? And I said you would call him."

I sipped my espresso, and picked at the croissant. "Did you see anyone else?"

"Oh my God, I almost forgot to tell you. That hideous boss of yours was circling like a buzzard. I know she was trying to find you even though it's Saturday."

"Mary? Oh, I really should call her." I didn't have the energy to face her today.

I stepped into a long linen dress of blood red. If I had any more accidents, at least I would be color coordinated.

"What about Harry? Has anyone gotten an update?" I felt selfish for not thinking of him before now.

"His condition is unchanged. Devon spoke with Pam this morning. Harry is conscious, but groggy. Clarke still has a police guard on him but who knows for how long."

I nodded ruefully. "Clarke believes the murders are solved."

"He wants to believe it even though he knows it isn't true. That murderer is still out there. That's why I got you this."

Therese reached into her purse, and presented me with a bag. "Here's a little gift I picked up for you at a store in Crystal City."

I pulled open the wrapping paper saying, "Oh you shouldn't have."

When I saw what it was I repeated. "Oh you really shouldn't have. What in the hell is this, Therese?" I held the bottle out to her.

"It's pepper spray—police strength, and thoroughly tested. Don't give me a hard time about it either."

"What am I supposed to do with this stuff?"

"The way your luck's been running you just may need it. Go on, Grace. Keep it in your purse."

I had to admit it would have come in handy dealing with Cyrus.

"I can never find anything in my purse as it is. I'm not even sure this stuff is legal in D.C. You better take it back."

Therese snorted. "Screw that. You need to protect yourself."

I smiled smugly. "I have Patrick to protect me."

Therese made rude gagging noises. "Five minutes ago you were bawling, now you're a Stepford wife." She stuffed a piece of bread in her mouth, almost choking. "Oh, they had the cutest pair of hand cuffs in this store. The guy said it's a big seller around Valentine's Day."

"I'll bet. Hey, when are you going back to Chicago?"

She gave me a coy look. "Not for awhile. Maybe never."

"WHAT!"

"Devon and I want some time together. My firm has a branch here, so a temporary loan of an ace accountant like moi, is no big deal."

How ironic that the murders had spawned two romances. I suddenly recalled my main goal—finding the Mole.

"I never asked you. Did you get anything more out of Braddock or Cates?"

Therese shook her head. "Nada. Even Devon drew a blank with them. I think they're sitting tight hoping the whole thing blows over."

"Shit! They may be right." I felt both restless and useless. "Let's take a walk and see the neighborhood," I suggested. "New surroundings may inspire us."

We started down the stairs, almost colliding with Chen who was carrying my luggage. He wore another white suit and an impenetrable smile.

"Good afternoon, Ms. Quinn." He nodded politely to Therese.

"Patrick always has luncheon at 2:00 p.m. on Sundays. He asked me to check with you."

I felt like young Mrs. DeWinter in "Rebecca"—awkward and out of place.

"Anything you plan is fine with me," I said hoping to project an image of serenity. "Will there be other guests?"

"Just Miss Jie-ling," Chen said. "She comes here every week."

Fortunately I had a firm grip on the handrail.

"Steady, girl" Therese said under her breath. "Keep moving."

I nodded to Chen and followed her advice.

Therese rolled her eyes at me as soon as Chen walked away.

"I think we'd better postpone that stroll." She checked her watch. "Your guest could be here any moment."

My cowardice gene kicked in. "Wait! Don't leave me here alone!" I considered physically restraining her but rejected the idea. Therese worked out—she could probably deck me.

She gave me absolutely no sympathy. "Stop acting like a wimp. For Christ's sake, you're a Senior Executive not a galley slave. Buck up!"

She was right. I knew it. I had about an hour to steady my nerves and do a bit of snooping. I knew virtually nothing about Patrick's life except the bare bones sketch Mary Hagan had provided. Of course, I couldn't admit I'd had a dossier prepared on him and the Dragon Lady.

"I'll call you tonight," I told Therese. "You will be at the hotel, won't you?"

She laughed. "Not if I'm lucky! Call my cell. Devon's condo is just what you'd expect—an appalling bachelor pad complete with a black leather chair and plaid sofa." She rubbed her palms together. "The boy needs work but there's so much of him to work with!"

She waved merrily and trotted off.

I had a million questions but with Chen around I had to be circumspect. I drifted aimlessly into the library to check out the selection. It was an elegant room, with carved walnut bookshelves filled with hundreds of books bound in red Moroccan leather. The desk, credenza and distressed leather sofa made it very much a masculine room. I could feel him in it.

The credenza housed a collection of snuffboxes, mostly jade. It also contained some answers to my questions. Silver frames held family photos. Two handsome young men, mirror images of one another had Patrick's face. So this was the twin brother! A middle-aged couple in formal attire had to be his parents. Mrs. Fong, she of the red nightdress, was an elegant woman with intelligent, piercing eyes. I didn't relish being interrogated by her! The man in the photo was Patrick's father—had to be. He was a hunky vision of his sons in twenty years. I liked what I saw although it was a bit overwhelming. The final picture showed Chen holding two large herding dogs—some kind of shepherd breed. They had show ribbons attached to their collars. So, these beautiful creatures were the pets referenced in Mary Hagan's dossier. I had just leaned over to study them when I heard a noise. Jie-ling Chow was standing in the doorway, hands on hips. She wore a tailored pantsuit in white silk and looked untouched by the rigors of last night.

"Meeting the family, I see. I hope you are feeling better, Ms. Quinn."

Would this bitch ever lighten up? "I'm very lucky," I said. "Thanks to all my friends, I'm back to normal."

She walked to the credenza and picked up the photo of the twins. "Have you met Patrick's brother, Ms. Quinn? His name is Justin. He's a psychiatrist."

Justin Fong—what a great name. "No, I haven't met him—yet."

Jie-ling made a sharp sound that passed for a laugh. "Oh, I forgot—you really don't know Patrick, do you?"

Don't let her get to you, Grace. Remain calm. "You know it's strange, I feel like I've known Patrick forever." I managed a bright smile that would have made Therese proud.

Jie-ling turned and faced me. Her expression was impossible to decipher.

"I misjudged you Ms. Quinn. I was afraid you would ruin our operation. You saved it instead. I thought you were a typical Caucasian woman but your actions were very brave. Thank you."

I was floored—Dr. Chow was human after all. I wasn't crazy about her slur against white women but under the circumstances, I let it go unchallenged.

"I tried to warn you off, you know. Make you go away. What I told you about Patrick—the engagement—was part of our cover story. Patrick has had many romances but with you it's different. He's never been so ... taken ... with a woman. I can sense it. I know him so well."

I could feel my face getting warm. Jie-ling kept speaking.

"He was curious about you at first. We wondered if you were any ally of Cyrus."

"ME!" I said. "Why on earth would you think that?"

"Out of nowhere, you found the body and the Abacus. Then you showed up at the Association questioning Patrick. It seemed so unlikely."

I chuckled. "Come to think of it, I suspected both of you of murder, so I can't complain."

She came closer to me, almost too close. "Do you ... care ... for him as well?" she asked. Her eyes reminded me of a raptor studying her prey. I resisted the urge to flinch and stood my ground.

"I love him," I said simply.

She gasped. "You just met him! That's ridiculous."

I'm no doctor but this babe had either breathing problems or heart trouble. No pills could cure the heart trouble she had. I couldn't believe that I'd said it aloud—to Jie-ling Chow no less. I loved him! Saying it made everything seem so official.

The library doors swung open and Patrick glided in. He wore a summer suit of taupe linen with a striped silk shirt. My God, he was magnificent! I felt that tingling again.

"Oh, there you are ladies. How about some lunch? I'm starving."

He escorted us out to the patio where Chen had arranged the table.

"Is this too hot for you, Grace? I know you hate the humidity."

You're the only thing that's too hot for me and I want all I can get. Burn, Baby burn!

"No Patrick, this is fine."

"Ms. Quinn was looking at Justin and your parents, Patrick." No more snarky lines, Jie-ling was all peaches and honey. Bitch!

He raised an eyebrow and looked at me. "You were, huh? Wait 'til you meet Justin. He'll charm you like he does everyone and he'll love you just like I do!" Patrick bent over and kissed me on the cheek. Now Jie-ling was the one who flinched.

"Did you trace the Abacus yet?" I asked. I couldn't trust myself. If he kissed me one more time, every dish on the table would go flying—Jie-ling be damned. Crime was a more neutral topic.

"Yes Patrick, did you find anything?" Jie-ling twisted her napkin in her lap.

"Not yet, but we will."

"What about Madelaine?" I asked, hoping the old bat was in a straightjacket.

"I'm going over there after lunch." He turned to Jie-ling. "Maybe you should go with me. She knows you."

"What about me?" I asked quietly. I hope I didn't whine.

He had a mischievous glint in his eyes. "Since she tried to kill you twice I think we can safely assume you're not welcome there."

Jie-ling shot me a look of triumph.

Something was bothering me. "Will she be able to stay at home with her nurse?"

Patrick shook his head. "Without Cyrus there I'm afraid that's impossible. The best solution would be to sell their home and pay for professional care."

I bit my lip. Patrick looked at me in amazement. "Don't tell me you worried about her?"

"Not really, but Patrick, I'm worried about Whistler."

Jie-ling tilted her head and said, "Cyrus returned all the Whistlers to the Freer."

"No, I mean their cat."

"A cat! You're worried about a cat?" She gave a dismissive snort.

I ignored her and grabbed Patrick's arm. "Could you make sure he's okay? I'll find a home for him or take him myself. Please."

His eyes softened, "Don't worry, Baby, I'll make sure he's okay."

They were almost out the door when a thought struck me. "Oh Patrick, if you see my Bottega tote, will you bring it to me? I still think Madelaine has it."

He laughed. "You and your purses. You have a thing for leather!"

Jie-ling was fuming. "We'd better leave, Patrick," she said, clutching his hand.

Before the gate closed, he ran back to the table. "Promise me you won't get into any trouble while I'm gone." he tweaked my chin. "Save your energy for me."

CHAPTER TWENTY-FIVE

I didn't break my promise. After lunch, I grew restless and decided to take a little stroll. Harry Hawkins was in George Washington Hospital a scant five blocks away. It was my Christian duty to visit him. I felt clothed in virtue.

Chen was lurking somewhere. Even though I couldn't see him, I knew Patrick had deputized him to watch me. I grabbed my purse, and calmly called out: "Chen, are you there?"

He materialized from nowhere. "Yes Ms. Quinn, may I get you something?"

For some strange reason I hated to deceive him. It didn't stop me but I felt a pang of guilt.

"No thanks. I think I'll take a walk around the neighborhood. The homes are so lovely."

His expression was blank but in his eyes I saw a first class bullshit detector.

"I will drive you anywhere you like. Patrick says you dislike the hot sun."

Full marks to Chen. The subtle reminder about Patrick was nicely done. No wonder this household ran so smoothly.

"A friend of mine is in G.W.U. Hospital. I plan to visit with him for awhile." I headed toward the gate. "I'll probably beat Patrick home."

Chen nodded, radiating disapproval. "We usually dine at eight. Will that be convenient?"

"Fine, thanks." No mousey Mrs. DeWinter—now I was REBECCA!

I walked up to M street, desperate for a shady spot. It had to be at least 110 °F degrees in the sun. The Hospital, one of Washington's finest was famous for treating President Reagan's gunshot wound. It was still the place of choice for anyone like Harry with heart ailments.

Harry's room was easy to find—no one else had a police guard. The cop was an edgy white guy of middle age whose manner bordered on rudeness. I had to drop James Clarke's name several times before it impressed him. Finally, he allowed me to visit my friend.

Harry was alone today, hooked up to a machine that emitted a constant beep. I cringed at how pale and shrunken he looked amid the stark white sheets. Hospitals had a way of diminishing even a rough and tumble guy like Harry.

"Hey Gracie, good to see you." His voice was a bit weak, but still the same old Harry.

"Hey yourself." I went up to his bedside and gave him a hug.

"Whoa, don't do that to a heart patient! This ole beeper will go wild."

I gave him a playful punch and pulled a chair alongside his bed. "Where's Pam?" I asked him.

He tried to sit up, grunted, and settled back in the bed. "I'm still sore as hell. Pam is taking a break. She went back to the hotel to freshen up, and get some rest."

"You gave us quite a scare you know."

Harry gave a crooked grin. "I guess I should thank you for saving my life."

I shook my head. "Not me, my friend, thank Jonathon Grey. He was amazing."

"Jonathon—I don't remember anything. I was waiting for you, and ... then I woke up here."

I didn't want to be pushy, but time was short. That officious nurse outside might evict me at any time.

"Harry, do you remember anything? Even a small detail would help."

He blinked, and closed his eyes. "He must have come up behind me. I was sitting on the deck chair, then WHAM."

"Did you hear him approach?

"No, I was staring straight ahead and—wait a minute!"

I tried to be patient, but I was tempted to shake the words out of him.

"I smelled something. Some kind of perfume or cologne, that's what it was! It made me start to turn, and that's why the docs say I didn't break my skull." Harry looked triumphant! "There—does that help any Grace?"

I clasped his hand and squeezed. "It just may, my friend. Now, what did the cologne smell like?"

He curled his lip. "Oh I don't know. I'm no good with that kind of stuff. Pam knows every perfume and scent in Neiman Marcus. I just pay for it."

I tried to be patient, but it wasn't easy. "Was it pungent, unpleasantly strong?"

Harry thought about it. "It was strong—I didn't like it. I know I've smelled it before on someone." His face brightened. "That's it! My allergies kicked up—I sneezed."

Only one name reverberated in my head—the king of cut-rate cologne himself—Kelvin Cates. Just this week he had slapped on enough of some noxious brew to kill lice.

I couldn't stop now. "Harry, do you remember who you spoke with that afternoon."

He looked puzzled. "About the Mole, you mean? Just Kelvin and Ev. They told me to stop meddling and shut up." He averted his eyes. "I'm afraid they kind of blamed you Grace."

"Big deal! Those cretins blame anyone with a brain."
I looked at my watch—five in the afternoon.

If I stayed too long, Chen would track me down with a pack of bloodhounds or at the very least two Belgian sheepdogs. I gave Harry a kiss, and turned to leave. Suddenly, a thought popped into my head. "Harry, when Pam gets here, ask her about that scent, or cologne or whatever. Call me if you think of anything." I gave him my cell number.

"Are you still at the hotel, Grace?" Harry asked, looking at the number.

I turned away when I felt my face get warm again. "No, I'm staying with a friend. See you Harry."

I had to tell my news to someone, but who? Therese couldn't do anything about it, she'd just flap her arms and go crazy. Clarke didn't want to hear it, and Patrick would only worry about me. As I exited the Hospital, my answer came walking up the street. It was Jonathon Grey!

He was shocked to see me but very curious. Naturally, he was too well bred to pry, but he wasn't above hinting.

"I've been trying to reach you," he said. "Therese was very mysterious about everything that happened with Cyrus."

I craned my neck, looking for Chen. "Why don't we go across the street and have a coffee?" I asked. "There's a Starbucks only a few blocks away."

Actually, I miscalculated. It was five long city blocks away. The heat, humidity, and guilt made that a most unpleasant walk. Surviving heatstroke became my major goal; Jonathon didn't even sweat.

We snagged a table, and ordered iced coffees. By the time I told him my entire saga at the Freer, Jonathon's eyes were glassy.

"Do you mean to say that Cyrus was the murderer?" he asked. "That's odd. I was positive it was related to this IRS Mole thing."

"I agree. Let me tell you about my visit to Harry."

I related our conversation ending with the peculiar fragrance Harry had recognized.

"It has to be Cates, it all fits so perfectly. You know that creature practically bathes in cheap cologne." I was convinced, but Jonathon was noncommittal.

"That's not much to go on, Grace. Lieutenant Nelson will need more proof before he arrests Kelvin."

"I'll help him get it. I just don't know how. Yet."

Jonathon was cautious. I'd forgotten that he was a CPA.

"Now Grace, stop right there. Haven't you had enough trouble lately?"

The wimpy part of Jonathon reared its ugly head. I chose to ignore it.

"Isn't Chris still involved in the operation? Surely he wants to find the Mole."

Jonathon nodded. "That's true. I'll mention it to Chris."

I could just imagine how well Charming Chris would react to my conclusions. Maybe they were right—I should back off. Then I remembered the flash drive and the note Maude wrote: "We were never close friends, but you have integrity. I know you'll do the right thing with this."

I really had no choice, even though it would be safer and more convenient to quit. I owed it to Maude.

"I got involved to find Maude's murderer. I can't quit now."

I checked my Rolex, and jumped up. It was almost six-thirty, and I had to beat Patrick home.

"Jonathon, please excuse me. I've got to run. Thanks for listening."

He stood up like the gentleman that he was. "How can I get in touch with you?" he asked.

"Through Therese or call my cell. I'm sort of a transient right now."

He pulled me into a hug, and wished me luck. I walked briskly back to "P" street, praying the BMW would not be there. It was my lucky day. I had enough time to shower and make myself presentable before dinner. I decided to dress formally like the heroine in all those British mysteries. I chose a red silk blouse, long black skirt, and pearls for a touch of innocence.

It didn't fool Patrick for a minute. He was waiting for me in the library, reading the Sunday *Washington Post*. I'd never seen him with his glasses on and the effect was dazzling! He glanced up, gave me a quizzical look and headed for the bar.

"You're beautiful tonight, Grace. May I get you a drink?" His voice was stiff and formal. Oh, oh!

"Scotch straight up." I said, surprising even myself.

"Hard day?" he asked, staring down at me. "Chen tells me you went to visit a sick friend."

"It's my day for good deeds," I said piously.

"What good deed did you do for Jonathon Grey?"

"Huh?"

"You didn't think I'd let you wander around without protection, did you? You were never out of Chen's sight, you and Jonathon Grey."

Patrick was a simmering caldron of anger and jealousy that I found thrilling. I went over, and threw my arms around him.

"I'm so glad to see you," I said kissing his ear. "Don't worry about me. Jonathon is just my friend. Anyhow, I can take care of myself."

He put his arms around my waist and drew me to him. "I saw that at the Freer last night. You could have been killed! Don't you see—if anything ever happened to you, I couldn't live with myself."

He pulled me on to his lap and stroked my hair. "I love you, Grace Quinn, I really do. But you make it damn hard." Patrick began to rock me back and forth in a strange, soothing rhythm. "I didn't plan for this to happen. You came out of nowhere." He gently kissed my ear. "I told myself I was being cautious but you sneaked through all my defenses."

"I love you Patrick," I whispered, snuggling up to him.

No more coy remarks or evasions. I had finally taken a stand and it felt so good. Liberating.

He slowly unbuttoned my blouse and ran his thumb up and down my collarbone. The sensation was so exquisite that I gasped. The man was a magician! Every place he touched was on fire! If he kept that up, we wouldn't make that eight o'clock dinner. Patrick must have realized it too. He raised his head and gave me a mischievous grin.

"To be continued," he said. "Now, tell me about this mission of mercy you went on today."

"You first," I said. "I need some time to recover."

I hoped he would spare me any mention of Jie-ling. Fat chance.

"We spoke with Mrs. Day and Madelaine's physician. Fortunately I have power of attorney for her. I thought it was odd when Cyrus asked me but now it makes sense."

"Maybe he knew something like this might happen," I suggested.

"Maybe. Anyhow, Mrs. Day will stay with her tonight and tomorrow, they'll take her to a skilled care facility where she can live and get treatment."

"Are you going with her?" I asked.

"No, Jie-ling is. We're meeting a real estate firm tomorrow to get the house on the market. It'll sell right away—they always do in that area."

"What about the Abacus? Any word?"

Patrick frowned. "We've narrowed the list to three individuals—all on the West Coast. I'll probably fly out there next week."

"Speaking of that, I need to find a new hotel or an apartment."

Patrick leapt up so fast that he almost dumped me on the floor. "No, it's not safe yet." He stared into my eyes. "Promise me. You can stay a few more days—or forever."

I kissed him. "Oh Patrick."

I don't know what my answer would have been. I was saved by the bell—the dinner bell. A gong sounded and Chen entered the library.

"Are you ready for dinner, Patrick?" he asked.

Chen was the perfect servant. He never acknowledged that his master was sprawled on the couch with his shirt undone, and a half-naked woman in his lap.

"Yes, Chen," Patrick said calmly, "we'll be right there."

He helped me up, and opened the adjoining door. "Before we go in, I have a surprise for you. Two surprises, actually."

I followed him and saw Whistler, reclining on a velvet cushion, grooming himself.

"Oh Patrick, you found him!" I hugged his waist. "Thank you!" I ran over to Whistler, and patted his silky fur. "Oh, he's beautiful!"

Whistler gave me the feline once over. While he clearly considered his new surroundings adequate, he reserved judgment about me.

"One more thing. Close your eyes." Patrick reached into the closet and put something heavy in my arms.

I jumped when I felt the strap. "My Bottega bag! Unbelievable! How did you ever find it?"

He gave me a wicked grin. "Actually Jie-ling found it in Madelaine's closet. You have her to thank."

I reached up and put my arms around his neck. "I choose to thank you."

As we walked to the dining room, Patrick said, "You know you've got Jie-ling all wrong."

"Humph!" I sniffed.

"Yeah you do. She's never been romantically interested in me." Patrick's smile was mischievous. "It's YOU she's attracted to."

I was speechless, unable to utter one word. Then Patrick took pity and winked at me. "I was only kidding. You're safe. Jie has no designs on you."

We spent the evening making plans and drinking Krug. I believed I was close to finding the Mole, but Patrick wasn't convinced.

"You need to tell Clarke," he said. "The police can check everyone's alibi for the night Harry was attacked. Stay out of it. Let them handle it."

"I'm afraid Clarke may take the easy way out. With Cyrus dead he can close two cases. That'll help his clearance rate."

Patrick pinched my cheek. "Don't be so cynical. Clarke's one of the good guys."

He filled my champagne flute one more time. "Let's drink a toast." We touched glasses, and took a sip.

"To Grace Quinn, the real Abacus prize." he whispered.

I don't remember much after that—great champagne goes straight to my head. Patrick dimmed the lights and put some sweet sounds on the stereo—Coltrane, I think.

"You know, I've never danced with you before," he said. "Tonight's the night."

He took my hand, and led me to the middle of the floor.

"I like to dance," I said. "It's almost as good as making love."

Patrick smiled down at me. "There's plenty of time. We can do both."

CHAPTER TWENTY-SIX

We slept late on Sunday. I must admit my head ached but the memory of last night made everything worthwhile. I told myself that the staples not the Krug caused the pain. I'm such a liar!

Chen brought breakfast and the newspapers up to Patrick's bedroom. We lounged in the sitting room, drinking espresso, reading the *Post,* and debating the next steps in solving Maude's murder. It was a one-sided debate since Patrick refused to participate.

"There are no next steps, Grace. You're officially out of the murder business."

"Why?"

Patrick scowled. "How many attempts on your life are enough for you? It's time to let it go."

I can be stubborn too. "I started this alone, and I guess I can finish it that way. Cates can't get away with it, Patrick. I won't let it happen!"

He folded his newspaper and slapped it down on the floor. "I can't be with you every minute. Who's going to save you the next time?"

"Save me! I did pretty well on my own."

"Right! You're hell on wheels against an old man and his senile sister. Cates and Braddock are grown men, mean ones at that."

"Okay, I'll find someone to help me," I said. "Let's see, there's Therese and there's always ... "

"Don't say it." Patrick interrupted. "Don't you dare say Jonathon Grey's name."

I jumped up and put my arms around his neck. "I was going to say Mary Hagen. After all, she's hot to find the Mole too and it could help my career."

He didn't believe me for a second but he swung me into his lap, and held me tight.

"Don't do this stuff to me, Grace. I just can't take it."

"I love you, Patrick. Don't worry about me."

He gave me that little half smile. "You're really a brat, Ms. Quinn, do you know that? I think I may have to give you a spanking." He grabbed me and put me over his knee.

"I'll scream! I'll scream for Chen." I said.

Patrick laughed. "Go ahead. Chen's hearing isn't what it once was."

We'd never made love in the sunlight before and Patrick insisted on opening the drapes. I was kind of creeped out by it.

"You really are a little convent girl, aren't you?" he teased. "Something this beautiful should always be done in the open. I want to look at you."

"I guess I should be glad you're not filming this."

He raised his eyebrows. "Who says I'm not?"

I squealed and dove under the covers. Fifteen years of Catholic education had left its mark.

◇ ◇ ◇ ◇ ◇

I called Mary Hagan's office at nine. She was unavailable but her secretary told me the Boss had been asking about me. Damn! I explained about my injuries and said I wouldn't be back to work for a few days.

"What *really* happened, Grace?" Shirley asked. "We've all been dying to know."

"There was an incident at the Freer," I said. "Dr. Worthington had a heart attack."

"Oh," she said. "We thought it was something exciting. Devon Hall said someone tried to kill you. Again."

"Nothing that dramatic, I'm afraid." Damn that Devon, he was getting just like Therese.

"Please tell Mary I'll call her cell. Bye!" I hung up before Shirley demanded a contact number. I needed a few more Mary-free days just to remain sane.

It took me awhile to get ready. Patrick was sitting on the patio, reading the *Wall Street Journal* and eating breakfast. *He* looked untouched by last night's activities, carefully dressed in a navy pinstriped suit with Hermes tie. He looked so good I wanted to rip off that starched white shirt and ravish him. Fortunately good sense and the looming presence of Chen restrained me.

"Good morning, Ms. Quinn, May I serve you breakfast?"

Chen never cracked a smile. He reserved such favors for the charming Dr. Chow.

"Just espresso and orange juice, thanks."

Patrick put down his paper, rose and pulled out my chair.

"Good morning," he said. That man could infuse more meaning into two words than anyone I'd ever met. Our eyes locked and he kissed my forehead.

"I've had to change my plans," he said. "They want me in San Francisco tomorrow morning. Don't worry—I'll be home Wednesday."

I was disappointed, not worried. I was hoping for a return engagement with the Krug.

"No problem. I have a lot to do myself. Therese is going with me to have my staples removed."

Patrick frowned. "Are you sure that's all you two are up to?"

"Absolutely."

I know he didn't believe me but for once I was telling the unvarnished truth.

"Chen will be gone all day but he'll be here tonight." Patrick smiled fondly at his friend. "Monday is his day to visit the Temple."

"Temple?" I said. "I didn't know he was Jewish."

Patrick laughed. "You nut! Chen is Buddhist. He goes to a temple in Maryland."

I shrugged my shoulders. Anything was possible these days.

"Oh, you're going to love this. Tonight you get a big surprise." Patrick smiled mysteriously.

Actually I wanted an encore of the big surprise he gave me last night. I looked up at him, and said, "What is it? You know I love surprises."

"You'll finally get to meet my dogs, Sun and Tzu. Chen's picking them up at their trainer's place this evening."

"I can't wait! I love dogs. How will they react to Whistler?"

"Not a problem. They were raised with cats." Patrick looked at his watch.

"Hey, I've got to run. Will you be okay?" He took my hand and kissed each finger. "Will you miss me?"

"Every second."

It sounded corny, but it was true.

Get a grip Grace. This isn't real.

Therese was ecstatic. "I found the neatest apartment right over in Dupont," she said. "I'm renting it furnished for six months."

I noticed the coy expression on her face. "Does that mean you'll be seeking something more permanent after that?"

"Who knows?" she said.

"If you have any influence over that boyfriend of yours, tell him to button his lip. He's blabbing everything he knows."

Therese looked offended. "Don't be silly. After all, he's a special agent."

"Yeah, yeah, big deal. They're worse gossips than any bunch of women."

Chen appeared suddenly. I swear I saw a puff of smoke whenever that man beamed in. It was downright spooky.

"Ms. Quinn," he nodded at Therese. "Ms. Harding, may I get you anything?"

"No thanks." I said. Patrick had probably given him our full itinerary.

"I'll be leaving soon, when the maid arrives. Patrick said you'd be home for dinner."

"Yes. Enjoy your day, Chen."

He nodded and left the room. Why did I always feel guilty around him?

"I found out something," I told Therese. "Let me tell you about Harry."

She squealed when I mentioned Cates and the offending scent.

"It has to be Cates! That lummox wouldn't think twice about snuffing Harry."

"Snuffing?" I said. "You must be watching reruns of the Untouchables again."

"Elliot Ness *was* a Special Agent you know," she said dreamily. "There's just one thing. I still can't see Cates as a criminal mastermind. He's managed to hide any signs of intelligence for years."

"I know, that's been bothering me too. Well, we'd better leave."

We took a cab to the American University area of the city, where Patrick's personal physician removed my staples. He'd insisted on that, rather than another trip to the emergency room. Dr. Irene Liu was a petite Asian woman in her fifties. I liked her friendly smile and no nonsense manner. She took a peak at my back too while I was there.

"My goodness, that looks like a stab wound." she said.

"It's a long story," I said. "It's not infected, is it?"

"No, but I think I'll change the dressing. Patrick would never forgive me if I didn't."

Patrick seemed to have a lot of influence, more than a mid-level State Department guy ought to have.

We stopped for lunch at La Chaumiere, one of my favorite French restaurants. To my surprise, Therese insisted on paying the bill.

"You've survived three attempts on your life this week," she said. "You can live with being in my debt." She waited a minute. "I guess the big question is, can you live without Patrick?"

"What?"

"Face it, Grace you're going to have to make a decision. Patrick loves you and he wants you. BUT—" She lowered her voice, "he's very strong. You'd have to make some big changes in your life. Are you ready for that?"

"Look who's talking. You've already disrupted your life for Devon."

Therese shook her head. "It's not the same thing. Devon and Patrick are polar opposites."

I knew she was right but I didn't want to think about it. Not now, not when my head hurt.

"Come on, I need to get back to work and you should lie down." She flagged a cab, gave me a hug, and sped away. I walked slowly back toward "P" street, dodging the noxious rays of the sun. The humidity and Dr. Liu's tweezers had given me a headache. I decided to get my book, and curl up on the leather sofa in Patrick's library. I dropped my purse on the floor and settled in.

I must have been dozing. The ring of the doorbell made me leap off the couch. Damn! Who could be outside? I peered out the window and saw a black Jaguar XJ-6—my dream car. Oh shit! The driver was Mary Hagan. That woman would track me to the ninth circle of hell.

After I waved her in, she lingered in the foyer surveying Patrick's beautiful home. I swear I saw dollar signs on her eyeballs. As usual, my Boss was a model of perfection—melon silk suit, paisley shell and five-inch heels. She carried a taupe Chanel bag with the big CC logo.

"Well, you certainly know how to convalesce in style," she said. "You look remarkably chipper for someone at death's door." She enveloped me in a cloud of Creed and gave me a European hug.

I couldn't get over the car. "That Jag is incredible," I said. "How'd you manage to get it?"

Mary narrowed her eyes, "That's an odd question coming from someone whose boyfriend is a millionaire. Men enjoy giving us toys, Grace. You just have to ask them the right way."

She put her hands on her hips. "Am I going to be invited in or do I have to melt in this heat?"

I was still transfixed by the car. "I'm sorry," I said guiltily. "I was resting in the library. Please come in."

I looked at my watch. Three o'clock—Patrick's plane must have just left.

Mary was busy inhaling every bit of his home. I thought I heard the Ka-ching of that cash register she called a mind.

"How'd you find me, Mary?" I asked. "Not that I didn't want you to. I just haven't had the energy to move."

My bid for sympathy fell flat: Mary saw right through me.

"You've been amazingly energetic for an invalid. Get back on your couch, I don't want you to faint." She laughed. "Remember, I've done a full security check on Dr. Fong. I had his address."

"I forgot." I should have known she was the only one sneakier than me.

Mary eased into one of the club chairs. "Okay, tell me exactly what happened, and I mean *everything*."

I started with Cyrus, Madelaine, and the Abacus.

Mary was dumbfounded. "You mean that old man heisted the Golden Abacus right under everyone's nose! Incredible!" She giggled. "How does Patrick feel about that? Wasn't that his responsibility?"

"Not really. He's just a cultural attaché."

She gave me a look of pity. "You really believe that? Grace, Patrick Fong is one of the highest level intelligence operatives they have at the State Department."

She saw my confusion. "Oh, I guess he forgot to mention that. He works for one of those alphabet agencies, specializes in the Asian theater. He must be bullshit about losing that Abacus!"

I was finding it hard to process everything. That pain pill I took had fogged up my mind.

"You didn't mention that when you read his dossier," I said.

Mary rolled her eyes. "Of course not, you nitwit. It wasn't in the official record. That stuff is buried deep. Remember, I have my own sources."

I remembered Patrick looking me right in the eye, telling me he was a "nerd." That rat!

"So Cyrus Worthington murdered Maudie and the security guard? Go figure." Mary shook her head in wonderment.

I held up my hand. "Wait a minute, Mary. That's not right. Cyrus was crazy not homicidal."

She crossed her legs at the ankles. "Didn't you just tell me both he and his sister tried to kill you?"

"Well, yes." I said reluctantly.

"In my book, that makes the entire Worthington clan homicidal. Now, let's move on to more interesting topics. What about the Mole?"

I shrugged. "No real progress. However ...."

I told her about Harry, and his olfactory clue. "There's only one answer. It's so simple it was staring us right in the face. Kelvin Cates.

"What! You've got to be kidding." Mary said. "Cates is an imbecile. He couldn't lead a horse to water let alone run a sophisticated scam."

"But his noxious cologne, the smell."

Mary opened her purse and started rummaging for something. I loved Chanel bags, but they were way over a thousand dollars. Maybe Patrick ....

"Hello, Grace. Planet Earth calling." Mary had her pen poised to record in her Gucci notebook. "Does Jonathon Grey think Cates is the one?"

I hated to admit it. "Not really. Neither does Therese. In fact, Chris, Jonathon and I worked out a criteria for the Mole."

"And?"

"It doesn't fit Cates. We stipulated that the Mole must be intelligent ...."

"There goes Cates," she interrupted. "Proceed."

I reached for my juice. It was empty. "Do you want anything to drink?" I asked. "I'm so thirsty."

Mary waved me away. "For Christ's sake, I'll get it," she said. "Is there any sparkling water in the bar?" She answered her own question. "Of course there is, Pellegrino, right? Enjoy the service now, Grace. I promise it won't last long." She poured both of us a drink and sat down.

I gulped down my drink and regrouped. "Okay, the Mole must be wealthy, or have access to funds. Remember the bribe to Kingman."

"How much was it?" Mary asked.

"Fifty Thousand." I said.

"Yikes! That money was wasted on a slug like Kingman. He could barely feed himself."

"I didn't know you knew him." I said. "Kingman, I mean."

"They're all of a type, security guards. Gung ho, cop want-to-be, not too bright. Keep going."

My head felt really foggy now. If only she would leave and let me sleep. With an effort, I focused on my task.

"We also listed these qualities: knowledge of the tax system, access to inside information, part of the IRS landscape, manipulative and technically competent."

I beamed, proud that I had remembered it all. Mary wasn't impressed.

"If you find anyone who fits that laundry list, I say hire him. We could use a little duplicity." She drained her glass of Pellegrino. "Okay, where does this leave us? Maybe we should consider Evan Braddock instead of Cates. He's marginally smarter."

"Yeah, and he's as mean as a sewer rat. But he doesn't wear cologne."

Mary snorted. "That's where caveman Cates would come in handy. Brawn not brains."

"You know, I never thought of that." I gave Mary my best sycophantic smile, "No wonder you're the boss."

The sharp ring of the phone broke my concentration. I slowly dragged myself up to answer it.

"Let it ring," Mary ordered. "We're finally getting somewhere."

"I can't. What if it's Patrick?"

It must be love. You actually defied your boss!

I answered on the last ring. It was Pam Hawkins, Harry's wife.

"Grace, I'm sorry to disturb you, but you said to call. About that fragrance Harry smelled."

"Of course. Hi Pam, how is he doing?"

"He's having surgery tomorrow, but the doctors are very optimistic."

"Great."

"Anyhow, Harry is hopeless about any kind of perfume or cologne. But I talked with him, and I really think it was perfume he smelled. There's only one kind he's allergic to no matter what he says—Creed. He bought me some in Paris, and broke out in hives the first time I sprayed it on. Now he practically wears a mask whenever we go near a perfume counter. I hope that helps."

"Sure Pam, thanks for the update."

CHAPTER TWENTY-SEVEN

I hung up, pasting a big smile on my face. If I could just think clearly, everything might work out. I stumbled back to the couch and sat down. Mary Hagan was silent, her eyes like lasers.

"Was that Harry's wife?" she asked. "Patty or Pam. Something like that."

I replied with forced cheer. "Yeah, good news about Harry. His surgery is tomorrow."

She took out her compact and freshened her makeup. "Harry is a decent guy. Too bad he almost died."

My mind was working overtime. How stupid I had been! The criteria for the Mole fit my Boss perfectly—technically savvy, intelligent and right on the inside. Not to mention ruthless—I knew first hand about that. The Jaguar suggested a money stream far stronger than any man would provide. She always looked great, but I thought she was just a skilled bargain hunter. Some bargain!

"Are you leaving, Mary?" I asked. "Shirley said you had tons of meetings today."

She rose slowly and stood with arms folded.

"I think we both know better than that, Grace. You've become a liability."

I felt so tired; I could hardly keep my eyes open. A great time for Narcolepsy!

She watched me with the ghost of a smile on her face. "Don't fight it Grace. I gave you a nice dose of Valium in your juice. I'm afraid Patrick will find his true love dead, a probable suicide. You're a mystery buff, you'll appreciate this. Sleeping *The Big Sleep,* isn't that what Chandler would say?"

Forgive me if the finer points of detective fiction eluded me right then. I could only look at my boss, a person I had admired and ask one thing. "Why, Mary?"

She was amused. "I find your naïveté endearing. It was always part of your charm."

I glanced at the telephone. Too far away I could never make it.

"How could you murder two people? You're not a monster."

"It was a business necessity. I calculated the risks and decided to do it." Mary was very much the rational CPA, evaluating an investment strategy.

"Maude?"

She actually laughed. "Now, there was a bit of pleasure in that one. I always hated that brazen cow."

I suddenly remembered Chris Grey's words. Maude had bragged about bringing an executive down.

"She found out about you, didn't she?"

Mary's face grew hard. "Can you believe it? She actually figured it out. Who knew she'd been staking out Cates and Braddock."

"Did you intend to kill her? Your weapon was ... unusual."

"I met her to see how much she knew. When she told me about that recording, I had no choice. Nosey bitch. She brought it on herself. There was glass all around and I found a shard that was just the right size.

You should have seen the look on her face!" Mary laughed. "She fell like a Sequoia."

I fought to stay awake but I knew it was a losing battle. Maybe if I kept talking, Chen would come back.

"You better leave—Chen will be here soon."

"Nice try, Grace, but I don't think so. I followed him for a while. He's busy praying."

I blinked. Maybe if I stood up. I tried, but I couldn't trust my legs.

I looked at my watch. "Therese is due here at four o'clock," I lied. "She'll know something's wrong."

Mary shook her head. "I hope she does show up, that bitch. I'd enjoy it." She walked over to the couch, and felt my forehead. "Somehow, I think we'll have all the time we need.

"I suppose Kingman was blackmailing you."

"Can you imagine, that stupid rent-a-cop thought he could outwit *me*. I gave him $50,000, just to buy his silence. Then, he got greedy."

"He saw you kill Maude?" I pressed my nails into my arm, hoping pain would keep me from passing out.

"He saw enough."

"And Harry?"

Mary walked over to the credenza and examined the Jade. "Dear Harry. In his own blundering way he was getting too close. I took a tire iron, gave him a little love tap. He never even saw me."

"Yeah, but he smelled you. Creed was a poor fashion choice that time."

She frowned. "Very amusing, Grace. You always had a quick wit. I'll miss it."

She looked at her tiny-jeweled watch, and grimaced. "This is taking longer than I planned. I have a meeting at Treasury in an hour." She picked up a pillow and started toward me. Fear gave me a jolt of adrenaline.

"Just one thing. Why did you get involved with tax fraud?"

She laughed. "That's so very Grace—you really are a true believer, aren't you?"

I hauled myself into a sitting position. "Yeah ... I guess."

"The answer is simple—*Money, lots of it*. We're not so different, you and I. We both l-o-v-e spending it."

"Liking nice things, and killing for them are two very different things," I retorted.

If I lived until tomorrow, I would examine my conscience. I wasn't like Mary—was I?

She gripped the pillow and reached down toward me. "I'm going to have to help you sleep, I see."

Suddenly, the front door swung open. Mary and I both froze.

Patrick Fong burst into the room and called out. "Grace, are you there? Who owns that Jag?"

"Patrick!" My voice wasn't loud, more like a whisper. Mary wheeled around to face him.

"What's going on?" he asked, his body tense. "My flight was canceled, and I thought ...."

Mary Hagan drew a pistol from her Chanel bag and shot him in the chest. It was a fancy gun, all silver with a pearl handle. How could something that dainty hurt a big man like

Patrick? He collapsed, a circle of dark blood staining his beautifully starched shirt. I heard him gasp, trying to breathe. Mary walked toward him, ready to fire again.

I had to do something, anything. I saw my purse, and remembered Therese. I dumped everything on the floor until I found it. I tore off the cap, crawled off the couch and hobbled toward her. She never saw me coming. I sprayed Mary Hagan right in the face with my police tested, highly potent pepper spray.

She dropped her gun and tried to protect her skin, howling as the spray burned her eyes, and caused her to choke. I bent over and grabbed her gun. Some of the spray caused my eyes to water, but I gripped that gun with all my strength. I had to save Patrick.

Mary sprang at me, wrestling me to the ground. I enjoyed yanking that perfect bob as hard as I could. I gouged her eye while I was at it. The effects of the Valium made me sluggish, but Patrick's life was at stake. Somehow I was able to hold on as she clawed at my face and grabbed for the gun.

Another shot rang out as Mary fell to the floor, her mouth open with surprise or shock.

I crawled to my cell phone. Before I finished dialing 911. I heard the sirens. Shots fired in Georgetown brought the cops on the double.

Patrick was in shock, his face ghostly pale. I went to him, and used my hands to staunch the blood flow. There was still some light in his beautiful eyes but it was fading.

"Don't die—don't leave me," I begged. It sounds inane but that was all I could think of. I heard the sirens and paramedics, closer now—then blackness.

CHAPTER TWENTY-EIGHT

Patrick was lucky—he didn't die. Another two inches to the right and the bullet would have killed him. After they pumped my stomach I stayed with him, holding his hand throughout the night. Therese, Devon, Chen and Jie-ling Chow took turns keeping watch. Even Clarke joined the vigil.

When he opened his eyes, mine was the first face he saw. I kissed his hand, and spoke softly to him.

"Oh Patrick, my God. I'm so sorry. I didn't know ...."

He was too weak to speak but he squeezed my hand. I tried not to cry but I had to. If only I had minded my own business, Patrick wouldn't be there.

I got the chance to meet his family but not the way I'd hoped. The first time I saw Justin I almost fainted. When he strolled into the room, the living embodiment of his brother, he shook my soul to its core. I wasn't sure how they would react, if they would blame me. Justin walked right up to me and folded me into his arms.

"So you are the famous Grace Quinn," he said. "Don't worry, Patrick told me all about you." He winked at Patrick and held my hand. "We better not make him jealous. He always could kick my ass."

His mother was less sanguine. Dr. Fong was a professor at Stanford and a formidable presence. She was icily polite and remote, seeking comfort from her son and husband. She included Chen and Jie-ling in their conversations, always conducted in Mandarin. For all I know, she may have been exceptionally rude. I just couldn't picture her in that red nightgown.

Patrick's father was a judge. He was tall and athletic looking like his sons, with wavy black hair sprinkled with grey. He held out his hand and smiled. His warmth reminded me of Patrick or maybe it was his beautiful, dancing eyes.

"I know how much you mean to my son, Ms. Quinn," he told me. "Chen says you saved his life."

I was prepared for hostility. Kindness made me melt. I turned away, to hide the flood of guilty tears. Only Therese could fully understand the way I felt. I sat with her in the waiting room while Patrick's family was with him.

"Grace, you've got to stop this. No one blames you for that maniac's actions. I wish she had died!"

"I let her into the house, into Patrick's house. He almost died because of me."

"WRONG! He's *alive* because of you. You were incredible!" Therese rifled through her purse and found a mirror. "Just look at yourself. You're a mess! If you don't want to scare Patrick to death, go fix yourself up."

I shook my head. "My stuff's at Patrick's. I can't go over there again."

She jumped up. "Oh stop being a baby. I'll go speak with Chen." She whisked away, and returned with a set of house keys.

"Come on. Devon'll drive us over, and you can pick up your things. You're coming to stay with me."

I hadn't the strength to argue with her. We zoomed over to "P" street at break-neck speed, using Devon's police siren. I have to admit it *was* pretty cool. I noticed a small band of people ringing the front door.

"Reporters," Devon spat. "I'll distract them, so you can have some privacy."

He approached the newshounds while we headed for the back entrance. One enterprising fellow followed us anyway, shouting questions as he walked. "Ms. Quinn? Do you have any comment? Why did you shoot Mary Hagan? Was it a love triangle?"

A policeman stood guard at the door—it was a crime scene after all. He admitted us when Devon flashed his badge and dropped James Clarke's name. I tiptoed past the library, ignoring the ugly yellow tape. Clarke had retrieved my purse earlier that day. He overlooked the pepper spray but confiscated it, mumbling something about hazardous substances.

Therese grabbed my arm and helped me up the stairs. My knees felt so rubbery I had to cling to the handrail. The beautiful, empty house screamed Patrick's name at every turn.

"Go on, Grace. Take a shower, do your beauty ritual. You don't want that snooty Mrs. Fong to think you're not good looking enough for her son. Besides, there's a photographer out there."

Point taken. Even a fallen woman should look her best.

I fell asleep, curled up on the guest room bed. Therese was there when I awakened, her blue eyes electric with an over-caffeinated gleam. It took me a minute to focus. *Where was I? Oh my God, I'm still in HIS house! I can hear dogs barking.*

"What time is it," I cried. We have to get over to the hospital!"

Her expression was somber. "His mother wants to speak with you. She's in the dining room."

"What's wrong? Is Patrick okay?"

Therese slowly approached the bed. "He's fine. Buck up, Grace. Pretend Dr. Fong is just another irascible taxpayer. Don't let her get to you."

"Why, is something bad going to happen?" I whimpered like a small child.

Therese was never one to sugar coat a message. "She probably hates you."

I blanched. "I don't blame her."

"Oh bullshit, Grace. She wouldn't like you anyway. You're involved with her son, and you're … not Chinese. I read her as some kind of racist. Maybe it's just ethnic pride. Whatever."

I hauled myself off the bed, and headed for the bathroom. I have to admit, I primped a bit.

"Okay, let's see what she has to say."

I squared my shoulders and walked down the stairs to the dining room. Patrick's mother was seated at the table sipping tea, dressed in a chic red pantsuit. She half turned when I entered, and motioned me to a chair.

"You are feeling well, Ms. Quinn?" she asked. Her tone was clipped, but polite.

"I'm better, thank you. I'm getting ready to go see Patrick."

She compressed her lips in a firm thin line. "That's not advisable. Patrick needs time to recuperate—with his family."

I nodded politely. "Did he say that?"

The gloves came off. "Thanks to you, he's not saying much. I am his mother. I must ask you to respect my wishes in this matter."

"I know how much Patrick loves his family," I said, "but he's a man not a boy. He can make his own decisions." I stood up. "I'll go speak with him now. Good day, Mrs. Fong."

It took effort, but I managed to leave the dining room without lunging at her. After all, she *was* his mother.

Therese and Devon were already loading my things into Devon's car. She raised her eyebrows in a question. "Well, how did it go with your future mother-in-law?"

I made a face. "Do you guys mind dropping me off at the hospital. I'll take a cab to your place later on."

"Is everything okay? Do you want me to go with you?" Therese asked.

"Thanks, both of you, but no. I have to speak with Patrick."

We rode to Georgetown hospital in silence. As I got out, Therese pressed a key into my hand. "Here, take this. The address is on the keychain."

"Thanks." I felt a bit queasy but that didn't matter. I was going to Patrick.

EPILOGUE

On a beautiful September morning, I ran lightly down the stairs to the sunroom. Patrick was propped up in a recliner with a sheaf of papers. He was wearing a silk robe, reading glasses and a sexy smile. His dogs clustered around him, Whistler lay in his lap. I bent over and kissed him.

"You look content," I said. "Convalescence must be working."

Patrick raised his head. "Having *you* here is the best medicine, I could have." He took my hand and kissed it. "So, how did your meeting go?"

"I got my new assignment," I said. "They were pretty nice considering I took a month off."

He chuckled. "They should be. After all, one of their senior Executives is a homicidal maniac and you caught her. You did them a favor. Not to mention breaking up that Tax Champions business."

"I still can't believe Mary did that! I admired her, liked her even. She's really going to hate prison."

Patrick stroked Whistler's fur. "She's lucky. Clarke says they probably can't try her for the murders—insufficient evidence. She'll get nailed for two counts of attempted murder though."

Neither one of us spoke. Finally, Patrick asked me. "Where are they sending you?"

I swallowed hard. "It's not as bad as it could be. I mean they could have banished me to Fargo, or Cincinnati."

"Grace!" He wasn't quite as jovial now.

"I'm going to New York, just temporarily. There's a lot going on there."

He sighed. "Not too bad, not as good as staying here but not too bad."

"They said it was better that I leave, at least for now. Because of what happened ...."

Patrick's voice teemed with scorn. "Typical IRS—think of what's best for the organization. No loyalty to employees at all."

"I'll be in Washington a lot, probably half my time."

His beautiful eyes softened. "This isn't over. I love you and I'll never give you up. Never."

"I won't let you," I said. "I just need some time to think. Everything's happened so fast."

"Speed isn't always a bad thing," he said quietly, removing his glasses. "Loneliness is worse."

I looked away. "Since you found the Abacus, you'll be gone a lot. You may change your mind."

Patrick shook his head. "My mind is made up. They did mention something about Hong Kong, though. Cultural attachés are in demand."

I pulled up a chair and took his hand. "I've been meaning to ask you about that. We need to have a long conversation."

THE END